Praise for Ray Anderso

THE TRAIL is an intense psychological cat-an...
a bright new talent who is very familiar wit_ ...val strategies
and the unique and unforgettable setting that distinguishes this story.
Well-written and well-researched, Ray Anderson's debut novel will grab
you from the disturbing opening scene and hold you in its grip until the
grand payoff at the end of the trail.

—**Gary Braver, bestselling author of *Skin Deep* and *Tunnel Vision***

There's a particular darkness in the crimes of a middle-aged man. Murder's thought to be the medium of younger people with poor impulse
control, bad nurture and a hormonally-induced taste for the dark side.
But when a man at midlife commits murders on the Appalachian Trail,
the crimes open a window into something aberrant. **Ray Anderson captures this darkness with extraordinary skill.** He's in total control of his
prose, characters and a story that manifests the most disturbing crisis of
all—that humans can do these things, and we the readers, are human too.

—**Mike Hogan, author of *Burial of the Dead***

This book has more twists and turns than the Appalachian Trail itself . . .
a compelling, atmospheric thriller . . . Anderson captures the imagery
and emotion of the renowned trail like no one else.

—**Brett Ellen Block, author of *The Lightning Rule, Destination Known,*
and *The Grave of God's Daughter***

THE TRAIL perfectly captures the essence of the backpacker's lifestyle, and
the natural beauty of the outdoors stands in stark contrast to the violent
events that unfold.

—**Michelle Ray, author of *How to Hike the A.T.***

SIERRA

SIERRA

RAY ANDERSON

TURNER

FIC
Anderson

Turner Publishing Company
Nashville, Tennessee
New York, New York

www.turnerpublishing.com

Sierra, A Novel

Cover design: Maddie Cothren
Book design: Kym Whitley
Author Photo: Molly St. John

Library of Congress Cataloging-in-Publication Data

Names: Anderson, Ray, 1942- author.
Title: Sierra / by Ray Anderson.
Description: Nashville, Tennessee : Turner Publishing Company, [2016] |
    Series: An AWOL thriller ; 2
Identifiers: LCCN 2016007634 | ISBN 9781681626215 (softcover)
Subjects: | GSAFD: Suspense fiction.
Classification: LCC PS3601.N54475 S55 2016 | DDC 813/.6--dc23
LC record available at http://lccn.loc.gov/2016007634

9781681626215

Printed in the United States of America
15 14 13 12 11 10 9 8 7 6 5 4 3 2 1

TO NANCY—
THE BEST THING TO EVER HAPPEN TO ME.

ACKNOWLEDGMENTS

I **WANT TO THANK THOSE** readers who gave me helpful criticism. They include Joe and Fran Cucci, Susan Trausch, Virginia Young, Carol Chubb, Jennifer Harris, and others I may have missed here. Several readers also gave me detailed guidance and suggestions. These people are my sister Judy Carlson, Gus Borgeson, David Gardner, Robert Jones, John Lovett, Linda Santoro, Susan Shannon, David Miller, and, most of all, Alan Kennedy. My thanks to Hank Zulauf and his daughter, Holly Ciannella, for reviewing all the Spanish. Thank you Molly St. John, for my new back-cover photo. As many of you know, David Miller, who writes the A.T. field guides, also gave me permission to use his trail name, "Awol," for my protagonist throughout my hiking-thriller series.

I'm grateful that my agent, Sorche Fairbank, continues to represent and guide me. I would not be here without her. My thanks to everyone at Turner Publishing and particularly to the editors there who have taught me so much. My best to all the hikers I met on the Pacific Crest Trail. We saw some truly awesome sights. My biggest thanks to my family and especially to my wife, Nancy, to whom this book is dedicated.

I took a few liberties with scenes and locations so I could fit the timelines in the plot. But this was minor and most everything in setting and description, including the weather, came straight from my journals. I alone am responsible for any inconsistencies.

SIERRA

CHAPTER ONE

Valle de las Palmas, Mexico
April 2, 2007

LUIS ALVARADO LIFTED THE WHITE pawn and replaced it with his black bishop. "Check!"

Manuel's hand hovered over his king. His position was helpless. The banjo clock ticked, echoing off the veranda wall.

Manuel tipped over his king. "Bravo, señor."

"And now," Alvarado said, standing, "you will come with me."

The guard approached, hand resting on a holstered pistol. His thumbnail was missing, and a tattoo of a viper's head peeked from his sleeve.

Manuel, puzzled, looked at Alvarado. "Señor?"

Alvarado backhanded Manuel across the face. The guard stuck his pistol into Manuel's back and shoved him through the doorway.

A few minutes later, Alvarado watched the executioner strip Manuel and lock him in a holding cell. "I hate to lose chess players," Alvarado said.

Alvarado walked to the other side of the stone building, a former stable now converted into an interrogation room. He sat down at his desk, in front of a muscular young man seated in a chair. The man handed Alvarado a set of papers. "I hope—"

"Repeat my instructions," Alvarado ordered.

The man stood. "I will obey my field commander. I will complete my mission on time, every time. If injured or sick, I will find a way to complete my mission. I will never deviate from these instructions."

"Good. Now, listen carefully. Do you understand my instructions?"

"*Sí, señor.*"

Alvarado read through the papers down to the dated signature at the bottom. "From here on, you are called Barcelona. Your field commander is El Verdugo." Alvarado pushed a button on the desk intercom. "Bring him."

The man turned his head toward a growing rumble that sounded like something being wheeled on casters. Two men came into view, pushing someone strapped to a cross-shaped table. A man lay on his back, gagged. Metal troughs fastened under the cross extended on all edges below him. The men bowed to Señor Alvarado and left the room. A man Barcelona recognized as a guard entered with a machete.

"This scum you see here," Alvarado said to Barcelona, "did not follow instructions. He—Manuel—became distracted, then greedy." Manuel jerked furiously, but his arms and legs were strapped. Alvarado turned to his guard. "Proceed."

The machete swooshed down and separated the left arm at the elbow as Barcelona winced. The guard moved to the other side of the crosslike table and sliced through the right arm. Both stubs twisted and jerked; blood spurted from arteries, while the straps held the torso firm. Barcelona became weak and had to sit back down in the chair as the machete hacked the gagged man's right foot. After the executioner had severed both feet, he removed the gag. Screams reverberated off the stone walls. Blood drained into the troughs.

The three watched Manuel spasmodically jerk his truncated limbs. When Barcelona could stand the shrieks no longer and put his hands to his ears, Alvarado motioned to the guard. A few seconds later, the assistants returned to trundle Manuel out of the room.

As distance diminished the screams, Barcelona was unable to avert Señor Alvarado's stare. Both men heard a metal door heave shut and muted wails. All the while, Señor Alvarado continued to stare into Barcelona's eyes.

"I shall ask you one last time: Barcelona, do you understand my instructions?"

CHAPTER TWO

KARL BERGMAN STOOD IN THE roseate glow of dawn at the Mexican border and the southern terminus of the Pacific Crest Trail. One of the five wooden pillars marking the PCT read 2,627 miles to Canada, but only the first sixteen miles were on Bergman's mind. Sixteen hot, arid miles that would daunt a camel. Twenty-one miles if Hauser Creek had gone dry, which his trail guide noted happened often this time of year. His dog, Blazer, sniffed the monument's sunken vertical beams, lifted his hind leg behind the tallest one, and peed. Bergman squinted south through the border fence. He half expected illegals to pop up out of nowhere, but all was quiet. The stars had disappeared; sand and sage stretched before him.

The beginning of a long-distance hike was normally a heady moment for Bergman, an experienced outdoorsman. But he didn't feel the anticipation he'd had when he thru-hiked the Appalachian Trail. Here the beginning sections were desolate and water availability a constant challenge. And he was uneasy, what with illegals trying to escape from Mexico into the United States, never mind all the other stuff about Mexican drug gangs and rival cartels. It looked like a forlorn land, and he was eager to be in mountains and forests and the Sierras, much farther north.

Bergman knelt down and adjusted the dog's saddlebags. "You ready to move out, boy?" He scratched the Belgian Malinois, mixed with a touch of shepherd. Bergman could feel the rising sun's warmth pushing away the last of night and was glad the animal wasn't too furry. He stood and planted his trekking poles on the marked path that headed north, and Blazer, sensing purpose in his master, moved ahead smartly.

He looked at the dog, but he thought about his wife, Linda. Six weeks ago, he'd gotten drunk and fought with her. He yanked a mirror off the wall, smashed it over a chair, slammed the door, and drove off—clean across his neighbor's front lawn, taking out a mailbox. An hour later he was arrested for DUI and disturbing the peace in a neighboring Massachusetts coastal town. He'd lost his license, again, and Linda—"Pack your shit!"—kicked him out. All over a couple of six-packs. Stupid thing was he'd reduced his drinking, and it was the first time he'd gotten drunk in over six months. He had been getting better.

The terrain was a flat, parched land of dun earth and sagebrush scrub. Dusty. The walking was easy, and Blazer took time to sniff rocks and tumbleweed. Bergman watched a helicopter buzz above the wire fence that separated Mexico from the United States. When he approached the town of Campo, a little over a mile north of the border, he stopped and watched two Border Patrol vehicles, spotlights still on, searching for illegals. He expected to be questioned and fingered his hiking wallet, which contained his permits. No one challenged him, though, and he and Blazer continued on until they stopped a mile north of Campo for their first water break.

"You thirsty, Blazer?"

Bergman bent down and removed a wide-rimmed Nalgene bottle from the dog's saddlebag. Blazer lapped the water. "Just a little now—we got a long day, Blazer."

Bergman looked back on Campo, a forgotten village cramped under the strengthening sun, as he unclipped one of four water bottles from the front of his pack belt. He stowed two more plastic liter bottles in each of the side pockets of his pack and an emergency bottle inside. Nine liters of water to hike twenty miles in ninety-plus-degree weather. His body hadn't adapted to the heat yet; two days ago he'd flown in from Boston, where the temperatures hovered at forty-five degrees. He turned from the morning sun and felt the cool water slide down his throat. His pack weighed twenty-five pounds, but that didn't include water, and each liter weighed over two pounds. Bergman, a Gulf War vet, was forty and as fit as he'd been in the army. He did push-ups and sit-ups every day, even after a hangover, and kept his weight at 180 pounds, packed solid on his sinewy frame.

They reached Hauser Creek in the afternoon. Blazer nosed around and found a trickle of water, but Bergman didn't like the looks of it and didn't bother pulling out his Aquamira treatments. After a long drink of the blackish water, Blazer rummaged through scrub and returned with a tattered poncho. "Watcha got, boy?" Bergman examined the blanket-like cloak; though stained and raggedy, the purple-and-brown stripes looked fresh and vivid. "Someone's been through here recently." Blazer scrounged further and found a crushed 7-Up bottle. His tail wagging, he brought it to Bergman. "Uh-huh."

That night, twenty-one miles north of the border, they camped at Lake Morena under the Big Dipper and a half-moon. Other campers were nearby, but Bergman could tell they weren't thru-hikers, those hikers who would attempt in the next five or six months to complete the PCT in one go. From where Bergman tented, angled and away, he saw a larger tent, glimpsed a frying pan, saw a flying Frisbee. He was surprised at the lack of hikers compared to the Appalachian Trail. He was starting his thru-hike at the right time of year, early enough before the desert boiled but late enough that accumulated snows would diminish sufficiently in the ten-thousand-plus-foot High Sierra by the time he got there. Whereas up to two thousand would try to hike the AT, only two to three hundred would attempt to finish the Pacific Crest trek to Canada before autumn snows.

Blazer was asleep when Bergman finished detailing the day in his trail journal. *Tired. Hot and bone dry all day. Thirsty, but for water as much as a beer.* Although too hot for campfires, several kids toasted marshmallows over a small flame in front of the large tent; hot dog and sausage smells clung to night air. He looked forlornly on the family gathered about the campfire. He couldn't help but remember the time, years ago, when he'd camped with his ex-wife. At the time, they'd been married less than a year. During a foolish argument, she'd tossed his beer into the campfire, so he got even by throwing her Kodak into the flames.

Now he'd blown it with Linda too. He was at the end of his rope. He couldn't drive for a long while, and he could only hope that his longtime partner, Tommy, would hold their kitchen and bath remodeling business together while he was gone. Bergman loved Linda. She'd been there when he needed it most. His only chance of reconciliation would be to square himself away over these next months and come back a changed man. By God, he would do just that.

Bergman turned and watched Blazer's belly twitch and wondered if the animal's dreams were troubled or pleasant. As a coyote yipped in the distance, he reached over and patted the dog's side, and Blazer squeaked out a tiny moan. At least she'd let him take the dog. They'd picked out the pup at an animal shelter two years ago. She was as attached to Blazer as he was, but Bergman had named him and always took the dog on hikes. He watched the dog breathe in comfort. As he continued to stroke Blazer, Bergman realized that whenever he hiked, he stabilized. The desire to drink would ebb and soon fold away. The excitement of adventure would take its place. Like the open backcountry road beckoning under a harvest moon, the unknown trail lured him, and he wanted only to move ahead, one foot after another.

FIVE DAYS AND SEVENTY-FIVE MILES later, Bergman saw the body. It was sprawled under a Joshua tree, thirty yards off-trail on the verge of the Anza-Borrego Desert. Just shy of noon, the body lay faceup to the sun. Blazer approached the corpse.

"Easy, Blazer."

The parched face, eyes open, was that of a young Hispanic. The right hand gripped a snapped branch, which Bergman assumed had been a hasty weapon. The branch was jagged at the end and stained the color of dried blood. Bergman crouched and looked behind him—he was alone. *Only a day*, Bergman thought as he recalled the time frame of rigor mortis. The body hadn't decomposed, so it could have been there less than twenty-four hours. The shirt was pulled up. Despite it being a crime scene, Bergman, cautious but curious, turned the body over with his foot. An X, in caked blood, scarred the man's naked back, and a hole was ground dead center into the X. Stabbed. The irregular wound was not from a bullet.

Unable to raise a signal on his cell, Bergman made notes as best he could. The man had no papers. Bergman and Blazer canvassed the area but found nothing. On his map, Bergman saw the community of

Warner Springs close to the trail, about twelve miles north. He looked up at the fulgent sun and down at Blazer, who lay watching the body from the shade of the tree. Bergman hadn't planned to hike a twenty-plus-mile day, but plans would have to change if he didn't want buzzards and coyotes to beat the authorities. He took a bandanna from his pack and covered the head with it and said a quick prayer.

That evening, calling from Warner Springs Ranch, he was directed to San Diego Homicide. He gave a report to the duty sergeant and left the ranch's phone number. Bergman had other complications on his mind and didn't want to have to deal with the matter on his cell phone. Later, after attending to Blazer, Bergman lay on the bed thinking about the dead man. Someone had had it in for this guy. And that someone wanted to send a message.

CHAPTER THREE

THE CAPTAIN OF THE SAN DIEGO Narcotics Division asked Detective
Vincent Sacco to give his report. Seven officers, including the captain,
were gathered around a burnished, worn oak conference table at headquarters. The day was sunny, and an empty coatrack looked lonely
standing in a corner.

"We all know new strains of coke and heroin surfaced in San
Diego about five months ago," Sacco said. "A few weeks later, we found
the stuff in LA and Santa Barbara. Then San Francisco. Our friends
up north tell us they've now seen it in Oregon—Ashland, Medford,
Klamath Falls."

"So what you're saying is," Captain Medina interrupted, "this stuff's
heading up the coast, and we don't have a clue as to how."

"Right, Captain."

Medina squared his notepad with the table edge and tapped the
bottom of his pen on the pad.

"It's Colombian, of course," Sacco said. "Thing of it is, this stuff is
purer and cheaper than anything out there and in greater quantity than
we've seen before."

"Why is it being introduced slowly?" an officer asked.

Sacco brushed a speck of white from his jacket. Dandruff, Medina
hoped, as he looked up at Sacco's full head of dark hair. Medina was
responsible for Sacco's recent promotion and was envious that he got to
travel and network with other departments.

"The pricing doesn't make sense," Medina said, tapping his pen on his notepad. "Shit's gotta cost bucks to be transported; its source would have to be sitting in our laps for it to be this cheap."

"Rising fuel prices alone would force the cost up," said one of the officers.

"Right," Sacco said. "Doesn't make sense. And we can't find it. We've confiscated drops all along the seaboard. This new stuff—it's not on the water. Our informants tell us nothing new is coming up I-5, and our arrests confirm this."

"It has to be airdrops," someone said.

"We've been checking everything," Sacco said, rolling closer to the table and leaning his six-foot-two body forward. "Airports—LAX on down to Podunk puddle jump. Bus stations, car rentals, trains, moving van companies. If something is capable of moving anything, we've checked it. So far, nada."

Others gave ideas and opinions while Sacco nodded and pursed his lips.

Finally, Captain Medina gathered up his folder and took a last sip of over-creamed coffee. "Well, Detective, now you know why they pay you the big bucks. Figure it out."

Later that afternoon, Sacco drove up I-5 to LA, where, as head of narcotics investigations, he would attend a similar meeting the next morning with the Los Angeles Police Department. After checking in to the motel, he headed to San Bernardino to meet his sister, Angela, for dinner.

Over ribs and beer at a local roadhouse joint, sitting at a checkered vinyl-covered table, he glanced at several framed pictures of fishermen on the wall next to him. With an array of colored flies pinned on their multipocketed jackets, the fishermen held up trout and beamed. The wall in front of him displayed photos of outdoorsmen in the San Bernardinos, the San Gabriels, and other mountains. One photo showed three hikers. He noted their backpacks—framed and shooting up behind them, with shoulder harnesses, belly strapped in front. The other side wall displayed actual fly rods, creels, and canoe paddles.

"So, Vincent, what's new?"

"Same old, same old. You?"

"Got a raise and a plaque celebrating ten years."

"Yeah?" Sacco raised his glass and clinked hers. "It's about time the skinflint came through. You're the best receptionist they've ever had. Cheers."

"Thanks." Angela fingered her black pageboy and sipped her beer.

Sacco was happy for his sister. Three years older than her brother and looking relaxed for the first time since her husband died, Angela had never reached out for the brass ring; she was content with a smaller life.

As if she read his mind, she said, "Are you ever going to settle down, Vincent, or are politics still going to take over?"

"I don't know. But I'll tell you this, as a free man, I've got little distraction other than my work, and I don't have to worry about scandals like some married men."

"You just haven't met Miss Right yet."

"I will, eventually." He looked down on his ringless hands, his clean nails. "But don't waste your time hoping to be an aunt."

She smiled.

"Have you thought about doing some traveling?" he asked. "Now that you have more time."

"Not really. It's been almost two years since I lost Matty, but I'd be lonely if I went off somewhere."

"I understand. Maybe someone else can make you less lonely."

"Maybe. We'll see."

After Sacco ordered coffees and a rice pudding with two spoons, Angela went to the restroom. Sacco sat there, looked around, and sucked on a toothpick as the waiter set down his black coffee.

He watched the waiter attend to a table of grizzled men who looked like they had just returned from an expedition outdoors. Their sunburned foreheads and tinged hair, combined with sweaty T-shirts and water-stained pants, caused Sacco to glance again at the pictures on the wall across from him. He thought of all the supplies and things hikers had to carry in those packs to last them a week or more at a time. Something began to shift in his brain just as Angela returned and sat down.

"I forgot to tell you," she said, "I found some old stuff of Matty's in the garage." She poked in her purse. "Here's a baseball from the NL championship the year before he died. Weren't you with him at the home games?"

Sacco took the ball. "I was for this one." He fingered the seams and became thoughtful.

"I'm sure he'd want you to have it."

"Very nice of you, thank you. Yes, I remember we won that game, and he was so excited he bought this ball."

In front of his sister's house, he leaned over to kiss her good-bye and then waited in the car as she walked to the bungalow and unlocked the door. Sacco worried the same sodden toothpick as he tried to nail down the thing in his mind bothering him.

CHAPTER FOUR

BARCELONA SUPPERED WITH HIS COMMANDER. El Verdugo, the evening of April 3. They were seated on the patio of Taqueria Paloma, a run-down joint in a barrio of Tecate near the US border. A shabby trellis of vines partially obscured Verdugo's view of the street, and he scraped his metal chair on scorched brick as he shifted to a better angle. Barcelona was forced to look on sage and cacti snagged with candy wrappers and scraps of paper.

"Test scores say you ran the 10K in thirty-two minutes, did eighteen pull-ups, and ninety-one push-ups," Verdugo said.

"*Sí*. Sorry, yes. I meant yes."

"And that you speak English with only a slight accent—when you remember to speak it."

"I had a boyhood friend who came from New Mexico. He spoke English perfectly, and I tried to match him."

Verdugo leaned toward him while swirling his rolled tortilla into spicy-looking menudo. Barcelona's mouth watered against his will. "I'm also told that you killed a man."

"Yes, but—"

"Doesn't matter to me. What matters is your mission."

Barcelona wished he could see Verdugo's eyes behind his sunglasses. Verdugo's charcoal hair was slicked back over his head, but Barcelona was convinced it was a toupee. He wore a gold chain around his neck and sported a large gold ring with an inlaid ruby on his left pinkie. Barcelona had at first felt lucky when he'd been plucked from prison—one of the chosen, he was told. But now he was a different kind of prisoner.

"You focus on your missions—one year of hard work, and you are a free man. Freed from that Tijuana shithole prison and flown with your wife and children to live in the great US of A." El Verdugo slurped and pointed the tortilla at Barcelona. "Manuel gave us nine months of good work before he got sloppy. He put us at risk; you could have been slammed in jail on your first mission." Verdugo shook the soggy tortilla in Barcelona's face. *"Enfocar! Comprendes?"*

"Yes," Barcelona said. *Focus!* The aroma of garlic in Verdugo's soup and the nutty smell of corn flour nearly made Barcelona swoon. Verdugo smacked his lips and sipped from his beer. Barcelona was offered no food, nothing to drink, given no money. He knew Verdugo enjoyed this display of power.

At three the following morning, Barcelona was fitted with his backpack. The owner of Taqueria Paloma had provided a small room above the restaurant's kitchen, which contained a cot, toilet, and a warped table with a lamp and a chair. Barcelona recognized the man who assisted Verdugo as the waiter at the restaurant and realized this was the waiter's room.

"Your trail name is Barcelona—any hikers you meet, that is what you go by," Verdugo said.

For over a week, Barcelona had studied southern sections of the Pacific Crest Trail. He'd been given maps to examine and had been educated and tested on where to expect water caches for hikers, natural water sources, the locations of intersections, side trails, and the usual hiker camps. At twenty-eight, Barcelona was lithe and strong with a face of angles. His legs were chiseled muscle.

"You will mule our desert routes. Do what I tell you, and you might get a change in scenery. You'll always have mules behind you and ahead of you, and you must keep the pace."

Barcelona looked up at Verdugo.

"You are one of many runners from here to Canada. I run teams down here. If you are late, or mess up, it screws up my teams. Then Mr. Alvarado calls us in for, shall we say, a visit."

Barcelona looked down to the floor and nodded.

Verdugo handed Barcelona an envelope. "Inside you'll find your California fire permit. You don't need campfires down here, but you are a long-distance hiker. If I send you to the Sierra, you may need a campfire there to accomplish your mission."

Verdugo hooked his thumbs under his belt, looked out the window briefly, and then turned back to Barcelona.

"You have your Spanish passport and your Canada entry permit in there. As trained, you are to blend in as a thru-hiker, who begins down here and finishes in Canada. Now take out the last paper and memorize it. That's your PCT thru-hiker permit. If a ranger stops you, that's who you are—Roberto DeLeon—a student from Barcelona, Spain."

"Again! What's your trail name?"

"Barcelona."

"If stopped by an official?"

Barcelona pointed to his permit and passport. "Roberto DeLeon."

Barcelona folded the papers and restored them to the envelope as he eyed a *cucaracha* scuttle beneath the desk. The roach stopped in the corner and twitched its antennae.

"In your pack, you have food for six days. You will meet me where?"

"Two hundred seven miles north of the border, Snow Creek junction, 3S01."

"When?"

"Seven days from now, April 11, at 4:00 a.m."

"I'll be coming from Palm Springs. You will rest up that day and the next—eat, drink—while another runner takes over from there. Then you will be taken to a different trailhead to begin your next mission. *Comprendes?*"

"*Sí.*"

Verdugo slapped Barcelona's face. "Barcelona! Concentrate. You speak Spanish again, I won't just slap."

The slap concussed Barcelona back to prison and to Brocomante, the inside enforcer. That's how the vicious fight had started, when Brocomante slapped him upside the head a day after Barcelona arrived.

"Okay. I meant to say *yes.*"

"You are nervous; that I don't mind. I do mind when you don't focus and talk like an illegal."

"It will not happen again, El Verdugo." Verdugo's nose reminded Barcelona of a toucan's beak, and he wanted to smash it.

Verdugo looked at his assistant and pointed to the box on the table. The assistant carried the box to Verdugo. Verdugo pulled a shiv from his boot and cut the bindings. Inside the box was an opaque, cylindrical plastic container, eighteen inches high and nine inches in diameter. It weighed twenty-seven pounds.

"Explain what this is," Verdugo demanded.

Barcelona felt the sting on his left cheek and could see the beginning of a hand-shaped mark when he glimpsed his reflection in the mirror facing him. "It's a food vault, to protect food from animals. The cover seals to keep odors contained. My mission is to deliver this on time, every time, as instructed by my field commander."

At 5:00 a.m., El Verdugo's assistant delivered Barcelona to a squat building at a dirt road a quarter-mile south of the US border. The assistant handed an envelope to a female security guard in a San Diego Gas & Electric uniform. The woman, whose name tag read Yolanda, shoved the brown envelope under her shirt and pointed the direction to Barcelona.

Three minutes later, Barcelona stood at the five short wooden pylons that marked the Pacific Crest Trail. He read the carved lettering and looked back at the wire barricade bordering Mexico and the camouflaged tunnel exit he'd just crawled through, dragging his pack. He felt a lump in his throat as he stared across toward his homeland—*I love you, Juanita, Trini, Roberto!*

CHAPTER FIVE

TULIO LOMBARDI, SHADED UNDER A felt hat, sat in the passenger seat of a green Ford Expedition. His driver, Frank, was taking him to a cabin in Sierra Meadows, California, twenty-five miles southwest of Reno and six miles due east of the Pacific Crest Trail. Lombardi and his three commanders controlled mules along PCT routes in northern California, Oregon, and Washington. He lived in Reno and reported directly to the family in New York. This afternoon he would meet with Luis Alvarado, who, with his two commanders, controlled southern and central California and answered to his cartel chief in Mexico.

"Not like the old days," Lombardi said to Frank.

Frank smiled and flicked ashes from his cigarette out over the top of the window.

"Thirty years ago, you would have picked up the spic and driven him to me. We would have spent the evening in Vegas at a front-row show. Had our ladies beside us. Now this is what it's come to—Jesus Christ, Frank, where the hell are we?"

"Should be there in a few minutes, boss. The Sierra Nevada's pretty secluded."

Lombardi shook his head as they passed another ski area. The rugged spruce, pine, and white-barked aspen followed the contours of ski trails snaking up toward a distant peak still covered in snow. "It's a young man's game now. The other day this new guy, Magnante, shows up from New York. I take him to Ponte's; he doesn't even look at the menu—says he's a vegetarian."

Frank chuckled.

"Magnante's the guy who suggested these arrangements. He looks at me with those Rodney Dangerfield eyes and tells me to take a field trip—'Check on things at the front,' he says. So now I gotta meet the spic."

At the mountainside cabin, Alvarado and Lombardi excused their assistants and got down to business. The day, May 14, was sunny and unseasonably warm at sixty-five degrees. On the cabin's screened porch, they sat at a table in rustic cushioned chairs overlooking a subalpine meadow splashed with multihued wild flowers and bear grass, large olive-colored clumps with their own stalks of creamy-white flowers. Snow-mantled peaks faced them to the north and south. Alvarado sipped tea, his mustache disappearing as he tipped his cup. Lombardi drank black coffee.

"Here's what I know, Tulio. We started this scheme nine months ago. You've crossed over into Washington State. In a month, we'll have a continuous operation—except in winter—from Mexico to Canada. Are your people happy?"

"So far," Lombardi said. "But the number of moving parts worries me."

"We have a series of routes that stretch north. A breakdown in one route doesn't kill the overall operation." Alvarado smiled.

Lombardi sat back. His paunch contrasted with Alvarado's wiry frame, but they both sported gelled gray hair combed straight back over their crowns. "But really, how long can this crazy idea last?"

Alvarado took the remark as an insult; he was, after all, the creator of the scheme but allowed that Lombardi was ignorant of this fact. Without showing any sign of pique, he deposited the remark into his memory bank.

"As long as we don't get greedy," Alvarado said.

"When I first heard about it, I thought it was someone's idea of a joke. It's nuts."

Alvarado clenched his toes. He wanted to gouge out the brown mole on the side of Lombardi's nose. "Ah, but it works." He took another sip of tea. "And we needed to do it to outflank the Cordiero cartel."

"They will figure out what we're doing."

"They may. But what can they do? War with us in the US?"

Lombardi thumbed an ant next to his saucer and flicked it off the table. "What if they expose our scheme to the feds?"

"I'm taking care of that. We are tracking their US people. I know Cordiero. He will first threaten to expose us—if he finds out. And he will understand that if he exposes us, we will also give them up, every last person. Cordiero is not a foolish man; he will be upset he hadn't thought of the idea first."

"That animosity may worsen when they see how much we've cut into their profits."

"Some, I'm sure, but my sources tell me we are getting new business, particularly in Oregon and Washington, your neck of the woods, where they aren't established."

"That doesn't worry you?"

Alvarado smiled. "The US market is enormous, enough for everybody." He tapped a forefinger on Lombardi's wrist. "And down road we'll have the jump on Canada."

The two men sat quietly and sipped their drinks. Alvarado thought about his new man, Barcelona, one of forty mules in south and central California and one of seventy-eight on the entire PCT. Barcelona was put on the first route, a 207-mile stretch from the border to a drop point near Palm Springs. Five other mules were also hauling on the same route. Each of these six men hauled a million dollars' worth of drugs. Only one of the six vaults would make its way to British Columbia three months later. Another would end up in Palm Springs in a week. The other four vaults would find their ways to LA, Reno, Vegas, Tacoma, depending on demand. And Alvarado—the chess player, the master of secret moves and traps, a man of prodigious memory—ran his part of his creation as a ringleader in a circus. Verdugo was his lion tamer. Alvarado did the math in his mind again: Thirteen routes spanning both borders. Six mules to a route. Assuming thirteen mules at rest at any given time, sixty-five others were always hauling. Sixty-five million dollars! Yes, his boss and the Americans were happy.

Lombardi heard the sound of crunched gravel and saw a muddied Jeep Wrangler pull up as Alvarado looked at his watch.

"I have a surprise for you," Alvarado said.

A muddied, sweaty young man with wild hair and full beard stepped from the passenger side of the Jeep. A belt hooked with water bottles was strapped around his hiking pants, and he wore a ragged hooded fleece. Alvarado's central California commander, Jaime, stepped from the driver side and led the man onto the porch.

Lombardi looked at the smile of even teeth and into the man's eyes. "Mother of God—Nino!—is that you?"

LATER THAT AFTERNOON, LOMBARDI CROSSED the threshold into the den. Alvarado was seated at a table studying a book on chess openings; he had a chessboard with pieces set up in front of him.

"Thank you for the surprise," Lombardi said. "It was a pleasure to visit with my godson. I leave shortly, but you are staying here for the night?"

"Yes."

"Can I bring *you* someone?"

Alvarado smiled. "Sure. Send me a woman with big tits, who likes to fuck and is smart and classy. Oh, and who is an expert chess player."

CHAPTER SIX

As KARL BERGMAN WALKED OUT of the lobby at Warner Springs Ranch the next morning, the desk clerk, phone in hand, yelled to him. "Sir, it's the police; they want to speak with you."

Bergman turned back and took the phone.

"Mr. Bergman? Detective Sacco, San Diego Narcotics. I have a report in front of me that claims you found a dead man—stabbed—on the Pacific Crest Trail."

"That's correct."

"This says he was a young adult Hispanic."

"Correct."

"Mr. Bergman, I'd like to talk with you. I can be at the lodge at noon. I'll buy you lunch."

"Thanks, but I gave my full report. Can't we go over this now? I'd like to get back on the trail."

"Not on the phone—I'll be there by noon."

Bergman left his pack and poles in the lobby and went out to walk the ranch with Blazer. He squinted at a distant mesa already shimmering under the morning sun and stooped to retie a loose shoelace. Bergman planned to order a beer or two when the detective took him to lunch. He could drink on the government's dime. That would be a switch!

Bergman thought about his sons again. The divorce eleven years ago had been his fault. Again, a drinking problem had thrown the marriage on the rocks. His ex-wife claimed the problem stemmed from his army tours during the Gulf Wars and had requested that he get counseling.

He had, and he'd scanned a few brochures the counselors gave him on PTSD. But Bergman dropped out after only three sessions. He'd insisted that he was fine but admitted he did like to drink. After the split, Gloria took his two boys to a different ocean on the opposite side of the country. Passionate thru-hikers who complete the Appalachian Trail in the east gravitate to the Pacific Crest Trail in the west, a pull that worked out favorably for Bergman, who was eager to see his sons.

Before meeting the detective, Bergman had some time to soak his feet in the mineral waters of the town's namesake spring. The almost hot, sulfur-smelling spring felt luxurious, and his feet welcomed the roiling massage. Truth be known, Bergman wanted to become a "triple crowner," a coveted title bestowed on those elite thru-hikers who complete the three major long-distance trails in the USA: Appalachian, Pacific Crest, and Continental Divide trails. The PCT—a backpacker's dream hike, featuring exhilarating mountain scenery after the drylands in the far south—was officially dedicated on National Trails Day in 1993. So it was still relatively new, and Bergman was pumped. The trail crossed seven national parks, including Yosemite.

Sacco was nearly a head taller than Bergman and had a firm handshake and busy eyes. "Your dog?"

"Yes. Blazer. Where I go, he goes, even lunch."

"Would sandwiches from the grocery store deli be okay?"

"Perfect. I need to get some miles in today, so I don't have time for a fancy lunch."

They unwrapped chicken salad subs at a picnic table Sacco secured behind the store. Sacco broke off an end and gave it to Blazer. While the dog ate, Sacco rubbed Blazer's ears.

Bergman brushed some twigs from the table. "What can I do for you, Mr. Sacco? I don't have anything to add that wasn't in my report."

"Mr. Bergman, how would you like your newest DUI removed from your record?"

"How do you know about that?"

"Mr. Bergman, it's my business to know things."

They chewed in silence.

"I backchecked you, found your license suspensions, went from there. Look, Bergman, I'm not here to impress you or to threaten you. I need your help."

"So you know about the rest of it too."

"Resisting arrest. Three weeks in jail. Your arraignment. Yes." Sacco dropped another piece of his roll under the table for Blazer.

"The report says you fought off the first officer, splitting his lip, and it took two to subdue you. It's all there. Frankly, I'm surprised the judge let you off so easy when you could have been charged with assaulting a police officer. What's your version?"

"The report is correct. I spent time in jail. My wife wouldn't raise bail."

"No one else could bail you out?"

"I didn't ask."

"You're a decorated former army officer. Two tours in the Middle East. I'm sure that helped your case. Your file also contains a stern warning from the court judge, citations, and several letters of complaints from others." Sacco cocked his head at Bergman. "After a few drinks, it appears you get worked up. But I'm here to discuss other business. As I said, I need your help."

"What kind of help?"

Sacco glanced around to make sure their conversation was private and leaned in toward Bergman. "Okay. As I said, I'm with the narcotics division. I have a hunch that hard drugs and this trail are connected. Do you see packhorses or donkeys out here?"

"I'm not sure I like where this is going. But no, not here. Up in the mountains maybe."

"Uh-huh. A stabbed Hispanic trying to defend himself on the PCT makes me suspicious. We know this is a little-used trail that happens to stretch to Canada."

Bergman shrugged his shoulders.

"How would a cartel haul drugs out here? ATVs, dirt bikes?"

Bergman eyed him. "I have no idea. Maybe the PCT isn't connected at all."

"That's where I need your help. We can educate you on what to look for."

"Hold on a minute, Detective. I haven't done anything wrong here, and I didn't come out here to get educated."

"True. I'm moving a little too fast. My bad."

They finished their sandwiches without another word, but Sacco didn't take his eyes off Bergman. Blazer was asleep. Bergman broke the silence.

"Why me? Don't you guys have people?"

"Not experienced long-distance hikers—like those who've done the Appalachian Trail," Sacco casually added before inserting a potato chip into his mouth.

"So what else do you know about me?"

"Listen." Sacco leaned in. "Even if I had a department guy to do this, he would look like a cop. You look like a hiker and won't raise a red flag. And you have military training."

Bergman said nothing. Blazer napped.

"You can stuff a lot in those backpacks, am I right?"

Bergman frowned. "If you're going with this discussion where I think you're going, a hiker can't pack drugs. It would be too much. He has to carry food, water, and supplies, aside from his tent, sleeping bag, and pad. Pack weight is always the number one issue for a hiker."

"Guess how much ten kilos—that's twenty-two pounds—of pure coke is worth on the street?"

Bergman shrugged his shoulders.

"Eight hundred thousand dollars plus. And pure heroin isn't that much less."

"No. It's way too much. I keep my pack at twenty-five pounds. Add your twenty-two plus water, and you're at sixty. It's hard to go above forty. Too much to haul in these conditions."

"Okay, so maybe it's fifteen pounds at half a million. The point is I need to get this checked out. I have a hard time accepting the idea that a hiker would crawl over deserts and mountains for fun, but you're proof people do it. Maybe it's a stretch to think people would do it to smuggle drugs . . . yet it could be done. Am I right?"

"What about getting park rangers to help you?"

"I've thought about that. Two problems: They have individual areas of responsibility, so too many would have to get involved. And some of them may be abetting the operation, if my guess is right. Two months ago, we arrested a ranger who was doped out in Boulder Oaks

Campground. Tried to collect money from campers when there were no fees. No. I need someone like you. Someone who knows the culture, who isn't from around here, and who has reason to see this through with us."

"And you think I've got reason."

Sacco looked at him while wiping his mouth with a napkin. He put down the napkin but kept his eyes on Bergman.

Bergman gathered up his wrappings and wadded them as if making a snowball. "Well, I'll keep my eyes and ears open for you, but that's it."

Sacco looked at Blazer. "The dog smart?"

"Yeah. He's a good animal."

"Okay, look. You are in a position to help us as well as your country—"

"You don't have to give me the God and country pitch, Mr. Sacco." Bergman looked again at the mountains shimmering on the horizon. They called to him. He wanted to move to them.

"I read up on you and your service in Desert Storm, the Gulf. I lost a cousin in Iraq. Mr. Bergman, how about I get your dog trained to sniff drugs, and while that's being done, we can advise and train you in our end of the business."

Bergman looked at Blazer, who was stretched on his side. "Let me think this over. I'm not up for jumping off the trail right now—hell, I just got started."

"We'll put you up in a nice place, at our expense, and give you a per diem."

"I can't make a decision right now."

Sacco started to say something but closed his mouth and pushed some crumbs off the table.

Bergman stood up.

"Mr. Bergman—sit down a minute."

Bergman stood still. There was something different in Sacco's eye, and when Sacco spread his arm to offer him back his seat, Bergman sat.

"You come through for me, I'll get that DUI fixed, and we'll clean up your record. How about it, Bergman?"

Bergman eyed the dog and finally turned to Sacco. "If I were to do this, you'd have some things to learn. Like we all have trail names out here. I go by Awol. Just call me Awol."

"Trail names. How does that work?"

Bergman fidgeted, but if Sacco was to be successful, he had to know the basics.

"Long-distance hikers have adopted the convention of anonymity. I don't know how it started, but we all go by trail names instead of our given names. In some cases, that's all a hiker reveals. In the hiking culture, we don't probe into the lives of others."

"What a perfect setup for a mule. Okay, Awol, Mr. Absent Without Leave. Will you accept my offer?"

"Detective, this is not what I came out here for. I wish now I hadn't called and given my report. Can I at least have a few days to think about it?"

"Awol, the longer we wait, the more they become entrenched."

"Wait a minute. You don't even know if drugs are being hauled up the PCT. It's pure speculation, right?"

"All right, a few days. Call me at this number. Okay?" Sacco handed him his card.

Bergman—Awol—stuck it in a pocket. "And if I don't call?"

Sacco put his hand up. "Let's not go there, okay? I can get your life back on track. Don't throw that away, Awol."

Awol—watched Sacco disappear around the corner of the store. While Blazer still napped, Awol sat there contemplating his options. He figured his life was headed for renewed turbulence, but maybe for the good this time. Either way, the least he owed himself was a few days of quiet and peace on the trail.

CHAPTER SEVEN

TWO HOURS LATER, AWOL SWIGGED water beneath an afternoon sun. The thermometer on his watch read ninety-two, and it felt like he was surrounded by an open-fire furnace. Though he could see mountains to the east and west, the landscape stretching around him was dominated by thickets of chaparral, which in the hot sun smelled like a mix of creosote and turpentine and was known as greasewood because of its texture and explosive flammability. He opened Blazer's water bottle and held it for him.

"Don't be sloppy now." Blazer wasn't finished when Awol capped the bottle. "I know. Best I can do."

He took a minute to pull down the neck veil pinned on the back of his sun hat. *God, it's like Iraq,* he thought as he trudged the sandy, rock-strewn path. Blazer wasn't sniffing as much now, and he stayed on the trail; his tongue hung out as he panted. Awol had hiked five miles out of Warner Springs and had seen no signs of potable drink at Agua Caliente Creek, where he was now. The next sure water was Tule Canyon, twenty-three miles away. He pictured gullies of sweet flowing water as he and Blazer tramped by clumps of spiny-paddled prickly pear cactus and the feared jumping cholla, a cacti with brownish pads of spines that dare one to brush up against them. The needle-sharp spines attach to clothes, skin, shoes, and if you are sweaty—as Awol was now—the tips curve when making contact on skin, locking the spines underneath.

An hour later, Awol parked for a rest under a multibranched Joshua tree and watched Blazer pick the least sunny spot to lie down. Awol twisted his backpack and yanked the Velcro holding his small trekking umbrella.

He remembered asking the salesgirl in Eastern Mountain Sports, "Now what the hell is that?" He flexed the taut silver dome, nestled it among the tree's measly sword-shaped leaves, and was surprised at how well it blocked the sun.

That night, Awol forwent the tent and cowboy camped near two Joshuas, one of them bent over and hunched. He was a mere ten miles north of Warner Springs—Detective Sacco had made it a short day. Before he sat down to journal details of the afternoon trek, he poked about the campsite with his poles to ward off any snakes. He'd seen two rattlers today, one of them a sidewinder. Next to Awol's pack, Blazer lay panting. It was still a furnace out. After writing, Awol repacked the journal and watched a sliver of moon low in the sky. All was silent.

In the night, a combination of hushed voices nearby and something inching over his stomach aroused Awol. Blazer growled. Awol lay on his foldout pad atop the warm sand and eyed the creepy thing on his stomach. He gave the fist-sized tarantula a bat and watched its busy legs twitch and jump as it scuttled over him and away. Tarantulas were harmless, but the big spiders gave him the heebie-jeebies. Remembering the voices, Awol stilled and listened. Nothing, but then what sounded like a shout of Spanish up the trail. Hand on his Buck knife, Awol waited in a crouch, listening. They'd left; it was quiet. A moment later he heard scratching, and Blazer yipped and charged as Awol shined his hiking lamp. A javelina darted under a cactus, and Blazer gave up. Awol hoped that was all it was—he smelled the musky scent now.

He couldn't get back to sleep and lay on his back staring at the multitude of stars. He'd read about the grand, heavenly displays of the desert but didn't expect anything like this. He was at the bottom of an overturned bowl with a complete absence of artificial light and a 180-degree panorama before him. At first, Awol wondered at the vague white glimmer up to his right. *What's that cloud doing here at night?* He realized he was looking at the Milky Way. Not a cloud at all, but stars--stars upon stars.

He stared at the heavens, knowing sleep had also scuttled away, and considered his plight. He knew Linda loved him. He'd been able to help her through some rough spots and had paid off all her long-standing debts when they'd gotten married. He thought about Sacco's request. Getting this DUI expunged and his record "cleaned up" would be huge. A fresh start for both of them, if he could quit the drinking. She loved Blazer too, so he needed to bring him back safe and sound. But he also came out here because he wanted to reestablish a bond with his sons. And he'd wanted to hike the PCT for years. Getting in over his head was not new to Awol, and he knew it would happen with Sacco . . . but at what cost? As the heavens absorbed him, he relaxed but felt insignificant.

He awoke to Blazer licking his face. "Okay, I know you're hungry. Be patient." He rolled to his side and pressed the illuminator on his watch—5:15 a.m. He looked at the sky and noted the beginnings of light; still plenty of stars, but he couldn't make out the Milky Way anymore. When Blazer began to whimper, Awol got up and stretched. The temperature felt cozy, and that was bad news this early. He took out Blazer's food and watched the animal eat. When he packed up and went to the shaded trees for his water, two of his treated bottles were missing. "Fuck!"

Awol concentrated. Sand, chamiso, and sagebrush stretched to the massif and mesas on the horizon; hardly daybreak, and the earth felt parched. He'd cameled up at Warner Springs, and he had his emergency bottle. He rechecked his guide; eighteen miles to Tule Canyon. He remembered the voices from the night before. They'd swiped two bottles, and he'd used up three. That left him with four bottles, and Blazer would need some of that. "Shit!"

Late morning, and the sun in an empty sky starched the earth. He could smell the heat that rose in the clouds of dust kicked up as he tramped. Even Blazer, in front of him, stirred up enough swirls of sand to make Awol cough and spit. Halfway, nine miles out and doing fair with water, Blazer started barking a fit. Awol heard the rattles. The snake, a diamondback rattler, lay ahead and didn't move from its spot. Awol was amazed at the racket the reptile made. "C'mon, Blazer. Let's give this guy a wide berth." Awol—one eye on the rattler, the other on his new path— steered around, and finally Blazer did the same. "Good work, Blazer. Keep your eye and snout out." They both looked back and watched the snake slither to a dead yucca that promised lizards.

Awol knew he was getting close to water because the wiry desert chaparral, normally spotty and knee-high, was now invasive and nearly chest-high. Blazer started pawing at Awol, because whenever he barked for water, his master kept plodding. They made it to the canyon creek with half of the last bottle left between them. Awol, relieved to be at water, tottered to the creek and bent down at water's edge. He'd rationed wisely, but his muscles were depleted.

They had no sooner set up camp when Blazer's bark announced another hiker. A young guy hobbled to the creek with only a passing glance to the dog and Awol. He sat down, shoved off a tall above-the-shoulders pack, and removed his left boot and sock. He winced as he massaged his toes under the water. Awol wandered over.

"Got a blister?"

"Scorpion."

"Don't know much about scorpions, but I've heard—"

"Aaaach, Jesus."

"—that they aren't as bad as the black widow," Awol finished.

Blazer went over and sniffed the hiker's foot. The mutt wrinkled his nose and then proceeded to investigate the pack, whereupon the hiker shooed him away.

"Let me look at it," Awol said. The man's big toe was swollen and burned red. "Dude. You need to wash it, rest it, and give it air."

The man looked around. "I'll be all right. Need to move on."

Awol wondered what the hurry was; it was getting dark, and this was a good creekside camp spot. "Well, you should at least wash the sting and bandage it. Got antibacterial soap?"

"No." He looked at Awol for the first time then glanced at his watch.

Awol went to his pack and returned with a small plastic bottle of Mountain Suds wash and several Band-Aids. The man took the bottle and Band-Aids and washed the toe and rinsed it in the creek. Blazer ventured to the bare foot, sniffed, and when the man patted him, Blazer licked his face.

"What's the dog's name?"

"Blazer."

"How you doing, Blazer? You like this big toe?"

The man put two Band-Aids around it while Blazer watched. The hiker took a new sock from his pack and turned it inside out before putting it on then put his boot back on and tied it loose.

"Thank you very much," he said as he handed Awol the soap bottle and remaining bandages.

Awol took the bottle and gave him back two bandages, along with several Tylenol caplets. "You might need those; I've got more. You thru-hiking?"

"Yes."

Awol extended his hand. "I'm Awol."

"Barcelona," he said as they shook hands.

Blazer and Awol watched Barcelona deftly stone-step across the canyon creek and move to brush sixty yards upstream. He crouched, filling his water bottles. The man looked back at Awol only once.

CHAPTER EIGHT

BARCELONA WAS RUNNING LATE. If he ever wanted to escape the heat of the drylands and move to the cooler climate of the southern California mountains, he'd have to finish his missions on time. But the damn toe hurt. Even after he cut a hole in his boot to give it air, it throbbed and burned, slowing him down. At 4:08 a.m., after his usual seven-day haul, Barcelona staggered into the junction to meet El Verdugo. The Jeep lights blinked once, and Verdugo emerged.

"You're eight minutes late. What's the problem, Barcelona?"

Barcelona pointed to his toe; flesh stuck from his boot. "Scorpion."

"Get in," Verdugo said.

On the way to the town of Cabazon, Verdugo glanced at the foot Barcelona was massaging. "Don't you know enough to check in your boots?"

"It's my fault, Verdugo. I should have been more careful."

After a few minutes, Verdugo said, "You've done okay. That swelling will go away in time for your new route."

A half hour later, Barcelona was dropped off on the outskirts of town at a place that looked like a poor farmer's casa. The agave plants by the busted trellis looked marginal and crooked. A sego lily sagged by a forgotten wire fence. Verdugo grabbed Barcelona's backpack as a stooped ranchero slid out of the doorway.

"Mr. Gomez will get you what you need. I'll be back for you the day after tomorrow at four a.m. Study the next couple hundred miles, from 3S01 to Shady Gap."

"But you have my—"

Verdugo pinched Barcelona's shoulder and leaned his face within inches of Barcelona's eyes. "You listen more. I said Mr. Gomez will get you what you need."

Barcelona reviewed what Gomez gave him but couldn't get much information out of the man. Whenever Barcelona made the effort to converse, Gomez shut down. That evening, after Barcelona put his maps away, he asked Gomez where he was raised and if he had family. Gomez looked at him, slid a withered index finger along his Adam's apple, and skulked away.

Early next morning, while Gomez was sleeping, Barcelona discovered a PCT map stuck in an atlas. It showed the entire trail, but the nearest cities to the PCT were inserted in longhand—Palm Springs, San Diego, Los Angeles. Farther north, Reno, which was underlined in red ink. He looked up to the top and noted Klamath Falls, Bend, Yakima. Looking closer, he noted hand-drawn arrows and closed loops along the PCT and its access roads. All the arrows pointed north, and they multiplied near cities. No arrows pointed south. The closed loops looked like pickup routes resembling his own. *The stuff always moves north*, he figured.

AWOL AND BLAZER APPROACHED SADDLE Junction, 179 miles north of the border and 5 miles east of the biker/hiker town of Idyllwild, California. It had been four days since he'd seen Sacco, and he owed him a decision.

Blazer sniffed the air and Awol smelled a tinge of smoke and oil, immediately reminding him of Iraq. His stomach turned as memories of another time and place climbed into his brain. *I may have intentionally killed a man.* As they started down from the saddle on the Devil's Slide Trail, stepping over pinecones the size of his shoes, Awol heard what had to be Harleys and Hondas a few miles away. The sound triggered visions of Bradley M2 infantry fighting vehicles churning through dust and desert. *One of our own—a fellow American.* Two miles later, Awol and Blazer trudged down a rough road and came to a pullout; a jalopy of a red pickup was dropping off hikers with daypacks. Awol welcomed the reality that he was far from the Middle East, but he had apprehensions about going into town. He needed to keep his head on straight.

He was muddy and smelly and hadn't shaved in nearly a week, but he suspected the driver of the pickup was used to such wild looks. He approached, catching the driver's eye and looking hopeful.

"If you're going to Idyllwild, I'm heading there now," the driver said.

"All right! Today's my lucky day. Can my dog catch a ride too?"

Blazer looked sharp as he sat up on the seat and sniffed. Awol was proud of the animal. Awol's mind was full, and at least Blazer, so far, had been low maintenance. In no time, they were driven to the town center rotary and dropped off.

Idyllwild was a haven for hikers, but bikers took over on weekends. Motorcycles in all sizes and colors, festooned with saddlebags, mirrors, and antennas, were parked all around the village center. Standing in town, as bikers revved in and out of spots, Awol found it hard to believe that in over three days he had seen only one other person. An attractive thirty-something woman was standing by a bike he assumed was hers, and he thought about asking if he could take her bike for a spin. He would, of course, insist she go with him. He felt the growing in his crotch as he imagined her arms and hands circling his waist as he gunned her bike through town and up into the mountains. Blazer nosed his leg in the nick of time and jarred him out of his reverie.

He got a first-floor room at Idyllwild Inn, took care of Blazer, and then checked in with his business partner, Tom—Linda's brother—back in Boston. After Awol had been arrested, Tom had agreed to hold the business together until Awol returned from his hike in hopes the trip would help him get his act together.

"If that new bid in Quincy comes through," Tom said, "we'll have plenty of work. The crew is getting antsy."

"Sounds good. Listen, how's Linda?"

He wanted to hear Linda's voice, but she was clear about not wanting to hear from him other than accepting an e-mail with his location every couple of weeks. At least she wanted him alive, which was a start.

"Well, she's a lot more than pissed, I'd have to say. And she's done praying."

"I really fucked up."

"Yes, you did. And that's the same thing you told me the last time."

"Yeah. I know."

"You need to get it together. It might be too late."

A pause. "Tell her Blazer's doing great. Tell her that he misses her almost as much as I do. Okay?"

After showering away a week's worth of sand, dirt, sweat, sunscreen, and bug spray, he bought a newspaper in the Paradise Café and ordered food enough for two: salad, gumbo, tamales. He flipped through the paper, checking sports for news of the Red Sox, and began reading an article about marijuana being grown in California forests. The pot farms were run by Mexican cartels, the article said, and Mexican drug lords were sending immigrants to grow the marijuana. Sacco had been talking hard drugs, but this was also going on. He read further: "They are willing to kill anybody who gets in their way. . . .These aren't Cheech and Chong operations." An agent was shown clutching three plants purported to be worth twelve thousand dollars on the streets. "Plants grow under towering trees, preventing aerial view, and are a two- to four-hour hike from the nearest road. For years, Mexican drug cartels have used the remote forest to conduct and conceal their business. But pot production has intensified because it has become harder and harder to smuggle marijuana across the US–Mexico border." Awol looked to the mountains. He knew hard drugs were worth a lot more than pot. If these guys were hauling coke and heroin up the Pacific Crest Trail, then Sacco was on to something. *But slogging over the Sierra? The Cascades?* Only about three hundred miles of the total PCT could pass as level; the rest was up and down.

Awol sat there trying to enjoy the gumbo, fiddling with his spoon. The call to Tom troubled him. He couldn't go through another divorce. He loved Linda! *If Sacco could—*

"Is everything okay, sir?"

Awol looked at his waiter, not realizing he'd approached. He watched two men hoist Bud Lights at the table in front of him. "I'll have a Bud Light."

But as the waiter was walking away, Awol called out, "Wait! Never mind."

He pulled out Sacco's card and punched numbers into his cell.

Before he left town, he found a florist in the yellow pages and ordered a desert bouquet to be delivered with a note saying: *Blazer misses you too.*

CHAPTER NINE

Awol SPENT THE NEXT FOUR weeks off-trail in alcohol rehab. Sacco had made the arrangements. That was the only way Sacco could clear his DUI, he'd said. "Could or would?" Awol had countered. Sacco didn't flinch, and Awol had agreed.

With the approval of Sacco's new boss, they decided to keep Captain Medina out of the loop regarding this new recruit. Sacco had suspicions and convinced his chief that the PCT operation should be kept secret; only he and the chief knew.

During the four weeks Awol was in rehab and the two weeks following, Blazer was trained to detect cocaine and heroin and to respond to commands. "We'll give your dog the down and dirty on two drugs," Sacco said. "The good news is he's smart and eager. But we can't fine-tune him to make him a true drug dog—we don't have the time." And neither did Awol, who was antsy every time Sacco briefed him on operations and procedures in the final two weeks.

He reported to a cheap hotel conference room a mile away from Sacco's office. Awol felt cramped there, out of place. There was only one window, and he couldn't even see out of it, because he'd been installed at a table overlooking a closed door. He hated the hotel, which was also his home at night.

Awol was given a GPS, a satellite phone with turbo-dial direct to Sacco, and a PLB, a personal locator beacon, to signal his exact location in any emergency. When Sacco handed Awol what he thought was a notebook but was in reality a police log—"Just something you can scribble in to record details"—Awol reluctantly shoved it into his pack, not happy about the extra weight.

At the end of the last week, Awol was allowed to break away for a few days to find his sons. He hadn't seen either in ten years.

He took a bus and then a cab to meet his younger son, seventeen-year-old Gregory, after his classes at a private boarding school. Gloria, his ex, had given him the address and phone number.

To keep it informal, Awol suggested they take a walk around the campus. Gregory spoke only when spoken to and, although polite, walked with head down, hands in pockets, like he didn't want to be recognized. He had his mother's full cheeks and thin lips.

"So," Awol said, "how do you like it here?"

"You mean here at school?"

"Yeah. And out here in California too."

"I don't remember being anywhere else—than California, I mean."

"I see. Well, I hated to see you all go. I hope you know that."

Gregory glanced at him but didn't say anything.

"Do they make you wear that sport coat everywhere?"

Gregory removed the coat and carried it over a shoulder.

"You didn't have to take it off. I mean—"

"Are you seeing Kenny too?"

"Yes."

"And Mom?"

"Well, I don't know if that's a good idea. She told me your stepdad is ill."

Gregory said nothing, and Awol became frustrated because he didn't know what to say either, or how to act. After forty minutes of failed effort to draw him out, Awol put his hand on Gregory's shoulder.

"Well, I've bored you enough today. I can imagine how you must feel. This guy, my father, who I never see and don't know, drops by . . ."

"It's okay. Thanks for coming."

"Gregory, listen. You and your brother mean a lot to me. Your mother too. But you are my flesh and blood. I made some huge mistakes back then. The split with your mom was my fault, and I'll always regret losing you guys."

They had stopped in front of the main gate where they had started.

Gregory looked around him and behind him.

"I tried to keep in touch after you and Kenny left. You were both little. I went through hell. I got out to see you guys a couple of times, but . . ."

Gregory stood there looking embarrassed.

"It's just . . . well . . ." Awol wanted so much to hug Gregory, to bring him close even for a moment. He waited for some type of response, an opening.

Gregory put his coat back on and threw out a hand. "Thanks. I have to go."

Awol grabbed the hand as Gregory turned to go. "So, we'll stay in touch then?"

"Okay."

Awol took a step closer and saw Gregory stiffen and look down and away. "I know you'll see your mother this weekend." He handed Gregory an envelope. "Please give her this."

The next day, after a night in another cheap room, Awol tried a more informed approach with Kenny, now a twenty-year-old sophomore at UCLA. Awol showed up at the main campus and started walking around. After identifying himself at the bursar's office, he learned what residence hall Kenny lived in. Late that afternoon—after touring the athletic facility, the library, and the student union—he parked himself near the dining room of Kenny's dorm. Gregory had said that Kenny worked the dinner shift and was some type of manager.

Awol sat in the outer lobby. Earlier he'd procured a visitor day pass that allowed him to buy dinner at the hall. Two girls showed up and deposited a slotted, gift-wrapped carton on top of a table. They smiled at Awol and taped a poster to hang on the table in front of the green box. "GO GREEN" it said. "Petition your Congressman—stop wasting energy, and GO GREEN." He was about to ask them if they knew his son when he spotted a skinny boy coming through a side door near the inside serving line. Although it had been years, Awol felt an instant connection. He watched him set up money trays at the two registers and make notations in a pad. A few minutes later, the narrow-faced boy with Awol's curly, dirty-blond hair talked with the cashiers who seated themselves at their registers. His neck was pushed forward at an angle off his spine. He looked haggard, worn.

Later, after selecting his food and paying the cashier, Awol glanced around. He didn't want to distract his son from his work, so he chose a small table near the wall. Adjacent tables filled and, when abandoned, filled again as Awol nursed his food and pretended to read the campus paper. He refilled a Diet Coke and sneaked a glance at what appeared to be a small office near the kitchen, but he didn't see Kenny. After an hour, the hall had only a few occupied tables left. As Awol looked up, he saw his curly haired son loping toward him. His skin was white except for a tanned left forearm, and he walked lopsided. Awol absorbed the boy's hazel eyes and gulped when the boy grinned and stood in front of him. "Dad?"

Awol stood and shook his son's limp hand. "Hello, Kenny. Yeah, I'm your dad."

"Mom called me last night. Said she gave you my number."

"I should have called you."

"Not a problem." Kenny sat down.

For the next half hour, they talked about Kenny, his girlfriend, his plans for graduate school. "Biochemistry! Well you certainly inherited your mother's brains."

Kenny was interested in Awol's hike and kept coming back to it. "So you'll go all the way? A guy in my fraternity did the PCT in California but had to finish Oregon and Washington the next year."

Another half hour passed, and Awol sensed it was time to end their talk. They had both absorbed a lot of information.

"Listen," Awol said, "would you and your girlfriend like to join me for dinner tomorrow? And I'd like Gregory to come, if he is willing. You guys pick the place. And, if you don't mind, maybe you could drive?"

They had a friendly dinner the following night—Kenny got his assistant to sub for him—but Gregory, who had initially accepted the invitation, wasn't in the car when Awol had walked up to it.

"No Gregory?"

"He says he's sorry," Kenny said. "His Latin teacher has him in some remedial class, which is tonight. This is Jill."

Jill was a delight; shy at first, but articulate. It warmed Awol's heart to see her sit close to Kenny and focus on him when he spoke. Her presence emboldened Kenny, who spoke all the louder, with confidence and with measured enunciation, about campus sports, current events. Whenever Kenny turned to face her, she grinned.

"Kenny says you have a dog," Jill said. "I love dogs."

"Do you have one?" Awol asked.

"I did. But she stayed home with my mom, in Utah. Now my brother has her."

"What breed?" Awol asked.

"A springer spaniel. I named her Phoebe."

"I don't see spaniels much anymore."

Jill pulled out two pictures of the dog, one with her holding Phoebe beside Jill's mother.

"I know," she said. "Goldens and labs are all the rage now."

"Neat," Awol said as he looked at the other picture of the dog beside her brother, the brother on one knee, the butt of his shotgun on the ground between them.

"She loves to hunt with him. I'll probably let him keep her, now that I'm out here for three more years."

Later, while Awol had coffee and they had ice cream for dessert ("One scoop, two spoons," Jill had told the waitress), Awol sensed the only turbulence of the evening.

"You should tell your father about—"

Kenny stiffened and looked hard at her.

Jill shrugged her shoulders and looked away.

When Jill went to the ladies' room, Awol said, "You have enough to do without putting up with me, but I have one more night here. If you have a few minutes after work tomorrow, maybe I could see you again."

"It would have to be at the dining hall," Kenny said.

The following night, Awol read the campus paper and the local as he waited for Kenny to finish up. The academic year was winding down; earlier, he'd seen postings for summer classes. He was proud the boy was working, but it bothered him that his son looked peaked. Weak. Awol watched Kenny breathe through his mouth as he wiped a smear of OJ off the side of a Minute Maid juice dispenser. His T-shirt hung off bony shoulders, and he wobbled. Awol thought about Gregory and wished he'd not been so distant. But at least he'd reached out to Gregory and had made contact. He thought about trying to see him once more before heading back to LA, but Awol didn't know if he wanted to face more rejection. The flimsy excuse Gregory gave last night hurt.

Finally, Kenny slumped at Awol's table. He looked weary. He hadn't shaved, and Awol thought he smelled alcohol. He watched Kenny stick another mint into his mouth.

"Want one?"

Awol declined, now certain Kenny was masking his breath.

"You know, Kenny, hiking out in the forests and mountains"—Awol stopped for a second and refolded his napkin—"what it does is, it cleanses your soul."

Kenny was silent.

"I've learned some things out there. And it keeps you in great shape." Kenny smiled, and his father patted his arm. "You should try it. Come hike with me for a while."

"Sounds nice, but I can't."

"Why not? I'm only talking a few weeks."

Kenny looked down at the table and shook his head.

"You're quiet tonight."

Kenny pulled out another mint.

"Jill is terrific, by the way. How long have you known her?"

"Two years."

"What is it Kenny?"

"Sorry, I can't get into it."

"Is it something to do with Jill?"

Kenny brightened. "I wish it was." He played with a salt shaker.

"Now I feel like I'm talking to your brother."

Kenny smiled. "He's always been quiet."

"I love you guys." Awol started to tear up but caught himself in time.

"Thanks, Dad. So, I'll tell Mom you said hello."

"Kenny, is it alcohol?"

Kenny looked up. "No. It's nothing. Everything's under control."

Awol waited for Kenny to remake eye contact.

Kenny stood, but Awol stayed seated, his eyes not leaving his son. Kenny looked past his father. "All right. I went through a drug problem. I'm okay now, and a little drinking is a lot better than drugs. But I owe some people, and I can't just take off for a few weeks."

CHAPTER TEN

TULIO LOMBARDI HUDDLED OVER THE map with his godson, Nino. It was the middle of June in Reno, and this time Lombardi's driver had brought the young man to him. Lombardi had his arm around Nino's shoulder as they stood in the twilight in front of a man-made waterfall that accented Lombardi's hedges and gardens. The waterfall contoured around three planted spruces, pooled at each tree, and then finished its descent into a man-made pond filled with water lilies, carp, and koi.

"This is how we'll do it, Nino. Enough snow has melted; the southern Cascades are passable. From now on you'll hike from the crest to Route 89 and meet Frank at the river in Lassen Volcanic Park." Lombardi put a finger on the map. "Frank's picked a little-used trailhead, right about here."

Nino scratched at his neck. Mosquitoes were rampant on the trails, and he'd used up all his DEET. He looked like he had measles.

"Uncle Tulio, how come we can't drive it in like we've been doing?"

"Narcs are all over the place. This is a high distribution area. They know something is up and are ready to pounce."

"So we hike it up, over the crest."

"Right. The stuff will disappear right under their noses. They'll reduce manpower here and look somewhere else."

"What happens when the snows come?"

"We bring the shit back down." Lombardi squeezed Nino's shoulder. "But by then, you'll be out of here."

Nino smiled at Tulio. "How come they didn't tell you where I was?"

"This thing has been so secret, even your mother didn't know where you were. I knew you went on special assignment to Palm Springs, that you were expected back in the fall. Now I'm told you were given a choice."

"I didn't want to kill anybody, Uncle Tulio. I would have, to get made, but when they told me about this, that they needed an athlete, someone young—"

"That basketball thing was a fiasco—the coach should have been whacked!" Lombardi poured himself another glass of Marsala and rammed the cork back in the bottle.

"It's okay, Uncle Tulio. I wouldn't have made the pros. I'm too short."

"That's what they said about Ernie DiGregorio in my day. In the long run, you'll be better here. The NBA's full of crybabies."

BLAZER LOOKED LIKE HE WANTED to jump out of Detective Sacco's open rear window as they wheeled into a spot at the gravel trailhead near Idyllwild. A leashed German shepherd woofed at Blazer, but when Blazer emerged and stood his ground, the other dog sniffed him, ignored him, and lay back down in the dirt. A man in a car threw some food out the window to the shepherd and nodded to Sacco and Awol.

"Okay," Sacco said, "you know the drill. Give me a report whenever you come off the trail to resupply. If you have an emergency, use the beacon. I've got a chopper on call."

"Got it."

"I'm certain there's shit moving out here—just a matter of time before we nail 'em." He lowered his voice and stared hard at Awol. "Meant to ask, how's your boy at UCLA making out? It's Kenny, right?"

"How did you know?"

Sacco pumped Awol's hand and copped a look at the guy with the shepherd. "It's our business to know things, Awol."

"Uh-huh." Awol felt his pulse quicken. He eyed Sacco.

"Listen, I know you're upset and concerned about your son, but you need to stay focused out here. Your son was lucky to get out of the mess he was in. I'll keep an eye on him."

"So you've known about him all along?"

"Yes."

"Why didn't you tell me?"

"I was saving it for my trump card, if I didn't hear back from you when we parted at Warner Springs."

Awol continued to stare at him.

"I didn't want to coerce you into working with us, Awol. I felt it better for you to learn about the mess from your boy, not me."

"I only found out last night," Awol said. "What if I still didn't know?"

Sacco smiled. He patted Awol on the back and said, "If the time came," and then mimed dealing from a deck of cards.

Awol nodded and got out of the car. He stood with Blazer and watched Sacco leave. Awol had to admire Sacco; the man was a bull, and he knew his stuff. If what he'd heard was true, Sacco was preparing for politics.

"C'mon, Blazer," he said finally. "We have thirteen miles to go before sundown." A few seconds later, something made Awol look back to the trailhead. The man with the dog had his driver side door open and was resting binoculars on top as he scanned the mountains.

CHAPTER ELEVEN

IT HAPPENED JUST LIKE THE last time; Blazer announced another hiker while Awol was setting up camp. Awol looked up, and both men recognized each other.

"Barcelona, right?"

The hiker looked at the dog—Blazer was sniffing his feet. "That's right," Barcelona said, looking puzzled.

"How's that toe?"

"Much better."

"I thought you'd be up in the Sierra Nevada by now."

"What about you? How come you aren't up there?"

"Made some visits to friends and had other business," Awol said. "I was off the trail for over a month."

"Same for me. The foot was bad enough that I changed plans for a while. Are you still going all the way?"

"Yeah."

Barcelona looked north as Blazer sniffed him and wiggled his nose toward the pack. The pack was long, sticking up behind his head. Awol was suspicious, but Blazer didn't alert or set a fix.

"Well, nice to see you again," Barcelona said, extending his hand. "Have a good camp."

"Adios," Awol said.

Barcelona pushed off smartly and never looked back. Awol watched the man as he moved ahead, calf muscles clenching and bunching with every step.

That night, Awol made notes in the logbook Sacco had given him, noting first the man with the binoculars and then, "*Barcelona. Hispanic, mid to late 20s, 5'10", fit and muscular. Overly large pack; always in a hurry.*"

Finally out of the desert, Awol and Blazer climbed for five days over the San Jacinto Mountains, through forests of moss and green weedlike vetch and stands of ponderosa pine, California live oak, and firs. Awol stepped over pinecones and smelled a sweet aroma from the thick, cinnamon-red bark of the ponderosa. It was a welcome change from the desert. They descended to the San Gorgonio Pass, poked through canyons of desert scrub and small-leaved evergreen shrubs, and then hiked back up into the San Bernardino Mountains through forests of lodgepole pine and Douglas fir, finally reaching a canyon road from where they could hitch to Big Bear City. He'd met several day hikers, but other than Barcelona, no thru-hikers. By now, Awol was sure most PCT thru-hikers were ahead of him.

"So other than this guy, Barcelona, you have nothing?" Sacco said.

"Not at the moment. Just the guy at the trailhead." Awol closed his eyes while talking into the cell and massaged a calf muscle, annoyed that Sacco sounded disappointed.

"Hmmm. You'll call me when?"

"Wrightwood—ninety miles. Should be there in five days."

And five days later, parched and dehydrated, aching and ornery, Awol sat on a cot in a seedy motel room in Wrightwood, with even less for Sacco—he and Blazer hadn't seen a soul.

Three days north of Wrightwood, in the heart of the San Gabriel Mountains amid ponderosa pine and deer brush shrubs, Awol and Blazer approached Shady Gap near Pacifico Mountain Campground. Blazer limped into the camp. Awol took a look under the dog's right rear paw: an embedded thorn.

"Okay, Blazer. Let me get this." Awol stroked the dog's leg and gradually worked down to the underside of the paw. "Your paw will feel much better when this is out." But Awol couldn't grasp the thorn with his fingers. "I should have packed tweezers, Blazer." He looked to a small log cabin near a picnic table, and he and the dog ambled over.

"Stay." Awol left Blazer at the cabin door.

Awol found a bony man, partially bald, seated at a desk stirring his coffee. An igneous rock, peppered with obsidian, served as a paperweight on what looked like permits. Behind him, a large map was fastened to a wall; several spots were highlighted in yellow.

"My dog's got a thorn in his paw. Do you have any tweezers, by chance?"

The man kept stirring his coffee. "I might." He took a sip of the steaming brew, placed the mug back on his desk, and sat for a moment before he finally got up and disappeared behind a curtain. His manner reminded Awol of a captain he couldn't stand in the army.

"I'll need these back."

"No problem; I'm right outside with my dog."

A few minutes later, Awol reentered the cabin with Blazer.

"My dog is much obliged." He handed the man the tweezers. "How much is it to tent for the night?"

"Ten bucks, and I'll need to put—"

Awol followed the man's gaze to Blazer. The dog sat still as a sculpture, his nose pointing to a coat hung on a wooden coatrack directly in front of him. A ranger decal was sewn on the coat. The dog was a still life as he made a fix using the passive alert—the mode in which he was trained. The ranger watched as Awol collared Blazer and led him outside.

"Animal's been nutty lately—spooks at everything," Awol explained when he returned.

The man said nothing as Awol handed him a ten-dollar bill in exchange for a map directing him to his tent site.

That evening, after finding his site—the farthest one from the cabin—Awol set up his tent and leashed Blazer to a sapling next to it. He backpacked around to the other side of the campground to a hidden spot across the entrance road, where he could observe anyone approaching. He was sixty yards from the cabin. After pulling his fleece hat down to his ears and wrapping himself in his sleeping bag, he huddled beneath oaks, munching on gorp as a three-quarter moon rose in front of him.

The light was on inside the cabin, and the ranger passed by the tiny window now and then; Awol could see his shadow behind the curtain. Awol had seen only two cars at separate sites deep in the campground. He suspected the Cherokee at the cabin belonged to the ranger.

Awol pushed a button on his watch—2:30 a.m. The moon was almost behind him. The night was clear, and the light glowed behind the curtain. *Late hours for a ranger. Good that Blazer was quiet*, Awol thought. He recalled the dog trainer's comments. "Ideally, you and the dog should go through a 'finish class' as a team, but there isn't enough time, and I noted how closely you and Blazer work together. For what this dog is supposed to do, you should be okay. The dog has an excellent nose and is a fine animal." With nothing happening, Awol rezipped the bag and fell asleep.

An hour of intermittent sleep later, Awol awoke to that singular, rhythmic shuffle of hiking poles: thkk, thkk, thkk. A hiker with a headlamp and tall pack drew between him and the cabin. The man was taller than Barcelona and looked to be thinner. He ambled to the night-lit doorway. He didn't bother to knock, just swung open the door and shut it behind him. Awol saw a shadow pass behind the curtain.

Twenty minutes later, Awol heard a low rumble. Seconds later, a Jeep rolled up the hardpan, lights out, and stopped near the door. Under the dome light Awol could make out a driver and a passenger. The driver smoked a cigar but kept his hands on the wheel. Awol could see the passenger pointing to what Awol guessed was a map. After a few minutes, both men emerged. The passenger carried hiking sticks and dragged a backpack up the steps. Awol noted the time. Less than ten minutes later, the hiker who had walked in from the road stepped to the vehicle and swung his pack in back. The driver ground his cigar stub into the gravel, and they exited the campground. Another five minutes went by and then the other hiker, now with a headlamp on, stepped down from the cabin and poled in the direction of the PCT. As he faded into darkness, the cabin's lights blinked out.

Having worked his way back to his tent, Awol intended to get a few hours' sleep before heading out. After what seemed like only a short nap, he awoke to Blazer licking his face. He'd unleashed him last night and let him crawl into the tent beside him. Awol was tired and let Blazer clean his closed eyelids, but when the animal whimpered into his ear, Awol sighed and fussed to read his watch—8:10.

He got out Blazer's food and watched him eat and then cooked a breakfast of oatmeal and hot chocolate for himself. All the while he thought about events leading to this point. Without question drugs were around the PCT, and it appeared that he'd witnessed a drop-off. He'd thought something was up with Barcelona, but Blazer had sniffed his pack and ignored it. Awol made some notes in the log and thought back to his son Kenny.

Kenny had said that he'd been clean for over six months. He also said he owed some people. Awol wondered how much.

He decided to stay another night; this was a rendezvous for dealers, and watching the cabin was more important than following the runner from last night. He'd go to the cabin, pay for another night, and hopefully draw the ranger out, get what information he could. He thought of Sacco's advice: "Remember, let us handle any type of investigation. Don't get in over your head."

As he hoofed it to the cabin, watching a beginning rain peck at the pond next to him, Awol practiced in his mind what he intended to say, how he would be casual, unsuspecting. He didn't notice any cars at the campground. When he got to the cabin, he saw something taped to the door. In a transparent protective cover, the ink-scrawled message read: "We are closed the next several days. Use the honor system for the rates posted below. Take an envelope and slip the money under the door. Thank you." The note wasn't even dated.

CHAPTER TWELVE

AWOL CALLED SACCO ON THE satellite phone.

"What do you have for me?"

Awol explained what he'd seen.

"Okay. Here's what I want you to do—stay put, hide, whatever. As soon as the ranger returns, call me. I've got your location."

"And if they make another drop before you get here?"

"I don't think that will happen, but if it does, follow the mule."

"These guys fly all hours of the night. Bring your track shoes."

"Just keep me updated."

"Right."

"Awol?"

"Yeah?"

"You're doing fine."

Nothing happened for the next three days, and Awol was concerned—he and Blazer were nearly out of food. Today he was due in Agua Dulce to resupply; instead, he was forty-one miles and two full days away. He approached a camper and managed to yogi a few granola bars and some cheese. When a lady offered water, he said he had plenty of that but was hungry. He tried to look forlorn. She handed him a useless bag of unpopped Jiffy Pop, then she and her girlfriend busied themselves unpacking.

He camped hidden behind oaks and boulders a good hundred yards away but still within sight of the cabin. He shared pieces of granola bars with Blazer and was happy to see him nibble and swallow the popcorn kernels. Blazer wasn't getting any exercise, but his paw was fine and he looked settled.

At 2:00 a.m., Awol awoke to a light patter of rain. Blazer nosed the side of the tent, and Awol unzipped the screen to let him in. Twenty minutes later, a downpour beat on the tent. Awol couldn't get back to sleep and peeked out the flap toward the cabin—nothing. Whenever he rationed food, invariably that was all he thought about, and his stomach rumbled as he opened the tinfoil containing the last of the cheese. He figured he'd beg the ladies for food in the morning, offer to pay them, but at the last second he wrapped the cheese back up and stuffed it into the pack. Rain thumped on the tent the rest of the night while Awol twisted and turned, his mind stoked with hunger and frustration. *Why did I have to get involved?* Yet he knew he wouldn't turn away; he owed it to Kenny. Awol knew how addiction worked. His hatred built.

He crawled out into the mud and drizzle at just before eight, intent on finding the campers to ask for more food. Blazer trotted beside him. He was nearly to their site when he saw their car pull out—they had packed up and were leaving. In the foggy drizzle, he held up his hand. The ladies smiled and waved from their car and kept on going. *Shit!* On his way back, he heard a vehicle and turned to see the ranger driving in with his Cherokee. Now he'd been spotted, wandering around without his pack. He wished he'd thought to slip money under the cabin door. He and Blazer crossed the squishy gravel road after the ranger gave him a wave. One way or another, he had to reach Sacco.

Awol had just stowed the satellite phone in his pack—Sacco was on his way—when he heard the crunch of twigs and footsteps.

"What's going on in there?"

Awol crawled out and stood in front of the ranger.

"How much do I owe you?"

The hardmouthed ranger stared at him. Blazer sniffed but didn't set an alert. "What are you doing camping over here?"

"Okay. Sorry. I was trying to use the facilities but didn't want to pay."

The ranger peeked into the tent and walked around it. "Let me see your ID."

Awol dragged out his wallet, pulled out his license, and handed it to him.

"Those ladies that left said you were scrounging for food. They said you made them nervous." His stare burned through Awol as he handed the license back.

"Sorry. My bad. No harm done."

"Mr. Bergman, you pack up your stuff and move out of here, or I'll report you. Okay? And that will be thirty dollars."

There was something in his tone that tripped a lever in Awol's brain.

"Can I buy some shit?" Awol asked.

The ranger stiffened and took a step closer. "Now look, I don't have any idea what you're talking about. But if you're not out of here in ten minutes, I'll have you arrested."

Awol knew that he blew it. After packing up, he headed for the agreed rendezvous, one mile out from the camp road at the stream. At least he remembered to have Sacco bring food for him and Blazer.

From his window, Ranger Larson watched Bergman leave. He remembered the incident with the dog. He needed to call Gomez and have him alert Verdugo to the possibility of a shakedown, but Larson was afraid Verdugo would find out he'd been using. Larson had been told about the execution back in the desert. He put the phone down. Then he realized Verdugo wouldn't find out because Verdugo's man, Gomez, sold him the shit—and Gomez was scared to death of Verdugo. If Larson didn't alert Gomez, who was coming tonight, the feds could make arrests; he'd be accused, and Verdugo would get him later. So he decided he'd say something to Gomez about an attempted break-in and police in the area, but he wouldn't mention the guy and the dog.

"TELL ME THIS AGAIN," SAID Verdugo. He was taking a call from Gomez. After he listened to everything a second time, he was silent. "Okay. Tell the ranger you ain't coming. Tell him to stay and run the campground like he's supposed to. And you do nothing 'til you hear from me. *Comprendes?*"

CHAPTER THIRTEEN

AWOL WATCHED AN UNMARKED TAN Ford Excursion pull up to the turnaround
at the stream. The giveaway was the two antennas protruding from the
roof. Sacco emerged from the driver side, clearly out of place in his
pressed khakis and spit-shined boots. As Awol walked to him, two more
men got out, one stretching while looking upstream. The banging of
doors flushed a flock of starlings from several aspens behind the vehicle.

"Did you bring food?"

"I did," Sacco said.

"And for the dog?"

"Of course."

Sacco introduced his associates and patted Blazer. "Let's find a spot
less exposed." Sacco drove west by the stream and pulled into a copse of
firs. After tending to Blazer, Awol described the cabin and the location
in between bites of his tuna sub. Awol, knowing he couldn't go back to
his former spot, suggested that he tent north of the campground. That
would allow him to stay in sight of the cabin and be near the PCT. Sacco
agreed and said he would stay with the vehicle, hidden on the approach
road. He told Awol to stay out of the planned raid on the cabin but to
leave his phone on vibrate.

Sacco, rotating with his men, watched during the day and at night.
The Excursion was set up for two to sleep in back. Awol slept in his
tent during the day and spied at night. Two days later, after watching a
number of campers come and go, Sacco had a fit.

"Awol, am I missing something here? What gives? Nothing that warrants a raid is happening. My men are tired, and now we're out of food!" Awol had to hold the phone away from his ear. Even Blazer perked his ears up at the blast from the phone.

"You're not the only one who's pissed. All I know is Blazer traced a fix, and the ranger knew it. A guy hiked in with a big pack and went into the ranger's cabin in the middle of the night. Then another guy is driven in by Jeep, goes into the cabin too, and that guy hikes out with a big pack—all within twenty minutes. I saw it happen."

"I'm pushing the envelope here, but we're going in tomorrow morning at four. We'd better find evidence inside."

At 4:00 a.m., Awol felt the vibration and pulled out his cell. *Just bring the dog over.*

Hidden, Awol watched as Sacco pounded the door of the cabin. One of his men stood next to Sacco; the other stood at a rear entrance. Sacco pounded again, with Blazer beside him.

"Open up!" Sacco shouted.

Awol didn't like the idea of not being involved. But he knew he'd blown it and figured Larson would lie and make egregious accusations about him. Sacco said stay out, but dammit . . .

The inside light came on and, shortly after, the door opened.

Ranger Larson squinted through the screen and blinked his eyes. "What's this?"

"I'm Detective Sacco, with the San Diego Police. Step aside please."

"So, what's this all about?"

Sacco flashed his badge. "I'm with the narcotics division." He and Blazer stepped inside. Awol came in right behind them.

"Well, that's interesting," Larson said. "This supposed hiker over there, who's been scrounging food off my campers and scaring them off—never mind hiding his tent site on a state campground without paying—asked me to sell him drugs. I didn't know what the fuck he was talking about, or why in the world he would be asking *me.*"

Sacco glared at Awol as Blazer lay down on the rug to watch the proceedings.

Sacco turned to Larson. "What the fuck we're talking about is coke and heroin. Hikers with big packs coming in and out of here at weird hours. Four-by-fours wheeling in and out at four in the morning."

Larson didn't flinch. "That's total bullshit."

"Let me see your ID, and I want the names of the people you report to."

Larson calmly walked to the curtain while Sacco followed. "C'mon, Blazer. Ranger Larson would like you to check out his inner quarters."

They weren't in there long, and Blazer didn't alert.

"You satisfied, Detective?"

"No, I'm not—not at all. And lying to government agents will get you in big trouble."

"Like I said, I don't know what you guys are talking about." Larson held up his palms, looking more confident now that he had put on pants.

Sacco looked at Awol, as if he expected him to say something. He looked at the dog and back to Larson. "I'm going to ask you one last time to give me the names of the three people who showed up here at this time five days ago." Sacco took out a notepad and thumbed through it.

"I don't have a clue as to what you're talking about," Larson snapped.

"As you wish." Sacco closed the pad and headed to the door.

Awol stared down Larson, who finally looked away and went behind the curtain.

Outside, Awol and Blazer followed Sacco to his vehicle. Sacco stared at Awol while holding open the front passenger door.

"All I wanted was the dog. Thank you for exposing yourself in this total fucking fiasco."

Awol pursed his lips and didn't say a word.

"Do you mind telling me, Mr. Bergman, what he was referring to when he said you'd asked to buy drugs?" Sacco skidded out onto the gravel road and looked right at Awol.

"I'm sorry. He came over to my tent and got me so goddamned mad . . ."

"Do you realize what you did? Awol! We need to get some things straight. One—as I told you, you don't lead investigations. You don't ask questions. You leave that to us. Two—when I give instructions, I want them followed. I didn't want you in there. Three—you could have saved yourself, me, and my men three wasted days if you'd told us about this conversation with the ranger up front. And now they know we're onto them."

"You are right. I apologize. But I figured Blazer would give me away anyway. He saw my dog."

Sacco pulled the Excursion over to the side. He shut down the engine and cut the lights. "Look." Sacco huffed and banged the steering wheel with his palm. No one said anything for over a minute.

"Okay," Sacco said. "We know he's lying, but I've got nothing to go after him with, and he knows it. We know they're hauling north, right?"

"Right."

"You said you're two days out of Agua Dulce, right?"

"Right."

"Charlie here is going with you as far as Agua Dulce. We need to get a fix on how this drug thing is done. At best, the two of you meet up with a runner. Charlie will know what to do; he's packing. At worst, I have another set of eyes and ears, and one of my guys gets used to this trail."

"Guess I really fucked up."

"You did. But don't take this as punishment—Charlie may be needed, and you're giving my man field experience."

"Right." Awol stepped from the vehicle and kicked a stone.

Charlie had already hauled out his backpack, which Awol hadn't noted the other day. "Don't worry, we called in for food and had someone bring it out," Sacco said as he pointed to Charlie and his pack. "I'll meet you both in two days in Agua Dulce."

Later that morning, the two hikers and Blazer approached the Mill Creek Summit ranger station. "Let me go in with your dog," Charlie said. "You continue on by a few minutes after I go in so they don't connect you with me or the dog."

Charlie walked in, and the ranger, who looked like a teenager, pushed a clipboard in front of him.

"We need you to sign in," the tanned young man said. "And we'd like to see an ID."

Charlie took the clipboard. The page listed several male names that appeared to be all in the same handwriting. "I saw two women ahead of me; how come they didn't sign in?"

The boy hesitated, "Guess they just walked on by."

Charlie looked at him. "This bit with the IDs. That something new?"

The boy appeared tongue-tied, and Charlie wasn't helping matters by giving him hard looks. The young ranger mumbled something as Charlie walked to the window and looked out. Awol had just passed.

"Have a good day," Charlie said as he scribbled his signature and placed the clipboard on the counter.

Outside, Awol ignored Charlie's mutterings and tightened Blazer's carrier straps.

An hour later, they were ascending to a rocky side trail bordered by scree. Awol, tired of answering Charlie's questions, gave him the lead figuring that would keep him quiet. The trail was faded but obvious.

Charlie stopped yakking, and Awol lost himself in his surroundings. Looking at a distant valley stretched green with firs under a late-morning sun, he felt stress leach from his body. This inspired a renewed commitment to working with Sacco—for Kenny's sake.

They reached the steepest point on the trail—evident by Charlie's huffing—and stepped through a section of scattered rocks and boulders the diameter of Jeep tires. Awol had stopped to look down on the rock piles and scree three hundred feet below him, when several boulders, rounded from windblown sand, tumbled from above. Blazer barked and jerked back. The boulders loosened other boulders and rocks, sending flying chunks of stone and detritus down the trail. Awol lurched sideways, blinded by the dust, unsure if he should run or stay fixed. A boulder missed him by inches and blew his trekking pole right out of his hand. Awol heard a sickening smack, and through the dust glimpsed Charlie tumbling off the side of the trail. Awol crouched, covering his head and closing his eyes, and prayed.

After another eternal minute, as smaller stones continued to bounce by him, Awol opened his eyes. But it took a minute of rubbing and dabbing them with a water-soaked bandanna before he could see.

Awol wobbled over to the side and saw Charlie's twisted neck and caved-in head, the rest of his body covered by rocks and scree. Awol turned to where Blazer was barking some twenty feet ahead. He followed the dog's gaze to a figure scrabbling off the arête in front of them, headed toward the road. Awol snapped to, grabbed his binoculars, and focused. No pack or sticks, but the tanned body looked strong as the man deftly cleaved down the rubbly slope, heading to cover in scrub and pine. Even from the back, he looked vaguely familiar. The legs. Chiseled. Awol could see the calf muscles bunch and contract, just like Barcelona's.

CHAPTER FOURTEEN

AWOL PHONED SACCO. HE WAS coming back with officials, and Awol dreaded his arrival. After he doctored up a bruised arm—Blazer didn't have a scratch—he unburied Charlie's body, turned him away from the sun, and draped him with his poncho. Awol took off his hat and closed his eyes for a moment before angling around rubble, away from the sun.

Like the calm after a storm, it became quiet. Even Blazer lay in a heap behind Awol who, eyes glazed, sat on a boulder staring at the rubble before him. It was as still as a snapshot. Awol felt defenseless, useless, broken.

The medical examiner who came with Sacco asked questions and filled out a form. Sacco scouted the area and made notes.

"So what do you think happened?" Sacco asked Awol.

"Probably an accident, and we were in the wrong place at the wrong time."

Sacco listened.

"But I did see a man, without hiking gear, scrabbling toward the road after the slide stopped."

"Describe him to me."

Awol gave him the details. Sacco didn't ask if the man looked familiar, and at the last minute, Awol chose not to tell Sacco that it might have been Barcelona. He just couldn't bring himself to do it; he felt miserable enough already.

Seated on a rock, Sacco put his pad and pen away as Charlie was carried off on a stretcher. "There goes a good man," Sacco said. "A damn good man."

He looked at Awol. "I may have erred in asking for your help; you're not trained in police work. But this was no accident. It has to be connected. You know it, I know it, and the man upstairs"—he pointed above his head—"knows it."

Awol just looked at Blazer, who sniffed up-trail, eager to move.

Sacco angled his head at Awol. "I'm going to pay another visit to that ranger station back there. And right now I don't want you to do anything. Okay? Hike on. Stay alert. Call me when you resupply. Just do not do anything on your own."

THAT AFTERNOON, ALVARADO LISTENED TO Verdugo on speaker phone as he moved a rook on the chessboard in front of him. Alvarado was replaying a game annotated in the book on his lap, *Capablanca's Best Games.*

"This man, Sacco," Alvarado said, "can he be bought?"

"No. Medina says he's on a fast track—wants to go into politics."

"Then Medina has failed us. For the second time." Alvarado captured a bishop with his knight and silently mouthed *check.*

Verdugo knew Alvarado was losing patience with Medina. He was too. Medina had said he would turn Sacco; that wasn't going to happen.

"Has Medina outlived his usefulness?" Alvarado asked.

"We need him to control Sacco, feed us info."

"Mr. Sacco, if politically inclined, would like to make a name for himself—at our expense. He'll be too hard to control and a menace to us."

"Do you have something in mind?"

"I do. And you know what that is. You tell Medina he has one last chance to redeem himself."

"Okay," Verdugo said.

"Meanwhile, what do you suggest we do about the immediate situation?"

"Refigure some routes, change the drops, see what they do next."

"What about the guy with the dog?"

"The ranger said he wasn't with the feds. Barcelona says he's clean."

"Why the dog?"

"Just a dog. Some hikers bring them for company."

Whenever Alvarado studied chess and simultaneously thought of other matters, he would apply chesslike thinking to those matters; he did so now. The man with the dog was suspicious, and he and his dog intrigued the chess master. At the moment, they were a nuisance. Looking ahead, just like the great Capablanca, he visualized a time when they might become of special use to him.

"Do you like Barcelona?"

"He's a bull. And smart."

"Start sharing information; see if he can be trusted. Plant seeds now for later."

"*Sí.*"

"And keep your eye on Gomez. His eyes were shifty the last time I saw him."

"He's due for a beating. Don't worry, he owes us, and he's got nowhere to go."

"Did Medina put the lid on the traitor, last seen in the desert?"

"*Sí.* He saw the X; he got the message."

"Something else. Keep me informed, good or bad, about my counterpart up north—Lombardi. I don't trust him."

CHAPTER FIFTEEN

Awol CALLED SACCO WHEN HE reached Agua Dulce, two days later.

"Did you learn anything new back at that ranger station?" Awol asked.

"No, I didn't."

"Anyone talk to the young ranger Charlie and I saw there, or Larson again, back at the campground?"

"That young ranger you and Charlie saw has disappeared. We're working with head rangers on Larson, but they don't know squat."

"I'll call you when I reach Mojave. Figure three days."

Awol hoofed it to a well-known hostel in Agua Dulce and chose a cot in a large tent that accommodated six. After seeing to Blazer's needs and then taking a shower, he borrowed one of several bicycles available for hikers and pedaled into the village.

Ordinarily he would be overjoyed to be in town, to be showered, to be eating pizza. But he sat at an outside plastic table in a plastic chair, drinking a Budweiser, and watching the last glimmers of daylight recede, feeling like shit. Rehab had taught him not to drink, no matter what, one day at a time, but he didn't care. He felt responsible for Charlie's death. No matter how he tried to turn the conversation in his mind, he always came back to the point that he should have used his head. That he should have camped farther away at that campground; that he should have kept his mouth shut with Larson. That he fucked up. Again.

So he ordered another Bud. And then three or four, and more after that. When the joint closed up, he had trouble mounting the bicycle. He left it on the patio, with a curse and a crash as he rolled into some chairs. He lay there for a while, then picked himself up and lurched back to the hostel without the bike. As he meandered, he thought about Huck Finn, who got into trouble every time he left that raft on the river. *When will I learn? When?*

Next morning, the sun was out, promising a nice day. Green everywhere, as spring had moved into summer. Awol could hear a lawn mower while he massaged his temples and wished it were dismal and rainy. He didn't feel like engaging with anyone or anything—except for Kenny. He pulled out his cell, got Kenny's answering machine, and was about to leave a message but couldn't think of what to say or how to convey his feelings. He called Gregory.

"Kenny told me he'd had a drug problem. What can you tell me about it?"

"He won't talk about it. He got messed up."

"How?"

"He got behind in payments."

"Does he need money?"

"He says he has to make payments."

"How much does he owe?"

"I don't know. But he also bought for some friends who blew town and never paid him back. He doesn't like to talk about it."

"Why?"

"I think the mob threatened his girlfriend."

"Anything else you can tell me?"

Gregory blurted, "Kenny OD'd and almost died."

After he ended the call, Awol was about to jump out of his skin. He went beside the tent and alternated thirty push-ups with fifty sit-ups, performing this combination three times. He found a tree, did ten chin-ups, walked around the tree a couple of times—his head thumping from the previous night's indiscretions—jumped up again to the limb, and finished with ten pull-ups.

After his exercises, he thought about calling Sacco to check in on Kenny, but the idea made his stomach churn. He'd screwed up Sacco's life enough. Awol spent the day drying out, promising himself he wouldn't go back into town. He'd learned the hard way again. They pounded him in rehab to not think about tomorrow or the past but to stay in the present—*just for today*. And today he would not drink.

Late afternoon, Awol ambled to a stationary trailer, complete with rolled-down awnings, and ducked inside to the hostel's makeshift kitchen hangout. Hikers were playing cards, cooking popcorn, and gaming. Awol sat down, exchanged a few words, and watched the handful of younger people. Two college kids arm wrestled on the kitchen table to the cheers of girls. The video-gamers were locked in what appeared to be a death match. When the popcorn was ready, the gamers quit and turned up the TV. Three card players continued to flip cards.

Awol watched the news. When a story came on showing arrests made in southern California forests on hidden marijuana farms, only one other person so much as glanced at the TV. Linked with the story was footage showing arrests made at the Mexican border; helicopters and Border Patrol vehicles were shown scouting the area, just as he'd seen the morning he started his hike. A few more of the hikers in the room turned their attention to the TV. A girl hollered, "Hey, that clump of sage looks familiar," and a few laughed. The card players continued flipping cards and didn't even look up.

That night Awol left Kenny a message saying that he would always be available for him, that he was proud of him. He asked him to relay his best to Jill and Gregory and left his cell number. He paused, wanting to say more. "Kenny . . . I love you."

The following morning was overcast and wet from a night's rain. Awol and Blazer moved into Sierra Pelona Valley, 460 miles north of the Mexican border. While he poled through the grass-covered vega, he imagined Ranger Larson standing in front of him and how he would love to beat him senseless. Awol looked at Blazer and wondered if animals had such feelings.

CHAPTER SIXTEEN

ALL DAY—THROUGH GREEN AND fuzzy foxtails, through pungent grassy meadows of yellow and purple mustard—Awol and Blazer hiked a stretch of modest ridges and canyons. Within the first hour Awol had settled down, and by midday he felt cleansed. This happened every time he hit the trail after a bout of drinking. After eating lunch under triangular-toothed leaves of cottonwoods, Awol and Blazer wound in and out of small ravines and, in the late afternoon, climbed to a firebreak on a cuesta. The natural firebreak began where fireweed and charred trees abruptly ended before the red-rocked cliff. Below, twenty-five miles north of Agua Dulce, was San Francisquito Canyon Road. Awol squinted through his binoculars and searched but saw no one walking. He'd heard of a hostel near this area, and when they reached the road two days later, fortune smiled; they got a direct hitch.

It didn't take long for Blazer to reach a tizzy. He wanted to alert everywhere. A hiker had curled into a fetal position on a decrepit outdoor sofa and didn't bother to open his eyes when Blazer sniffed and alerted in front of him. Awol tugged his dog away only to have him sit in front of another hiker, who looked as if he was asleep in a hammock. This young man did open his eyes and turned over to his other side. Awol noted a can of Turks hashish. The dog sniffed the pungent Latakia but moved away; Blazer alerted to only coke and heroin.

"Okay, boy, you've made your point. Settle down now."

The owners had big hearts and opened up their hostel to all hikers—the young, the older, the sick, the hikers in need. They passed no judgments and offered each person a shower, food, a place to stay and sleep, all for a modest donation of the hiker's choosing. Awol declined the shower and found a place to set up his tent out back, where he and Blazer could stay separate from others. The entire place smelled of pot and rot. A small group of hikers were using it as a drug haven. After tethering Blazer to a juniper, Awol went back, even though he knew he would get himself worked up.

The guy on the sofa was awake and sat with another hiker. They were sharing a joint.

"Dude, you've been here for two days. When you leaving, man?"

The hiker who had been sleeping on the couch smiled with glassy eyes. "When they kick me out." He chuckled and, as if in slow motion, drew the joint to his lips.

"What will you do then?" asked a hiker sitting in a director's chair across from them. He rolled a joint using hashish from the Turks can.

"I'll head over to Hikertown."

"And when they kick you out of there?"

"I'll come back here," he said and shrieked a laugh into the night.

Inside, Awol dined from a buffet of burritos and tamales and a vegetable salad with assorted dips, salsa, and Doritos. After leaving the gracious hostess a twenty-dollar bill in a ceramic pumpkin set aside for donations, he pulled aside her husband.

"Where do these kids get the hard stuff?"

The host looked at him.

"You know, coke, heroin?"

"Damned if I know. But one way or another, they'll always find it. Lately the stuff's been everywhere."

Back in his tent, Awol listened to laughter and shouts. Someone beat bongos; later, he heard girls singing. He could smell the doped-up air even at his tent. He thought back to his thru-hike of the AT. The few dope smokers he'd encountered were discreet. Here it was all open. California was, well, California. Nevertheless.

Next morning, at the first trills of birdsong, he and Blazer were the first ones up and out. After trudging a mile, they got a hitch back down Canyon Road to the trailhead. He noticed from his guide that Hikertown, off Highway 138, was only thirty-nine miles away. He initially had no intention of going there, but when he approached the highway three days later, he thought it would be a good place to replenish his water. As he drew near the highway, he heard gunshots and dove to the ground. Once he was down he realized it was just a vehicle backfiring. He got up and crossed the road knowing he was going to Hikertown for another reason—whether fueled by his son, pressure from Sacco, or his own deepening curiosity and concern—an obligation to learn more about the drug culture.

Hikertown, a hostel consisting of a few small outside sleeping shacks, was borderline neat and isolated from the highway by a chain fence. A middle-aged man in sunglasses identified himself as the caretaker and allowed Awol to get water from a hose attached to an outside faucet. It was just after noon.

"We have sleeping space if you want it," the man said.

"Thanks for the offer, but I'll sit, have a snack, and move on."

The man walked away, and Awol saw him look back at him.

On impulse, Awol asked, "Do hikers sometimes switch back and forth between here and the Nelsons' hostel?" Awol pointed behind him.

The man stared at him, turned, and continued walking without answering.

A few minutes later, Awol walked by a shed as the door squeaked open. A college-aged boy in skivvies meandered over, while Blazer alerted at the shed.

"Has the mail come yet?" he asked. He scratched his armpit with one hand and knuckled an eye with the other.

"I don't know. You okay?"

"I need my fucking mail."

Awol saw Blazer go into the shed.

"I need to get my dog," Awol said.

Awol walked in and was overcome with a stench similar to that of the opium den he and two other lieutenants had found in the Middle East. Here the odor, which rode up his nostrils, was mixed in with rot and decay. Candy wrappers lay on the floor along with torn magazines; a sweat-yellowed pillow without a pillowcase lay bunched on the narrow cot. *How in the hell could the boy stay in here?* he wondered.

"I need to know if you're staying or not," the man in sunglasses said. He'd returned and stood at the door behind Awol.

"My dog is agitated." Awol led the dog out and faced the man, who'd backed out of the doorway. "You have any idea what that's about?"

The man crossed his arms and stared back.

"Where's my fucking mail?" the boy hollered. "I need my meds and my fucking mail!"

The boy sat down in the dirt, and Blazer growled.

"You know," the man said to Awol, "we don't have room for you. Why don't you take your dog and go."

Awol looked at him and crossed his arms. "Maybe I'll just stay right here and make a big fuss, whether you like it or not."

The man looked at the dog, while the boy wandered back to his hole and closed the door. "You like your dog?"

Awol continued to stare.

"Reason I ask is, I wouldn't want anything to happen to him."

Awol watched him walk away and not look back. He called Blazer and headed out.

Awol missed the shade of trees, the scenic forests of red fir and pines. They had dropped north from Liebre Mountain into the heart of Antelope Valley, the western arm of the Mojave Desert. For whatever reason, owners of the immense Tejon Ranch, which lies astride the Tehachapi Mountains, didn't allow right-of-way for PCT hikers. The Tehachapis would have been the perfect segue to the Sierra; instead, hikers had to trace the Tejon Ranch's boundaries along a hot, waterless, and ugly multimiled stretch.

A few miles later, at two in the afternoon., Awol and Blazer sat under the stingy shade of a paloverde tree surrounded by long pointy stemmed yuccas and watched dust devils swirl to the east. The temperature had reached 101 degrees, and Awol was again thankful for the compact silver-domed umbrella. He mulled over what transpired at the hostel and was about to dig for the phone to report it when a dust devil blew right into his face. He tasted the grit stuck in his teeth and covered his eyes. He'd call Sacco later.

That night he camped waterside at Oak Creek Canyon, 530 miles north of the Mexican border. Too hot to tent, he laid down his pad and hoped the scorpions and spiders would leave him be. After a meal of Ramen noodles sprinkled with gorp, he reached Sacco on the second try.

"Got some info for you," Awol said. But after he relayed the details of the two hostels, Sacco didn't appear excited.

"Nice to have the info, but unless this is a drop-off point, what can I accomplish?"

"Kids here are getting shit from dealers."

"Yeah, and I end up tipping my hand again. Reports about me will be sent up the line to the people that matter. We need to establish a runner, a mule on the PCT—then I've got a solid piece of their operation to work with."

Awol frowned. "But these hostels should be either cleaned up or shut down before some kid ODs."

"Think of prostitution," Sacco said. "The cops come in and raid some street corners. They round up some women, bring them to town, read them the riot act. A few days later, the prostitutes go back to work the same corners. Nah, I need something substantial."

Two days later, Awol resupplied in Mojave, California, a town that lay along a flat highway in blinding sun. He understood why siestas were popular in this part of the country. This highway was built through a desert, and from noon until two, you were at risk of being baked alive. He huddled next to closed window blinds in a taco joint fortunate enough to have A/C and nursed Diet Cokes packed with ice. He didn't bother to call Sacco; he had nothing to say.

He did call Kenny.

"Kenny, level with me. How much money do you owe?"

"Twelve thousand dollars."

"Christ."

"Don't worry about it. The past is over and done with; I got this under control."

"Kenny, listen to me—you get in any trouble, you call me. Understood?"

Three days later, on a dirt road leading to Robin Bird Spring, Awol spied something hanging from a tree. It looked like somebody's fur coat. Blazer trotted up to it, sniffed, and stepped back, barking. As Awol drew closer, he could make out an animal's legs, and ears furled from the back of a head. "What the fuck . . ."

The full-grown German shepherd was hung by the neck and gutted. The underside had been sliced from the throat to the crotch; blood and guts had drained and formed a pool of offal beneath the animal. Awol noticed a piece of paper stuck under the rope at the dog's neck. He pulled it out and unfolded it—staring at him was a large handwritten "X."

CHAPTER SEVENTEEN

Barcelona was at the appointed pickup spot an hour early. Adrenaline continued to course through him as he sat on a hillock dotted with oak and pine near a gravel path and waited. He'd followed Verdugo's instructions to the letter but was beside himself about it. *Only for my family . . . Juanita, Trini, 'Berto.* What bothered him was that he had over ten months to go, and already he'd killed a man and gutted a dog. He began to pray aloud in Spanish but stopped, feeling like a desperado who only prays when cornered, when his life is about to end.

An hour later, lights winked on from the road. He shouldered the pack and paced to the vehicle.

"You look frazzled, Barcelona."

"I . . ."

"What!"

"The guy with the dog. When I was bit by the scorpion, he helped me with medication, bandages. Verdugo, he suspects nothing."

"What's your point, Barcelona?"

"I just thought, Verdugo, that . . . maybe . . ."

Verdugo looked at Barcelona. "I give you some advice—only once. Don't question me or Alvarado. Ever."

"Okay, Verdugo."

"You're lucky to be here. Don't fuck it up, 'cause your family means nothing to me or Alvarado."

"Okay. I hear you."

"Since you know this man with the dog, you will continue your normal work but will keep heading north, just like him. Depending on what he does next, you may be taken from your duties and given a special assignment. Do you understand?"

"Of course, Verdugo."

AWOL CUT THE ROPE AND dragged the animal away from Robin Bird Spring. Blazer watched him as he rolled the carcass down a small embankment and covered it with branches and leaves. He sat down a few yards away and pulled out his guidebook. Awol figured someone was tracking him, watching him, and he wanted that person to know that he'd gotten the message and was bailing—for now. He noted in the guide that a half mile north he could access Jawbone Canyon Road. That gravel road, twenty-six miles later, would take him to a visitor center at the junction of State Highway 14. He footed back to the spring and filled up the water bottles.

Late in the afternoon, he and Blazer hiked east down through the Piute Mountains. He had no fear; if he was going to be attacked, they would have gotten to him by now. Down, down they went, having started out at almost seven thousand feet. Every step for seven miles, Awol felt his knees throbbing and his quads burning until he finally bottomed out at the crotch of the mountains into Kelso Valley. At 8:30 p.m., after three more miles of desertlike terrain, Awol could go no farther. It had been a much longer day than he'd anticipated; originally, he had intended to camp at Robin Bird Spring. He laid out his pad and scrounged in his food bag for oatmeal, a granola bar, and gorp. At 9:30 p.m., he set his watch for 2:30 a.m. The time to hike this terrain was at night. He was following a gravel road; all he needed was moonlight and his headlamp.

Awol couldn't stop thinking about that poor shepherd. In his mind he accepted that human value is normally worth more than animal, but he thought less of humanity after seeing that gutted dog. He wanted to pound someone.

CHAPTER EIGHTEEN

JUST AFTER MIDNIGHT, AWOL WAS wakened by the sounds of a vehicle. It was moving west slowly, and a searchlight combed the sides of the road. He put one hand on Blazer's head and palmed his knife with the other. "Quiet, boy." They lay together off the side of the road in the scrub. As the vehicle drew near, Awol could see the searchlight moving back and forth. The dark pickup crawled by them, and the searchlight beamed on Awol. The truck stopped a few seconds as Awol froze and closed his eyes. Then it inched along, and Awol felt the shine move over him. After a minute, he turned and saw a white canvas spread over something in the bed of the truck. Spooked, he watched the pickup fade into the dark.

"C'mon, boy. Whoever they are, they're going west, and we're going east, right now."

In five minutes, Awol was packed and ready to move. Blazer sensed the urgency and whined. Awol adjusted his headlamp and poled down the gravel road. Two hours later he was groggy and exhausted, more from nerves than muscle soreness. He would take a breather. With a pole strapped to each wrist, he sat in the middle of Jawbone Canyon Road, leaning on his pack, facing east.

Two hours later he woke, not remembering where he was. The stars overhead looked like snowflakes about to fall; he watched and waited. A few minutes later, he saw a tinge of light on the eastern horizon in front of him. Blazer was snoring beside him. Awol stood, grateful to have made it out of the night alive.

They hiked east, winding through low exposed hills. The day would be another scorcher, but he hoped to arrive at the junction by midmorning. He figured he had eight or ten miles to go and that they would make it with just enough water. A short while later, Awol heard a rumble and turned to see a familiar black pickup, white tarp sticking up in the back. No lights were necessary as the vehicle crawled along. Awol stood to the driver's side with Blazer and waited.

The truck rolled to a stop, and a beady-eyed man looked out the window at Awol. He grinned, displaying a browned snaggletooth. "Seen any rattlers?"

"Can't say that I have."

"Rattlers are all over here. I hunt 'em."

"You hunt rattlers?"

The man grinned again, flashing the brown tooth. He wore a white T-shirt, and a tin of Skoal sat on the dash. "Bang one of those poles on the canvas back there."

Awol, relieved that he wasn't in this man's crosshairs, whacked a pole on the canvas and then leapt back into the ditch. "What the . . . !" An instant cacophony of buzzing took his breath away.

The man placed a chew in his mouth with a yellowed pinkie and smiled at Awol. His cheek bubbled up, and spit drained from his lips. "Don't worry; I got 'em in cages."

"Jesus! What do you do with these things?"

"Sell 'em for food. Mexicans'll buy 'em for all kinds a reasons." He spit a quid into the ditch and grinned. "I'd give you a lift, but I got no room for the dog."

"Not a problem. How far am I from the visitor center?"

"Six miles. Watch out for rattlers," he said as he chugged off.

CHAPTER NINETEEN

Sᴀᴄᴄᴏ ᴡᴀs sᴇᴀᴛᴇᴅ ɪɴ ʜɪs office reviewing the latest drug busts on the West Coast, when Captain Medina rapped on the doorjamb and entered.

"Any news?" Medina asked.

"Just the usual. And the Mexicans are growing more marijuana in our forests."

"Vincent," Medina slapped a folder in his hand and sat down. "What happened to Charlie? Give it to me straight."

"It appears to be a tragic accident. He was at the wrong place at the wrong time."

"What the fuck was he doing on a hiking trail?"

Sacco shifted in his chair and looked at him. "We heard a rumor about a ranger up in that area dealing. He went to check it out."

"Incognito."

"Incognito."

Medina pursed his lips. "So what's your plan now?"

"There is no plan. The ranger's clean."

AᴡᴏL ᴛᴏᴏᴋ ᴏᴜᴛ ʜɪs ᴍᴀᴘs and guidebook; he had decisions to make. At the visitor center—where he arrived after he stood on Highway 14 trying for a hitch for over an hour, watching vehicles whiz by—the lady working the information desk took heart when he returned to get out of the sun and offered to drive him to Ridgecrest when she finished work.

Now, sitting at a small table in his room at the Motel 6, he concluded it was dangerous and foolish to trudge along the PCT in this section. One, someone was tracking him and had threatened him. Two, he could be of no help to Sacco here; the thugs would be careful. Three, if drugs were being hauled up the PCT, there were other mules ahead of him. So he decided he would jump ahead. That way, if he was being watched right now, they would conclude he had bailed.

The thought of going home was out of the question. The hung German shepherd had tripped another lever in his brain. These people had killed Charlie and were responsible for Kenny's mess; they had to be stopped. He wished he had been friendlier to Charlie, and he felt bad for his family knowing that two little girls were without a father. But he didn't know what to do about Sacco. If he told him about the dog, Sacco would tell him to bail, that he would take it from here. But Sacco still had nothing substantial, as he had termed it. Awol was determined to find another mule, something Sacco could run with. He fingered through the guidebook and highlighted locations on his maps. He would leave what was considered southern California and bus to central California, to new terrain with cooler weather, and continue the PCT again at Kennedy Meadows, the gateway to the High Sierra.

CHAPTER TWENTY

TWO DAYS LATER IN THE High Sierra—after a motel employee, trying to impress Awol with his new Wrangler, whisked him up through soaring granite cliffs to six thousand feet—Awol climbed north on the Pacific Crest Trail from Kennedy Meadows Campground. The landscape had changed again. Jumping ahead in season, he expected to see snow. He was lucky that much of it had melted. The clovered path alternated between views of expansive snow-spotted alpine meadows spotting stalks of fire-red snow plants along with the cabbagelike corn lily and forests of red fir. Blazer was happy to be out again as he romped around pinyon and Jeffrey pines and sniffed the twined bark of junipers.

Fifteen minutes onto the trail, Awol experienced a headache that came out of nowhere. His gait slowed to a crawl; his legs felt rubbery. He pulled out his pad to take a brief rest and laid out flat for a half hour.

Feeling better, he climbed again, but the vertiginous ascent up the mountain shoulder affected his head, and he soon felt weak again. He forced himself to continue for another half hour. When he could go no farther, he pulled out his pad and rested again, flat on his back. Blazer drooped beside him.

For the first time in his life, he was experiencing altitude sickness. His head felt heavy and as big as a basketball. The Jeep ride up was the problem—too quick—and now he was trying to hike up farther using oxygen-deprived muscles that hadn't adapted.

He continued the pattern of hiking a half hour and then resting a half hour. At eight thousand feet, he'd had enough; he looked into the snow-patched, rock-choked gulch below him and the valley stippled with purple wildflower beyond and realized he simply couldn't walk another step. He set up camp in the scrub, took a Tylenol, and lay down in his tent. It was late afternoon, and he'd hiked only eight miles for the day.

He felt better after sleeping a couple of hours. Sitting outside his tent later, viewing the snowcapped rock spires in front of him, Awol understood that right now he was at one of the most pristine wilderness locations on earth. He stared at the expanse of bare, near-vertical granite walls supporting jagged, snow-topped pinnacles and thought of good and evil. *Did drug haulers absorb and appreciate this raw beauty?*

The next day he was still weak. He was able to hike for an hour and then rested for half an hour next to a gnarled pine, stunted by severe weather, and in this alternating fashion, he managed to complete thirteen miles. He'd learned a lesson and would never rush his body so quickly again. Tomorrow would be easier; eventually, his body would acclimatize. In the afternoon, he set up camp in a saddle at ten thousand feet. He had to admit the irony: the spectacular jagged peaks he was in the midst of were *literally* breathtaking. He gaped at the raw, natural beauty of the shadowed, craggy, snowcapped peaks to his left and the sun-washed crags to his right. The towering butte on his far right—fluted sides leveling into patches of sastruga, irregular grooves formed on a snow surface by wind erosion—looked formidable. And pristine. Just the same now as thousands of years ago. Not a soul was in sight. *Who would believe this?* Even with his diminishing malaise, he was experiencing beatitude.

In the morning, Awol smelled smoke. As he ascended to Forester Pass, at over thirteen thousand feet, he saw haze to the north. Forest fires had been rampant over the years in many of the lower sections, and he was sure this haze was from a forest fire. It was July, and it had been dry; no rain had fallen for a month. This morning he'd crossed several washes, kicking up dirt, pebbles, and dust in the dry beds of runnels. The forest was a tinderbox; twigs dry as broomstraw snapped into remnants beneath his boots. He hoped he wouldn't be stopped by the fires. He'd already resupplied in Lone Pine and was fixed until Bishop, a few days away.

Four miles later, when he descended into the basin, the haze had turned to wisps of smoke, and he started to question if he would be able to make it to Bishop Pass. He and Blazer camped that night with the odor of woodsmoke wafting in from the north and east. As he lay in his tent, he wondered what adjustments animals to the north were making, if mothers of young animals would fret and try to move.

Next morning, at Bullfrog Lake, it became clear that Awol wouldn't be able to hike over Bishop Pass. The smell of smoke filled the air; the haze hung, and already he'd tramped through extended patches of deadfall. He opted to hike east over Kearsarge Pass into Onion Valley and hitch to Independence. Less than a mile later, he encountered two hikers sitting on rocks at the junction of Kearsarge Pass Trail.

"Don't bother," one said. "You can't get through."

"I figured that," Awol said. "Are you going over Kearsarge?"

"I suppose," the other said, closing his guidebook. "I don't see any way to hike around."

"Nah, you don't want to bushwhack," Awol said.

Awol pulled off his pack, reached in for gorp, and sat down. "Where are you guys from?"

"Wyoming," they said, in unison.

The three of them were discussing Yosemite and Glacier National Parks when a hiker burst out of the trail behind them. Dark complexioned, young, and sinewy, he was in an addled state. He looked at them like a cornered animal, not knowing whether to step forward or remain fixed, ten yards away. Seconds of silence elapsed.

"Did you see the fire?" one of the Wyoming hikers asked.

The hiker looked behind him, peering around a larger than normal pack, and turned again to face them. He let Blazer sniff him and patted the dog, then he stepped forward.

"I saw flames. Had to come back—it's at Glen Pass."

Awol noted a slight accent.

"That's less than three miles up," the other Wyoming said.

The Wyomings, One and Two, introduced themselves.

"Madrid," he said. He still looked like he was in a muddle as he shuffled some twigs with his foot and glanced east to the pass.

"Madrid as in Spain?" the first Wyoming asked. "Are you from there?"

"Yes. I'm a student there, at the university. I have to go. Nice to meet you," he said and immediately started poling away toward Kearsarge.

"Madrid," Awol said to the retreating figure, "by any chance do you know a hiker who goes by Barcelona?"

"No, I don't think so." He tramped east and was out of sight in a matter of seconds.

CHAPTER TWENTY-ONE

STANDING ON THE COURTHOUSE STEPS in Independence, California, Awol watched the smoke and fire in the mountains. He and the hikers from Wyoming (he'd been calling them Wyoming One and Wyoming Two) had rooms in the Courthouse Motel across the street. Awol suspected that Madrid was also in town. Independence was a small place, so it would be hard to miss hikers waiting out a forest fire. According to the local news, the fire would be left to burn itself out. There was no danger, as no one lived up there, and the conflagration was headed for a man-made firebreak. Foresters and parks personnel had removed deadwood and undergrowth and dug down to soil, creating a quarter-mile-long path resembling a wide dirt road, which would, essentially, starve the fire.

Awol left Blazer by the motel and walked to the tiny library that adjoined the courthouse. He was reading California newspapers when two hikers entered. One could always tell a thru-hiker—the beard, the taut skin about the neck. But the craving for food, fats in particular, was a dead giveaway. One hiker had a bag of chips; the other a bag of donuts.

"You the guy with the dog? I'm High Octane," the taller one said, extending his hand.

"Awol. My dog is Blazer."

"Dreamwalker," the other said as Awol reached out.

"How did you know about my dog?"

"We met Madrid; he's camping out here somewhere," High Octane said.

"Uh-huh. Camping. Why not a room?"

"Who knows? Said he had to get to Bishop and didn't want a room."

The five thru-hikers in Independence concluded that the only way to avoid the fire was to hitch around it. They sat in Pines Café and, after a dinner of burgers, sausages, fries, and beer (but lemonade for Awol), High Octane and Dreamwalker announced that they would hitch straight up to Yosemite. "My girlfriend's coming down from Portland," Dreamwalker said. "She'll be in Yosemite day after tomorrow." The Wyomings would hitch to Bishop in the morning. Awol bought the last round of drinks, including his lemonade, and told them he would wait until midmorning to take the local bus up to Bishop.

"Here's to Canada," they all toasted. "Manning Park, British Columbia."

After things quieted down, Awol said, "I'm curious about something. This guy, Madrid, does anyone know him? What's his background?"

"Says he's a student in Spain," High Octane answered. "Couldn't get much else out of him."

A light haze hung in the air when Awol boarded the shuttle bus the next morning. As the shuttle pulled onto Route 395, he could see Mount Whitney, the highest point in the lower forty-eight states at over fourteen thousand feet. Blazer sat beside him, and when the dog spotted a coyote circling in lime-green corn lily, he yipped through the open window. The bus traveled north to Aberdeen and Fish Springs. In Big Pine, a dark-skinned lady with a short-stemmed red snow plant fixed in her sun hat boarded with two young children. The kids chose their seats, and when the boy came over to pat Blazer, the tiny girl followed. Gingerly she patted Blazer and then sat in the seat behind him to stay with the animal all the way to Bishop. Blazer loved the attention. Whenever he wanted another pat, he would lift his nose and wet-nuzzle her cheeks.

Bishop, 831 trail miles north of the Mexican border, was a good-sized town in the heart of the Sierra Nevada. Knowing that the Wyomings were staying at Motel 6, Awol had the shuttle drop him close by. He met them later for dinner at the Sizzler.

"Madrid asked about you," Wyoming Two said between bites of cornbread.

"He's here too? What did he say?"

"Wanted to know if you were here and where you're staying."

Awol nodded, and they ate in silence.

After a refill of iced tea, Awol wiped barbecue sauce off his lips and took a swig. "Makes you wonder though. What's Madrid hiding?"

"He is in a hurry. We ran into him in the grocery store lot. He'd been dropped off to get food, and a guy was taking him somewhere."

"What was the guy driving?"

"A Jeep."

Awol concluded that if the procedure was similar to what he had witnessed back at the campground, someone else had been taken back to the PCT and was poling north right now. A runner was ahead of him. The question was, where did this mule reenter the trail? *Near Bishop Pass on the PCT, where a mule was headed in the first place,* Awol thought. After checking his maps and guide, Awol selected the Piute Pass Trail, which was north. He'd scout the mule when he came north from Bishop.

Awol had no intention of calling Sacco . . . yet.

CHAPTER TWENTY-TWO

CAPTAIN MEDINA LOCKED HIS OFFICE door. His sweaty palms slipped along the top of the desk as he sank into his chair. *Kill him? How?* He tried to think of an escape. He couldn't do what they wanted. It was impossible. He pulled out an atlas from the credenza behind him and started flipping pages, then tossed it to the floor. Thump. *Where can I go? My money is tied up with them. I can't—*

The shrill ring of the phone made him jump. He lowered the volume on the headset, put it to voice mail, and a few minutes later listened to the message from Sacco: "I'm on to something. Need to rattle your brain on this. How about lunch tomorrow?"

Medina stared at the phone.

It had been the money. Seven years ago, there was no PCT operation other than some simple dumps from Tecate, Mexico, over the border into Campo, California. From there the drugs were smuggled to San Diego by dirt poor farmers in their pickups. Medina had been in charge of US Border Patrol employees from San Ysidro to Ocotillo, a sixty-mile strip right on the border. One night, when he had made an arrest himself and was confiscating the contraband, he received a call from Alvarado. To his surprise and dismay, he was reached on his personal cell number, which he'd given to only a select few. The message was simple: one hundred thousand dollars was his if he allowed Verdugo, whom he had arrested, to escape. The caller had barely finished his sentence when Medina heard a rap on the door. A Mexican policeman entered, sauntered to him, and handed him a takeout burrito box. Medina noted that the box wasn't warm when he took it, and there was no aroma coming from it. Inside was the money—all of it.

After the policeman left, Medina took the battery out of his personal cell to prevent tracking. He'd use another phone. Within two hours, the same Mexican policeman reentered and instructed Medina to put the battery back in his phone and to keep it there. The policeman held up his own police cell phone and displayed a picture, which he said Alvarado had received. The picture showed Medina counting the money from the burrito box.

Alvarado and Verdugo didn't spoil Medina; they gave him a taste of what was possible. But they owned him. They casually let him know that they knew the location of his two sisters, his brother, and all his nieces and nephews. They recited their full names. Just precautions, they said, should anyone think of contacting the US Marshals. Two days after he let Verdugo escape, he received an envelope containing several enlarged photos showing him accepting the box and counting the money. Verdugo called him regularly after that, but they'd kept his life simple, and he wasn't asked to do anything outrageous—look the other way here, miss an illegal there, occasionally let someone escape. For a year, Medina was taken care of. When Verdugo told him that they'd arranged an interview for him with the San Diego Police, he took the opportunity and got the job. He was told to create secret files on people he worked with, especially those he thought he could turn. The files were to contain the individual's hot buttons, family details, the names and addresses of relatives, and, in particular, the person's faults, debts, failings, addictions, wishes, and anything else that would make the person vulnerable. From such files, an occasional individual was "offered" Border Patrol duties, and Medina would be instrumental in that person's placement.

Within five years, Medina was promoted to captain. He divorced his wife, disowned his stepson from her previous marriage, and took in a pretty novia. But he couldn't stop gambling. He'd put all his money into it and was on the books—the Mexican books. Now, if Medina could pull off this outrageous request, to take care of Sacco, he would be handsomely rewarded. He could clear himself from their books; he could possibly escape. Otherwise there was nothing. He was a spider caught in his own web.

Medina arrived early at Carina's. The restaurant was fronted by the cartel; only he and a few others knew this for certain, but many suspected. More than one patron, as well as two waiters and a dishwasher, had been executed here over the years. Yet the food was superb, and everyone from the mayor on down came by to eat. A richly colored mural of bandidos and lush señoritas splashed over the back wall, adding to an atmosphere of secrets. A corrido mewled from hidden speakers. The first thing Medina noticed when he walked through the semicircular cobblestoned arch was Sacco, staring at him over his beer at a corner table.

"You got here early," Medina said.

"Wanted to be sure you had your special table," Sacco said. He didn't bother to get up. "Your drink is on the way."

"Sweet of you." Medina couldn't stand facing a wall with his back to everyone, and he knew that Sacco knew this. He sat down anyway.

Silence hung as a waitress poured Medina a Casa Madero Merlot. The waitress pulled out a pad and was about to speak when Sacco motioned her away.

"So what's on your mind, Vincent?" Medina adjusted his chair so he was able to glance better behind him.

"I was thinking of the last time we met here—and what you seemed to be asking of me."

"And what was that, pray tell?" Medina didn't flinch, but vibrations filled his belly.

Sacco stared at him and took a sip from his bottle. He nodded his head, in obvious contemplation. He played with the beer bottle and fingered the label. At last he spoke.

"I'm going to have to conduct an investigation, and I wanted to tell you in person. Figured I owed you that."

"Vincent, what the fuck are you talking about?"

"Took me a long while to see it, but two and two make four, four and four make eight. They've got you by the throat, don't they?"

Medina swallowed a mouthful of Madero and licked a lip. "Would you be kind enough to answer my question?"

"You recommended that Border Patrol guy who was executed in the desert. You got him the job, and when we tried to investigate the murder, the body and all the evidence conveniently slipped away."

"Let me stop you right there. That guy in the desert was on the take maybe, but no one, not a soul, knew that."

"Why was he executed?"

"Vincent, for Chrissake, you know how these things are. He either saw something he shouldn't have, or he was compromised, got greedy. He was probably holding out and dealing off the side."

"I've checked other BP hires you've recommended, and in each case we've had a problem or suspicions with the appointment. That's where four and four make eight."

Medina looked at Sacco and realized it would now be doubly hard to do the task requested by Verdugo; no doubt Sacco had made a file on all this and passed on his suspicions. *Maybe,* he thought, *I can use this new information to give me an out with Verdugo. If US feds suspect me and Sacco gets wiped out, the cartel would be vulnerable.*

"To think how much I've helped you," Medina said. "Who else is in on this investigation?"

"Why would you want to know that?"

Medina stared. "I see. Well, I guess I'll be going. Thank you for the drink."

"Captain Medina."

He turned to face Sacco.

"Is there anything you want to tell me? I will do my best to make this easier on you."

"No. There is nothing to tell."

"Then I'm not shutting down the investigation."

Sacco tipped the waitress and headed back to his office. He would use the afternoon to prepare the necessary papers. Pulling into his spot, he noticed Medina had already returned. Maybe Medina would change his mind. Sacco chose not to submit the request until the end of the day; he would give him a last chance. He knew Medina was compromised, had to be. Sacco saw how this could be a brilliant coup, how he would get mileage from the press, perhaps a commendation from the governor of California. Yet he felt sorry for his mentor. Sacco had never before betrayed someone who had helped him.

Sacco noted Medina's closed doors. He'd seen a lot of that lately, whenever Medina had been around. *Two and two make four,* he thought. He was surprised Medina's secretary had, apparently, taken a late lunch. Later, as he passed by the IT department on his way to use the bathroom, he learned she'd gone home early. He asked why, but no one knew. A more careful look around revealed locked file cabinets, shut-down computers, turned-off phones. Sacco went to his own office and tried to work, but he got antsy. Back at Medina's office, he put his ear to the door; he heard definite rustles and tears and the high hum of what sounded like a shredder. He knocked on the door and was ignored. He turned on the phone, hit a button, and heard the ring inside Medina's office. Again he was ignored.

On impulse, Sacco turned the thermostat all the way up but cracked some windows only in the reception area. Sacco could never understand why Medina kept an office without a window. If Medina was going to be difficult, Sacco would push right back at him. It was 3:40 p.m., and evidence was being destroyed—evidence that would assist his investigation. But he had to be sure. If it was all a ruse—merely the tearing up of newspapers or magazines, a setup baiting Sacco to make a move so Medina could expose him as a power-hungry, foolish narc—it would become a scandal. If he busted in without cause, he could be demoted.

Medina took the call from Verdugo on his personal cell. He had relayed the information he'd learned to Verdugo on his way back to the office. "Destroy all evidence and hold tight until I get back to you," he'd been instructed.

And now: "Take him out. And forget about two weeks—you've got twenty-four hours."

"Wait!" Medina had to remind himself to speak softly into the phone. Sweat coursed in his armpits. "You are asking me to kill Sacco in broad daylight?"

"I said, take him out. How you do it is your problem."

"Can I please speak to Alvarado?"

"He's not interested in talking to you. Says you blew it with Sacco in the first place, then you messed up with your guy in the desert."

"Messed up? I put myself on the line to get rid of the body and all the evidence."

"That's where you messed up! The body should have been taken care of before that hiker and his dog came along."

Medina began to cry. He squeaked into the phone in Spanish, between sobs. The heat coming up from the floor vents affected his mind; he couldn't think straight. Half in Spanish, half in English, he pleaded for his life.

"Twenty-four hours, or you'll end up like the piece of shit in the desert."

Medina hyperventilated as the phone went silent. When he recovered, he evaluated his options. He realized Alvarado had figured out a way to get rid of Sacco and him at the same time. By now, he suspected, Sacco had told everyone about his suspicions. If he all of a sudden suggested to Sacco that they take a ride, go somewhere to talk, Sacco would be wary. Even if he got that far and managed to kill Sacco, Medina would be hunted by the feds. *I might live, but for what?* He knew several people inside prison who would love to kill him. And the cartel—they could eliminate him at any time. He had, in fact, nothing. *God it's hot in here.* He could not negotiate with Sacco. That would deliver the dreaded X from Alvarado, which meant his family would also be murdered. Might not be tomorrow or next week, but the cartel would find a way; they always did. He thought of his sisters and brother and of their children. He'd have to let Sacco make the next move.

At five o'clock, Sacco couldn't stand it anymore. He had to do something. He no longer heard any sounds within Medina's office. This muted his frenzy, but Medina had no doubt destroyed evidence. He tried knocking again—and was ignored again.

"Captain! Are you okay? Please let me in. I just want to talk."

An hour later, two bulletproof-vested cops were ready to bash down the door. Sacco had put in the call to friends, and it had taken some convincing.

"Captain! We're coming in. Give yourself up, Captain," Sacco hollered. Nothing.

Sacco stood aside and gave the sign. The two cops rammed the door just as a shot fired.

Sacco peeked inside. Gun still in hand, Medina's blown-out head was slumped on the desk.

CHAPTER TWENTY-THREE

AWOL WAS IN POSITION, BUT Blazer was fully charged and eager to move up-trail.

"We have to wait, boy."

Blazer whimpered and scratched the duff with his paws. He looked pleadingly to his master as if he was waiting for him to throw a stick.

"I know, this sucks." He patted the dog's head and rubbed the ears. They were forty yards west of an open arête, which ended in the draw in front of them. The sun was behind them, giving them a clear view as they hid among the oaks and aspens. Blazer lay down at last, but Awol worried the dog would give him away. Madrid might have told his people about him and his dog. Awol rethought his location and moved forty yards farther off the trail onto mantle. He still had a clear view, but he and the dog were better hidden. He would not intercept but would try to follow as best he could. The thought of trying to keep up made him sigh. He fed Blazer and grabbed the bag of granola. He spied and waited.

Eight hours later, they both looked at a half-moon rise in front of them. At eight thousand feet, the temperature had dropped; Awol pulled out his fleece. He began to despair. If Madrid or someone else hiked at night with a headlamp, he wouldn't be able to follow him. Unlike the Appalachian Trail—which was full of roots and narrow, winding switchbacks of pits and angles, making it nearly impossible in most places to hike at night at more than a snail's pace—the PCT was exposed to the night and followed long and wide traverses. Awol's headlamp would be seen, and he couldn't bushwhack without it under a half-moon.

Awol could only hope the mule would sleep this night. He didn't think the mule had beaten him here. Where the hell was he? He tried writing in his journal, but his mind wandered. He needed to sleep, but he was charged up with thoughts about Kenny and Sacco. Sacco had reason to be upset and was getting impatient.

At 5:15 a.m., he and Blazer set out for the top of the pass, where there would be a wider view. Awol was setting up when he spied a hiker approaching a mile away. He looked through his binocs and—sure enough—extra-large pack, alone, moving smartly; this was the runner. Something made him take up the glasses again—*Barcelona!* Anger welled up in him as he watched Barcelona approach. He thought about the last time he'd seen him, back at the rockslide. Was he just going to let him glide by fifty yards in front of him? He could hardly stand it, but he stifled his emotions and was about to tuck into his spot when Barcelona moved to a large boulder on the other side of the trail and disappeared.

"Blazer," Awol commanded in a hushed tone. "Stay!" Awol held up his finger until the animal sat down. "Stay!" When the animal lay prone, Awol took out his Buck knife and sneaked down to the boulders.

Awol got to the front of the rocks and listened. He heard the pull of a pants zipper, and the silence thickened. Barcelona emerged.

"Did you gut that dog?"

Barcelona, seeing the knife, tucked under his full pack and brought his poles together in the military bayonet "ready" position. "I did, but I had no choice. I love dogs."

"You have a funny way of showing your love of animals." Awol was without pack and poles as he maintained a defensive position ten feet away.

"When your wife and children's lives are on the line, you have no choice."

Barcelona stared at Awol's knife and reached to unclip his pack harness.

"Stop! Keep it on. I'm not here to kill you, but you take that pack off, I will." Awol crouched and extended the knife in front of him.

"Where is your dog?"

"I'm keeping him away from the likes of you."

Barcelona lowered his poles. "I have to leave. Do yourself a big favor. Don't come anywhere near me. The people I work for like to chop off arms and feet and then watch those people bleed out and die. They want you gone, and I don't want to kill you." He poled off.

"Hold it! I saw you at that rock slide—you've already killed someone." Barcelona kept walking.

"Goddamn you, stop!" *Don't get in over your head,* Sacco had said. Awol heard the voice again. *Just don't do anything on your own.* For one of the rare times in his life, Awol restrained himself.

He watched Barcelona's calf muscles bunch on each step.

Awol spit and fretted after he scrambled up to Blazer and his gear. He shushed the dog as he yanked up the field glasses and watched Barcelona curve toward Florence Lake. He took out the satellite phone. For the first time, he could not reach Sacco.

He would be pressed to keep up with Barcelona. And to keep bushwhacking ahead of him would be difficult and exhausting at best. It also posed another problem: Barcelona would treat it as a threat and set a trap. As long as Awol didn't threaten him, he felt Barcelona would leave him alone. He decided to follow Barcelona at a distance, as best he could, and wait for Sacco to return his call.

Awol didn't sleep at all that night. He second-guessed every decision he'd made since coming West. As he twisted and turned on his pad, Blazer sensed the turmoil; from time to time, when his master grumbled something and sighed, Blazer would come into the tent and lick his face and nibble his ears. Awol would push Blazer away, and the dog would crouch down, lie on his belly, and look at him, waiting.

"Go to sleep, Blazer."

Awol stared into the blackness of the tent. He thought about Iraq. In Iraq he endured ennui mixed with periods of frightening horror. His stomach roiled constantly whenever he and his unit manned up. In a rearview mirror, he'd seen the army jeep behind him bounce into the air in flames. His own vehicle had missed the IED by inches, and the explosion made his ears hum for days. He'd never wanted to go through anything like that again, but here he was, engaging in dangerous scenarios involving drug cartels. And his stomach began to roil again.

At first light, Awol was mentally and physically enervated—so much so, he didn't feel like moving at all. His head felt light and heavy at the same time, and he wondered how that was possible. He all but threw Blazer his scraps. Awol ate oatmeal and did some light stretching but still felt like a zombie; he hadn't slept right in days. He checked the phone—nothing. After replenishing his water at Hilgard Creek, he thought about trying to reach Sacco again but didn't have the energy to face another unanswered call.

All morning, Awol trudged up the trail out of sorts. Vistas of rock-cragged buttes and snow-capped mountains were oblivious to him. They stopped for a snack by Heart Lake and Awol fell asleep, missing a bullhead jump up from the water in front of him. Three minutes later, after being nudged by Blazer, he was back on the trail.

Late that afternoon, coming down the steep north side of Silver Pass—as Blazer became a speck and still ran on ahead—Awol felt a shove. He was pushed over the east side of the pass. He tumbled over several times, clutching at rocks and scrub, and had just started to yell when his rib cage busted. He finally came to a stop but could no longer feel his left arm. He was vaguely aware of someone rushing to him and, with effort, he opened an eye.

"Listen to me. I am supposed to kill you." Barcelona showed his knife; the edge glinted in the lowering sunlight. He peeked around and spoke in a hushed tone.

"Get off this trail. This is your last chance. I have no choice; stay off this trail, or you are a dead man."

He rushed off as Awol lost consciousness.

Blazer lapped Awol's face again and again. Awol was aware of this, but try as he might, he didn't have the strength to move, to open an eye, to speak. Blazer went to his eyes, and Awol kept them closed. When Blazer nibbled his ears, Awol moved a finger, wiggled a foot. Blazer barked as a last resort, and Awol opened his good eye.

"You okay, Blazer? Good boy."

Blazer walked to the other side of him and gripped Awol's pack with his mouth and pulled. Awol felt immediate relief in his bad arm as he repositioned it. But his broken ribs made it barely possible for him to breathe. The animal barked again and scratched in the dirt.

Awol tried to roll to his less injured side but could make it only partway. Blazer understood, bit the lower part of his shirt, and pulled. "Not hard . . . go slow." Blazer tugged, and Awol was able to rest on his good side. That was the best he could do. He slowly took inventory. His left arm was broken at the elbow, he had busted ribs, his left eye was swollen shut, and his left leg, though not broken, was twisted grotesquely beneath him.

He managed to pull out Blazer's water bottle. *Thank you, God.* But when he went to untwist the cap, he bobbled it and the bottle rolled down into the pass and out of sight. *Fuck!* He looked for the nearest patch of snow—too far.

With Blazer's help, he twisted himself around so he lay uphill. Almost immediately, his head felt better as blood drained to lower extremities. But body pain was rampant. He got the pack off and noticed the ripped sternum strap, which may have saved his life; it didn't catch his throat. He reached up and felt a tender collar bone with a tumorlike bump below the neck. Awol was able to twist his neck only part way to the right. He pulled out his first-aid kit and uncapped the container of Motrin, gulping three tablets as he reached for another water bottle in his pack's side pocket. He saw that all his bottles—bottles he had filled at Mono Creek, three miles south—had been ripped from the side pouches on his pack. *Water!* He looked down into the pass; the bottles had tumbled to the bottom. He had some emergency water buried inside his pack, but the thought of twisting to get it was nearly enough to make him black out.

He kept the day's guide pages in his pocket and, looking around for the first time, noticed them lying among the rocks; these, too, had been torn from him in the fall. He crawled to one, straightening out his wrenched leg, and nearly had it in reach, when an early evening breeze shifted and floated it another ten yards away. The five-yard effort had taken a toll. He couldn't move another inch; just the thought of it was agonizing.

Ten minutes later, as the sun began to set and the chills of night began in earnest, the thought of attempting some type of camp on the rocky, exposed slope overwhelmed him. He couldn't find the emergency beacon but did manage to dig up the satellite phone. Holding it between his knees, he used his good hand to punch the turbo-dial for Sacco. This time Sacco answered.

CHAPTER TWENTY-FOUR

NIGHT CLOSED IN. CLOUDS COVERED the moon, and the wind felt like sandpaper rubbing his face. Awol lay on his side under his poncho and shivered. He'd managed to unfold his RidgeRest pad and roll his good side onto it, and he had turned his pack to buck the wind. Trying to set up a tent was impossible; the slightest exertion was like an ice pick shoved into his broken ribs, plus he was on a rocky slope. The wind itself was trying to roll him farther downhill.

"Hold on 'til morning," Sacco had said. "The chopper is on another emergency."

"Godspeed," Awol had rasped.

He didn't have the strength to eat. Blazer huddled by the rocks next to him but whimpered from time to time and peeked out at his master. Then the rains came.

BARCELONA NO LONGER HOPED HE would end up in purgatory; he convinced himself he was doomed to hell. The rain pelted his tent as he thought of the hiker and his dog. He should never have told Verdugo of their confrontation. And he should have killed the man, as instructed by Verdugo. He just couldn't. *I might have compromised my family.* With this thought, he wondered if he should go back, find the hiker, and finish the job. He had less than nine months to go to secure his family's freedom. He'd given up on salvation for himself.

CHAPTER TWENTY-FIVE

From DUCK LAKE, VERDUGO COULD see a chopper circle at Silver Pass. He refocused the binoculars and could make out a red cross. The helicopter dipped several times in the early light. *Has to be searching for a body*, he thought. It alarmed him that the feds already knew where the murder took place; one thing was certain, this man with the dog had been no ordinary hiker.

At a quarter after four the following morning, Verdugo picked up Barcelona north of Mammoth Lakes.

"Did you do what I asked, Barcelona?"

Barcelona looked at Verdugo. "I threw him off the pass, down into the rocks. He was dead where I found him."

"Good! Better that it looks like an accident."

Barcelona loosened his boots and wiggled his toes under the blowing heater.

"Alvarado likes you. It's time you learned more about our operations." Verdugo flipped him a manila folder. "Study up on that for the next two days. Give it back when I pick you up."

SACCO WAS LATE ARRIVING TO the emergency room at Mammoth Hospital in the Sierra, and he hurried to the ICU. Awol was in a coma. The doctor told Sacco he could not stay in the room, that he would be called when Karl Bergman revived. His three busted ribs, broken arm and collar bone, and sprained ankle weren't the primary problems; he'd been dehydrated and was suffering from hypothermia.

Three days later, Awol opened his eyes and saw his wife, Linda, reading in a chair. He eyed the cast on his arm, realized he was in a hospital room, and went back to sleep. Several hours later, he heard voices and woke up to Kenny and Jill. They and Linda got wide-eyed and closed in on the bed.

"Dad? Karl?"

"Hi. Where's Blazer?"

"Tied up outside, near the cafeteria," Linda said. "The nurse said animals aren't allowed in patient rooms. How do you feel, Karl?"

Awol's eyes glanced to Kenny and Jill and then back to Linda.

"Damn nice of you to come out. Thanks."

Linda came to the bed and leaned in to kiss him on the forehead.

"Gregory was here," Kenny said. "He just left."

Awol started to say something, teared up, and closed his eyes.

"And Jill bought you some of that ubiquitous, nutty fruitcake."

"The kind people try to give away at Christmas?" Awol said, eyes closed. They all chuckled. Awol looked at Jill. "Thank you."

After Kenny and Jill left and the doctors finished with rounds, Awol and Linda were alone.

"I treated you badly," Awol said. "As much as I'm happy to see you, I don't deserve it."

"Don't try to talk too much, Karl. You need to take it easy."

A minute or so passed. "Did Blazer take to the hike?"

"Yes. He's been terrific."

"I've missed him."

"Yes, I know you have. And thank you, again, for letting me take him on the trip."

"You can have the dog, Karl."

Awol frowned.

"I mean . . ." Linda stopped and forced a smile. "Sorry."

"I bought the dog for you. He's yours."

Karl tried to shift his position, and Linda came over to assist him.

When she leaned over to place her hand under his good arm, Awol tried to kiss her. Linda instead placed a hand on his cheek, and they looked at each other—saved from further conversation by a knock at the door.

"Well hello, Awol," Sacco said. He had Blazer on a leash. The dog pulled him to Awol's bedside, whereupon Blazer tongued Awol's outstretched hand. As Awol patted the dog, Blazer sniffed his body, the sheets, and got as near to Awol's face as he could without leaping up on the bed.

"How you doing, boy?" Awol said as he scratched behind Blazer's ear.

"I told the staff that Blazer is a police dog. They're allowing him to stay."

Awol looked to Sacco and then back at Linda.

"Detective Sacco came by earlier," Linda said.

"Should I come back some other time?" Sacco asked.

"No," Linda said. "You guys talk; I'll come back later." Linda patted Awol's arm and retreated. Silence filled the room.

Awol eyed Sacco. *For once*, Awol thought, *the man's at a loss for words.*

"How'd you get me out?"

"If it wasn't for your dog, we might never have found you," Sacco said. "You scrunched yourself in rocks, but Blazer jumped out and ran in the open just when we turned to look farther south."

"Yeah? Good boy, Blazer."

The tail thumped the floor, and Blazer rolled to his side begging for a pat on the belly. Awol tried to lean over to pat him but winced; the dog got up, sniffed Awol's face, and licked him.

"What happened to the PLB? I thought you were going to activate it after we'd talked on the phone?"

"I'd wedged it in the bottom of my pack. It was taking forever to find it—I wasn't thinking right and didn't have the strength. I felt ready to black out."

"I see. The phone had given me a location, but we couldn't see you, and without a beacon, well . . ."

"What's happening?"

"I wish I could tell you we made a bunch of arrests."

Awol remained silent.

"So tell *me* what happened, everything you remember," Sacco said.

"Were you in the chopper?" Awol asked. "I don't remember much."

"Yes. We lowered two men, who went down to rig you up on the stretcher." Sacco sat down. "You called me, of course. You were in agony, but we got the gist of what happened with Barcelona. What else do you remember?"

CHAPTER TWENTY-SIX

"**W**HAT DO YOU MEAN, HE'S alive?" Alvarado said.

Verdugo felt a chill creep through him. "I just got word from my inside man. He wasn't expected to live, but the gringo bastard is out of the coma and expected to recover."

Silence.

"Barcelona said he found him dead," Verdugo added.

"Have you been happy with Barcelona?"

"Yes. Physically, he's the best we've got."

"The man with the dog will quit?"

"Yes. He's in bad shape. And I'm told his head is scrambled."

"After Barcelona's next haul, shift him back down here. And keep him under your thumb. I won't tolerate another miscalculation."

Verdugo slapped the phone shut and sucked blood from his lip. Alvarado was never accidentally ambiguous; every word was calculated. The fact that he didn't indicate whose next screwup he wouldn't tolerate— Barcelona's or his own—meant they both were dispensable. It would take a while to get back in his cousin's graces. Verdugo understood one way of doing that would be to get information on Alvarado's counterpart— Tulio Lombardi.

DETECTIVE VINCENT SACCO WAS IN a quandary. He'd lost a colleague in the line of duty, his captain in a suicide, and now there was the Bergman fiasco—

all on his watch. He had just left the San Diego police chief's office—where he'd been summoned—and felt like Callahan in *Dirty Harry*. "Detective, show me your authorization for employing Bergman . . . It was never approved? Who the fuck is going to pay his medical bills? Any attorney will tell him to sue our ass!" At best, Sacco might escape with a letter of reprimand; he expected worse.

The following morning, he was taken off the case. He was handed an official letter from the chief outlining what he'd been told by him and ending with: *You are to concentrate your efforts on the illegal growth of marijuana in southern California forests*. When he tried to find out who would be handling the Pacific Crest Trail files, he was told that the decision was under consideration.

Sacco tried to take the turn of events with equanimity. He would have to lie low for a while and retrench. He still thought cracking the PCT drug operation would make his career. That evening he learned that Medina's counterpart in Los Angeles, Captain Cohee, would assume Medina's duties until a new person was assigned. Sacco expected to be passed over. But Cohee? Cohee was clueless.

CHAPTER TWENTY-SEVEN

Awol FELT STRONGER EACH DAY. At the end of the first week, his ex, Gloria, had come by with Gregory for a brief visit. She brought a vase of assorted flowers. After Linda shook her hand and placed the vase for Awol to see, she took Blazer for a walk. Gloria, whom he hadn't seen in over ten years, was as cordial as Gregory was quiet. Awol inquired after her ill husband, and they talked about Kenny and Jill and the boys' schooling, as she and Gregory stood at the end of Awol's bed. No one brought up the subject of drugs, and after twenty minutes, Awol was alone.

Several days later, Linda, who had been in Mammoth Lakes for nearly a week, announced she'd be leaving.

"I can't tell you how much you mean to me," Awol said. He looked at her sheepishly. "I'll make it up to you—I promise."

Linda turned and talked to the window. "Would you say these things if you were healthy, standing on two feet and drinking a beer, Karl?"

"I remember a scene in a movie where the girl says, 'Don't tell me you love me, just love me,' and I admit, I've failed you in that."

Linda, who was sitting by the bed, shifted her legs and crossed her arms.

"I've been meaning to talk to you about something else," Awol said.

Linda looked back at him.

"You remember what I told you about Kenny. I want to pay off his drug debt."

"With what?"

"We've got enough to cover it . . . in our account."

"Oh! In our account. Weren't we saving that for your promised big trip?"

"Linda. I have to do it. For Kenny, I mean."

"Let his stepfather pay. Why raid our funds?"

"His stepfather has other problems; he's dying."

"We have problems too, Karl."

"I can't fail Kenny again, Linda. My boy's gotten himself offtrack; this time I have to be there for him."

"So noble of you, Karl. And of course, I'm the selfish woman standing in your way." She stood and recrossed her arms.

"Jesus, Linda. Everything I do is wrong. Can't you see my side this time?"

"Yes, Karl, and your side's just one thing after another."

"I'm trying. I went to rehab. I've dried out. Sacco says—"

"I'm not interested in Sacco! Look at you! You never should have come out here in the first place. And don't think I'm stupid about what's going on with you and Detective Sacco. And now this—raid our funds to pay off your son's drug debt? You've hardly seen him in ten years."

"All the more reason why I feel obligated to do it," Awol said.

Linda sniffled and dried her tears with tissue.

"Linda, I've thought it through. You are, without question, the best thing that ever happened to me. Our problems have been my fault entirely. I want you to know that I've given up the bottle for good."

"The bottle is a symptom of a deeper problem, Karl. You have PTSD, and you won't get help."

"Linda." Awol tried to reach for her, but she remained standing beyond his grasp. "I can only do one thing at a time, okay? Right now, I want to pay off Kenny's drug debt."

Linda threw up her hands and gathered her things. Blazer, who had been quietly sitting at the bedside, perceived the change and padded over to her. Linda crouched down to pat him. Linda caressed Blazer and sighed. A full moment passed.

"We both love you," Awol said.

Linda said to the dog, "Karl is impossible. See to it that he keeps his head on straight, okay, Blazer?" And with that she gave the dog a final pat. Only at the door did she hesitate and come back to Awol. She closed her eyes, kissed him on the forehead, and went back through the doorway.

CHAPTER TWENTY-EIGHT

THAT NIGHT AWOL PHONED SACCO.

"What's this I hear about you being reassigned?"

"It's temporary. I'll be back."

"Looks like I really messed things up for you."

"You've gone through a lot more than I have."

"But you are on to something. I'm convinced you were right all along."

"Thanks, but it's back to square one."

"Listen, I'm going to pay off my son's drug debt. Anything I need to know?" Awol listened to silence. "Are you there?"

"Sometimes, in this racket, they want to keep a user hostage."

"He's done using. We're talking twelve grand."

"That's a pittance to them. If he tries to pay it all at once, they figure they might lose him."

Awol tried to sit, but gave up. "They won't take the money?"

"They do take his money, but not all at once; they bleed him on their own time. They meet him regularly for payments, figuring down road he will buy again, make a mistake."

"Those ruthless, fucking bastards."

"The way it usually works, if he gives them the total up front, they load on extra fees, vigorish, whatever."

The following morning, Awol made another call to his bank.

"Come over by the bed, Kenny."

His son was alone tonight, and he looked lost without Jill. Awol took an envelope from behind the pillow and handed it to him.

"Listen to me. You take this, cash it, and pay those bastards. If they question why you are paying all at once, you tell them you are leaving town, going to Boston, whatever, but that you need to square up now."

Kenny opened the envelope and stared at a check made out in his name for thirteen thousand dollars.

"Look me in the eye and promise me you will do this—that you will do it right away."

"Okay, Dad. I promise."

Awol began his physical therapy at the Sierra Clinic, which was associated with the hospital. He tackled the sessions with a positive frame of mind and pushed himself at every chance. Mentally he felt refreshed, like a burden had been lifted, and the staff admired his spirit as well as his progress. It had been two weeks since he'd left the trail.

After three more days, he was scheduled for discharge. He asked Kenny if he could arrange for him to get a room, temporarily, at his dorm. Kenny was happy to do it; the academic year was over, so a few rooms were available.

For the next few days, he kept moving. His right ankle was sore and his ribs hurt, but if he didn't cough or sneeze, the ribs held up. He paced about campus--wobbly at first, but kept moving.

Two weeks later, when he was doing much better physically, Awol called Linda. She was distant. "I know you're pissed off about the money," Karl said.

"You just don't get it, do you?"

"I know. I'd said twelve grand but ended up taking more."

"Karl! It's not about the money any more than your problem is simply about drinking."

"So what is it then?"

"We've been through it, Karl. You need some type of professional counseling."

"I don't have time for it. Look, I told you I've been to rehab. I told you I've given up—"

"Stop! Just stop!"

"Linda . . ."

"I'm not going to talk with you about this anymore. I don't want you to get hurt—physically—and I wish you well. But don't come back here unless you are cleaned up *in therapy* and 110 percent committed to our marriage. Good luck, Karl."

The next morning, Awol arranged for a dozen red roses to be shipped to Linda with a card saying, "Okay. I will be back! Blazer sends his love."

CHAPTER TWENTY-NINE

THE MORE LOMBARDI TRIED TO keep his cool, the more he wanted to spit into the phone.

"Mr. Lombardi," Alvarado said, "you need to concern yourself with your own territory, not mine."

"That's my point. Where that guy was thrown off the pass borders my territory. And besides, what you do affects the entire operation, all the way to Canada."

"I'm moving my man back down here. And let me be blunt—I don't take orders from you, and I never will."

What Lombardi wanted to tell him was to stick his goddamn chess set where the sun doesn't shine. He decided to drop his trump card. "Luis, I apologize; I'm out of line." He let that sink in. "Let's meet. And I promise no griping from me."

"I think we should wait awhile."

"I'll let you decide, but I haven't forgotten about the favor I owe you. I have what you've been looking for."

"You do?"

"Yes, Luis. I do."

CHAPTER THIRTY

IN JULY—AFTER WEEKS OF tramping around the outer campus with Blazer, often with a loaded backpack, and after ever more arduous physical therapy designed to strengthen his ligaments and abdominals—Awol felt he was ready to hike north again. His doctors advised against it, saying his particular trauma lent to slow healing and that any further breaks or tears would become a permanent problem. Besides, they said, why not local hikes? Why not easy ones? With that, Awol embraced his physical therapy all the more. His determination impressed his doctors, and they had to admit his recovery was not only strong but well ahead of schedule.

"Dad, I appreciate what you did for me. I'll never forget it."

They sat across from each other at an outside wrought iron table, next to the library. Students wheeled by on skateboards, one of them swinging his yo-yo. Four knockout coeds hovered nearby; each wore a single-lettered T-shirt, which from left to right read: F U K C. Blazer lay under the table as Awol reached over to his son and squeezed his shoulder. "You're welcome. Are you sure that you are free and clear, Kenny?"

"Yes. When I paid the collector, he tried to give me a packet of . . . I gave it back to him. It's over."

"Bastards!"

"Don't worry, Dad. I'm done, and the guy knows it."

"Good. Here's my next proposition. Join me for a while up in Oregon. Now that you can take some time off."

"Hmmm." Kenny pondered the idea and, for whatever reason, looked around behind him.

"Jill won't mind," Awol said.

"Jill just bought a dog."

"Yeah? What kind?"

"A golden retriever. She decided to let her brother keep Phoebe."

"Neat."

"Haven't you had enough of the PCT, Dad?"

"I came out here with a goal, to complete a thru-hike of this magnificent trail. The most difficult sections are behind us. You ready to leave this place and rough it with a military guy—your old man?"

On a July morning two weeks later, Jill drove Awol and Kenny to Ashland, Oregon. The previous morning, when she had picked up Kenny to go get the rest of his equipment, she'd introduced Awol and Blazer to Lulu, her newly adopted two-year-old golden. Blazer and Lulu sniffed each other thoroughly, and then the retriever took off across the courtyard by Kenny's dorm.

"Jill!" Kenny said, "Blazer's gone after her. Look at them go."

The two dogs romped for a full ten minutes, taking turns chasing each other.

"Figured if you were going to up and leave me," Jill said in a nonchalant voice, eyeing the horizon, "I'd get someone to keep me company."

The dogs now played in the backseat of Jill's car. Less than a mile into the trip, Awol slid over to let Blazer and Lulu sit side by side. Awol noted that Blazer protected his spot beside Awol and allowed Lulu the window.

It was full-on night when Jill dropped them at the PCT trailhead.

"Sure you'll be okay on the drive back?" Kenny asked.

"I have Lulu; I'll be fine. What about you guys? Are you camping right here?"

"First lesson, never camp at a trailhead. Kenny, get out your headlamp." Awol gave Jill a peck on the cheek. "We'll set up about a half mile in. If you camp at a trailhead, you lay yourself wide open to anybody and everybody."

She and Kenny said their good-byes while Awol played with the dogs by the back of the car.

"You guys say good-bye too," Awol said to the dogs.

As if on cue, Blazer barked at Lulu and playfully plunked his front down, then he followed Lulu to the door as Jill called her back in. As Jill turned her car around, she grinned and thumbed to Lulu, who was whining and pushing her nose up over the passenger side window.

Kenny and Awol watched as Blazer whined and yipped at the car until it disappeared.

The next morning, they stood next to each other on a bluff overlooking bottomlands. A clutch of blue grouse beat before them and swerved down to the river.

"You'll see a lot of game birds out here, Kenny. Grouse hang off timbered slopes and like to go to meadows near water."

Awol looked at cirrus clouds high to the west and motioned north as Blazer took charge and bounded along the path, stopping to sniff, looking back at them, then bounding again. You could sense the high intelligence of the Belgian Malinois. Blazer had a shepherd's ears.

"Beautiful animal, isn't he?" Awol said.

"Yeah."

That night they camped below Siskiyou Gap, in lower Oregon. After eating a meal of freeze-dried beef stew, prepared by Chef Kenny, under pine and hemlock, Awol looked behind him to the High Sierra.

"Some bad memories, Dad?"

Awol thought a moment. "Despite it being an awe-inspiring string of mountains and passes, the grandest outdoor spectacle I'll ever see—yes."

"Why?"

"Not now, Kenny."

A few evenings later, they sat by their tents, engaged in comfortable conversation. They'd gotten used to each other as hiking partners, and Awol's recovery needs matched Kenny's lack of fitness. After small talk was exhausted, Kenny broached the subject again.

"Linda and I—when Detective Sacco came to the hospital—we wondered about what really happened to you back in the Sierra."

Awol squirted on more bug spray. "How do you like Linda?"

"She's great, Dad. My mom liked her too."

"She's a winner. I'm glad you and your mom thought so."

"So—"

"Linda came into my life at the right time. As you and your brother know, I screwed up the first time."

Kenny hadn't expected this turn in the conversation. He wanted to know about what happened in the Sierra but now felt obligated to change course.

"Women," Awol said. "I think it was Richard Burton who said, 'They are a different species.' That's certainly true for me anyway."

Kenny smiled and leaned back on his elbows, while Blazer lay in front of them.

"Don't get me wrong. Jill is super. I'm talking about me and my experience."

"I know."

"And now I've screwed up things with Linda."

"How's that?"

"Well, that's enough sharing for one night, but know I love Linda. I'm going to journal, and I know you want to talk with Jill."

Awol got up and started to his tent.

"Dad?"

"Yeah."

"Never mind."

CHAPTER THIRTY-ONE

LOMBARDI FINISHED TALKING WITH MARIO Cedrone, the don in New York. He was delighted with the news and immediately phoned his godson.

"Nino! Get ready to celebrate," Lombardi said. "It's official; Oregon is yours."

"What's that?" Lombardi chuckled into the phone, "You'd better watch your step, or I'll tell your mother."

After a few more playful jibes, he congratulated Nino again and gave him his blessing. Then he called his trusted man, Frank.

"It's set for tomorrow night. Bring the woman to me in the afternoon, so I can brief her. And listen, not a word to anyone—make sure she understands that."

A day later, Frank introduced Lombardi to Paula and then excused himself. Lombardi could see at once that Alvarado would be pleased.

"I'm told you are a ranked chess player and you speak fluent Spanish—I'm sorry; let me fix you a drink. Sherry?"

"Sherry would be fine. Thank you."

He brought her the small glass and handed the drink to her with a napkin. "So."

"I played first board at an Ivy League school, and I've won some competitions. And yes, I minored in Spanish and spent a summer in Chile."

"But none of this is traceable, yes?"

"I have top-notch documentation and a whole false history in place to protect my identity. It's a smart idea in my business, especially once I leave it."

"What I have in mind . . ." Lombardi sat forward on the opposite sofa in the den of the Sierra Nevada cabin. "Well, let me put it to you this way--it may take several meetings for you to get close to this man and get information, but you will be well rewarded."

"How well?"

"Five thousand dollars for each time you visit with him and accomplish what I ask. Frank assures me that we can trust you. However, if I feel you are drawing this out or if my business is compromised in any way, I will do more than fire you."

She took a sip of the sherry and said nothing.

"I hope I make myself clear."

"Of course."

"One other important thing: do not, under any circumstance, let this man know that you understand or speak Spanish."

"Understood. What type of information am I looking for?"

"Tonight's goal will simply be for you to get another tryst. Accomplish that, and you get your first five thousand."

ON THE WAY BACK TO his San Diego apartment, Sacco thought about this newest change in his life. He'd been shunted. He knew that most legislators in California would like to legalize pot so they could tax the shit out of it and fill their coffers. Being stuck here would do nothing for his career and long-term objectives. His unease compounded until a few minutes later, on a last-ditch hunch, he pulled to the side of the highway, reversed direction, and sped back to his office.

He nodded to the duty clerk who had him sign in, a new procedure since the suicide. A few minutes later, Sacco accessed Captain Cohee's secretary's file cabinet. He pulled a Border Patrol personnel folder that contained the most recent appointment Medina had approved. He checked the wall map and found the closest Border Patrol station to Campo, California, where the PCT hikers begin their trek. *Yes!* He read from the file: *Yolanda Sanchez, formerly employed with San Diego Gas and Electric.* Medina, in a hurry to shred other records and evidence, had forgotten about this file, which was new enough to have still been with his secretary. Sacco put the file folder in his briefcase. It wasn't much, but it was a start.

CHAPTER THIRTY-TWO

ALVARADO TOOK IN THE WOMAN in front of him. She was young and beautiful with an incredible hourglass figure. When he'd joked to Lombardi that he wanted all this and an expert chess player besides, they both knew he was asking for the impossible. He wasn't sure what Lombardi had up his sleeve, but he was confident he could stay more than a step ahead. He'd figure out how to turn this to his advantage. But in the meantime, skilled chess player or not, she had other assets he could enjoy.

Alone, Alvarado and Paula eyed each other at the Sierra cabin. A fire crackled in the fieldstone fireplace as they sipped wine, and from beyond the picture window, into the gloaming, a tinge of spruce and pine feathered the inside air. Mahogany-stained eight-by-eight beams vaulted the cathedral ceiling of tongue-and-groove cedar. Recessed ceiling light was dimmed.

The day's meeting had gone better than expected for Alvarado; Lombardi was cooperative and even gracious as they discussed route adjustments and ways to be more efficient with drops. At the moment, business on the PCT was back to normal, and both agreed on the need to communicate. Lombardi had left before Paula arrived.

"How long have you been playing chess, Paula?"

"My father taught me when I was five, but I'd learned the piece moves before then."

Alvarado smiled and took a sip of wine.

"And yourself, Mr. Alvarado?"

"You may call me Luis. I too learned the game at five—so about twice as long as you." *A little less*, he thought, figuring her to be in her late twenties.

Alvarado went to the fire, put on another log, and used the tongs to tumble it back into the flames. He was aware of her watching him.

He turned to her and spoke in Spanish, saying, "I find it odd that one with such giant tits is a serious chess player."

Paula blinked her eyes. "I'm sorry, I don't understand Italian."

"Then how did you know I spoke in Italian?"

"I assumed it was. You are serving Italian wines; Frank and Mr. Lombardi are Italian."

"Well then"—Alvarado refreshed her glass—"let's see how good you are at the royal game."

Alvarado cleared the coffee table of newspapers and nudged the vase of golden poppies to the side. He placed a wood chessboard in front of her, with the dark square to her right. She frowned and turned the board ninety degrees, keeping the beige square on her right.

Alvarado said nothing. He grabbed two black pawns, one in each hand, put his hands in his lap, and waited.

Paula took a sip of her wine and rose to put her goblet on the fireplace mantel. She returned to the chessboard and addressed Alvarado.

"Luis, before I ask you to replace one of the black pawns in your hand with a white one, I would like to offer you a proposition. If you win, you own me for the night, and I shall do anything you want me to. If I win, you will do whatever *I* ask."

Alvarado couldn't help but smile. "My dear, I may have underestimated you. I accept your proposition. To show my good faith, I insist you take white," whereupon he set up the black pieces on his side.

She took up the Ruy Lopez opening, and at once Alvarado could see she was not an amateur.

Her beginning moves were assured. She handled her pieces with confidence and never touched a piece unless she moved it. On the eleventh move, Alvarado offered her a sacrifice, part of an elaborate trap he had worked out on the Ruy line several years ago. He stirred with anticipation as he looked up at her. Her skin was pristine, her lips full. She was pretty, but not stunning; better, she had an air of confidence and looked healthy, strong. She wore a necklace of polished ebony stones with matching earrings and what looked like a copper or bronze band about her right wrist, all of it understated in the right way. But the breasts! Her showpiece. Nestled in a low-cut oxblood wrap dress was cleavage full and firm. Luis went to the thermostat and adjusted it downward.

"Luis, ordinarily I'm not a smoker, but it does help me concentrate during a game. May I?"

"Of course."

When he returned with an ashtray, she had lit her cigarette and declined his sacrifice. She smoked quietly as Alvarado leaned into the pieces. This was the first time an opponent had refused a free bishop.

The middle game was a struggle. For the first time, Alvarado realized he would have to use all his skills to either find a combination to win it there or set up the endgame. Alvarado thought he could distract her, but she wouldn't flirt; she was all business. He was delighted with her play. The way she organized her forces was admirable. She was astute. But the endgame . . . ah, that was his specialty.

On the twenty-ninth move, locked in battle, Alvarado smelled a trap. But at the last moment, he saw a winning combination. The elegance of it made him swoon.

"Check!"

Paula responded with what he thought was the obvious move. Two moves later, he moved his knight to fork her rook and king. "Check!"

She moved her king, and Alvarado captured her rook. In the time it took him to drop her rook into the chess box, Paula had pushed her kingside pawn to the sixth rank.

He smiled as he brought over his rook behind it. *Surely she doesn't think—*

She tapped the board twice with her fingernail. "That's 'check,' Luis."

He looked and indeed it was, and now he remembered she had said something when the rook clanked into the box. When she had advanced her pawn, she opened up her fianchettoed bishop directly onto his king— the "discovered check." And now he looked back at her pawn; she would advance it again to the seventh rank.

Alvarado squirmed as he moved his king.

"Interesting, my dear. Quite interesting indeed."

She moved the pawn as expected. He was a piece ahead, and even if she pawned a queen on the eighth and final rank, he saw now that he would beat her by one remaining move. But she was treacherous—and Alvarado had never been so turned on.

The queens had been exchanged earlier in the middle game, and when she pawned two moves later, Alvarado went to the box for her queen. She was looking right at him as he offered it to her.

"I don't want a queen. Give me a horse."

Alvarado, surprised, put the queen back in the box and selected the knight, or horse, as she crudely called it. He replaced her pawn with it, and his neck flamed red as he realized he was in check by the pawned knight.

He stared at the board. Soon he looked up at her. "Checkmate in three," he said.

She nodded and reached in to topple his king.

After an invigorating discussion of chess openings, gambits, chess masters—over wine, cheese, and fruits—Alvarado rubbed his hands briskly and began to set up for another round.

"Can we wait until next time, Luis? My brain is fried, and I'm afraid I won't be at my best for you."

Alvarado hesitated, looking hurt. "All right."

"You are a serious and demanding player, Luis. You could be a champion."

"Funny *you* should say that. I shall never forget that brilliancy."

"But you have the strong mind, Luis. Your mind is made to last. I'm solid for a game. After that I disintegrate."

She swung her leg over the other knee. "And now, do you remember your promise to me?"

Alvarado spread his palms. "I'm yours, *mi querida*."

"Good. Go to the bedroom, undress to your briefs, and wait for me. Meanwhile, your flowers need water. I'll attend to it."

Alvarado lay on the bed in his briefs, listening to Paula water his plants. She finally entered and closed the bedroom door. The light on his end table provided the only light as she began to untie her dress. He moved toward her, and she put up a hand.

"Not yet."

He squinted at her and felt his prick rise as she undressed herself by the end of the bed, where she could see him. Her eyes watched him as she removed everything except her bra and panties. Alvarado sat up on the bed. Paula took off her necklace and bracelet, and only then, slowly, removed her bra. Alvarado moved to take off his briefs—he was a horny stallion.

"No," she said. "Not until I say."

She found his trousers, and as she bent to pick them up, her breasts were flush, almost rigid, causing his cock to stiffen even more. Paula removed his belt and folded it buckle to end.

"Stand up to the side of the bed," she ordered.

"What?"

"Do not make me repeat myself, Luis. Do as I tell you."

He got off the bed and stood beside it.

"Turn around."

He obeyed.

"Put your arms out on the bed and squat; don't kneel."

"My dear—"

"Quiet! You will speak when spoken to."

Alvarado wondered why he was still rock hard.

"Now you can pull down your briefs."

Alvarado hesitated.

"The longer you take, the worse it's going to be."

Alvarado did as ordered and braced.

CHAPTER THIRTY-THREE

OVER THE NEXT WEEKS, RUNNERS worked their routes along the PCT without incident. Routes in California, Oregon, and Washington operated under commanders reporting to Alvarado in southern and central California and Lombardi in northern California, Oregon, and Washington. Mules on various routes would make their drops on backcountry four-by-four paths, where the drugs were then taken to San Diego, Palm Springs, Los Angeles, Las Vegas, Reno, Klamath Falls, Eugene, Portland, Yakima, Tacoma, and Seattle. A package took three months to get from the Mexican border to Vancouver. It was as slow as the Pony Express of the Old West, but it was steady and virtually undetectable.

The "mail" continuously flowed. But it went only one way—north. After a drop, a mule was taken back to the beginning of his assigned route to prepare for a new run north. Keep it simple, Alvarado had said, and keep the money away from the mules. Alvarado had learned that lesson from Manuel, his patzer back near the border. Once, a mule bribed his driver to take him to a spot twenty-four miles north. The mule showed how it could be done by taking other four-by-four paths. The activity was spotted, probably by air; the mule, under doused lights, was able to jump from the vehicle with his pack. The driver was soon stopped and arrested as an illegal, but the mule had escaped. Any vehicle was suspect.

The Cordiero cartel, knowing Alvarado's boss had somehow developed new markets in the Pacific Northwest, strengthened their operations in southern and central California, and Alvarado, ever the chess player, advised his boss to let them. Alvarado had created the PCT scheme, and profits in new northern markets were rapidly increasing. Alvarado knew that the more the northern markets prospered, the likelier it was that he would be selected to succeed his boss, who had already hinted of retirement. For that reason, Alvarado advised him regularly and, without Lombardi's knowledge, laid out plans and timetables to build a future that would eventually have the Americans controlled by Alvarado. "Better to move around Cordiero," advised Alvarado. "We have larger opportunities. And by the time Cordiero finds out, our forces will be entrenched."

For hikers, mules or otherwise, the optimal seasons were spring, summer, and fall. Right now the operation was running smoothly. It bothered Alvarado that he had to share his creation, but he had to admit that the Mafia was better suited to administer the northern operation—at least for now—because of their long established market there. But he pressed the case that his creation would function best with one overall commander. He wanted the job, and he wanted Lombardi to report to him.

When Alvarado returned to Valle de Las Palmas, he felt achy but invigorated. Never in his life, never in his wildest fantasy, did he think what happened with Paula to be possible. Alvarado was sore from muscles he hadn't plied in years, sore from twists and contortions he hadn't experienced since youth. "There! Now that we are both sufficiently warmed, fuck me!"

He'd hoisted himself upon her, and she laughed and bear-hugged him and loved every minute of it. Less than two hours later, she crawled on top of him. "Now, Luis," she giggled as she rubbed her breasts against his face, "you wouldn't be thinking of going to sleep on me," and he'd rallied. And again in the morning. Alvarado came to believe everything was possible. He would have this woman. Next time he would defeat her in the royal game and own her. Was she Lombardi's plant? Most likely, though he couldn't be 100 percent certain. But he would test her again. Lombardi was not as mentally skilled as he; Alvarado would outsmart his rival.

What particularly invigorated Alvarado was that his plan for gaining information on Lombardi was shaping up nicely. *The dumb wop has the brains of a flea.* If Alvarado was to take command of his PCT creation, he needed to know Lombardi's operation, his people, his methods, his weaknesses. Paula, who looked forward to their next game, would be *his* mole, his entrée to Lombardi. He smiled as he thought of how he would accomplish this.

PAULA LIVED AND OPERATED IN Las Vegas. Although most of her clients were not mob associated, she was initially befriended by Frank, who had been instructed by Lombardi to search for a particular type of woman. Frank had called all his contacts and had put the word out about this singular woman he was looking for. When she was recommended, Frank was surprised that he already knew her—but he hadn't known she was an accomplished chess player. When Paula returned from the Sierra cabin to Vegas, Frank took her straight to Lombardi.

Paula counted the contents of her envelope. "Thank you, Mr. Lombardi."

Lombardi had already provided sherry for their private meeting in his den and told Frank to busy himself in the kitchen. Lombardi put down his glass and picked up his Siamese, who'd been arching her back by his shin. He placed the cat in his lap, whereupon the cat turned on her back so he could pat her belly.

"I've heard a rumor that Mr. Alvarado wants to take over my operation. I need to know who his contacts are, not only his main operational personnel, but his people within the San Diego Police Department. I want to know where these people are and what their duties are. And I want to know Alvarado's vulnerabilities—besides healthy female chess players. Did you whip him, by the way?"

"I did."

"You understand there is danger in what I'm asking of you."

"I've thought about that. I'm dealing with a calculating individual, and this information you are requesting . . . well, I'm not sure—"

"You will find a way. I'm doubling your fee. Consider it hazard pay and proof of my confidence in your ability."

Paula heard the cat purr and watched it curl its front and hind paws about Lombardi's wrist as Lombardi tickled its belly.

"This business we have together won't be for long," Lombardi continued. "I do know that chess players think ahead. He suspects a setup. Get in there and get this done."

"I'll do my utmost, Mr. Lombardi. But I don't think he trusts even his own people with some of the information you are requesting."

"As I said, you will find a way. You understand their language. Keep your eyes and ears open. I want anything and everything that you would need to know if you were in my shoes."

Paula put down her sherry and fiddled with an earring.

"When are you seeing him again?" Lombardi asked.

"This weekend in Palm Springs."

"Can your business handle this change of scenery?"

"I'm available to the escort service, but under the condition I make my own schedule and arrangements."

"That's unusual."

"It's the only way I will continue the work. It took me a while to reach this point."

"Good luck to you, Paula. I'll send Frank for you after your trip to the Palms."

CHAPTER THIRTY-FOUR

DETECTIVE SACCO WENT THROUGH THE Sanchez file a second time. Medina had approved it, all right; his oversized "M" was written on the corner of her personnel sheet. Sacco had Sanchez's home phone number, address, and background check information. Originally from Mexico City, she'd since lived in El Paso for three years; Tecate, Mexico, for fourteen months; and then moved back to the US, where she had resided in Campo, California, for the last two years. Her entire time in Campo, she worked for San Diego Gas and Electric. No other formal employment was listed. She had dual citizenship.

Sacco went directly to the chief's office the following morning.

"Chief, as you know, some of Captain Medina's past appointments caused us problems."

The chief moved forward in his chair. "Look, if this is about shit we've already gone over, I don't have time for it. You're off this case."

"Just read this, Chief. He forgot to shred the file of his most recent BP assignment."

The chief took the file and glanced at it. "So you think this Sanchez is working for the Mexicans?"

"Yes. I'd bet on it."

"But that's all we've got right now, isn't it?" He placed the folder in his desk. "I'll have Cohee stay on top of it. Meanwhile, you put your investigative skills to work on our marijuana problems. I'm reminding you for the last time, Detective—you are off the case."

Sacco left the office, the building, and the town feeling like the enemy.

He was glad of one thing, though: before leaving Medina's outer office last night, he had turned on the copier and duplicated the Sanchez file.

The next evening, Detective Vincent Sacco slammed his apartment door. Another pointless day in the southern California forest. He'd hoped for a success that would have eased him back into good graces with his chief. He stepped over his mail, which lay on the floor below the slot, and dumped his keys into a lathe-carved wooden bowl. After heading back to his bedroom to remove his grimy, sweaty clothes, he turned the A/C fan from low to high and stepped into a cold shower. Twenty minutes later he emerged, put a king-sized terry cloth bath towel on his bed, turned out the lights, and lay down on top of the towel. He lay without moving for another twenty minutes before getting up to put on briefs.

Five minutes later, he pulled a sheet of paper from a file in his leather bag. He picked up his cell and, after partially stuffing his mouth with a handkerchief, punched in the numbers for Yolanda Sanchez.

CHAPTER THIRTY-FIVE

AWOL, KENNY, AND BLAZER TOOK a snack break at a crest saddle, a morning-sunned ridge between the mountain behind and the one ahead. Fresh scat tinged the air as they looked downward; three bighorn sheep stood below the saddle in the draw. They seemed aware of the humans but kept to their own world. In the broad, green, creek-cut valley beyond, several pronghorn antelope browsed the grasslands. Kenny, out of shape and missing junk food and soda, tried to appreciate the view. The last week had been a struggle.

"You're doing fine," Awol said. "You need a couple of weeks to get all that sugar and crap out of your system."

"I'd actually like some sugar and crap right now."

"And be careful with that iPod. You need to stay alert so you don't stumble."

"Music relaxes me."

"You tripped twice yesterday and fell today; you won't feel so relaxed when you sprain an ankle or bang your head."

Awol watched a marmot peek out of the rocks behind Kenny.

"This morning you missed a golden eagle. By the time I got your attention, the bird had soared away. You also miss what's happening right around you," Awol said and pointed.

Kenny looked to his side and then behind him. A furry brown rodent, white fur around the nose, stared inquisitively at him, standing with its limbs hanging together in front. It looked like a woodchuck.

"Cool," Kenny said, throwing it a Craisin. The animal didn't move except for wiggling its nose.

Evenings, after setting up camp, Awol insisted Kenny join him in exercises.

"Got to do it, Kenny. Out here your legs get strong, but your arms and upper body atrophy. C'mon, get in the push-up position—ready, let's go. One, two, three . . ." Awol did his best, but his injuries still punished him.

"Jesus . . . can't we—"

"No. C'mon, Kenny, push . . . eight, nine, ten . . . keep pushing, son, push."

Too soon, Kenny's six-foot, 140-pound body collapsed in a heap.

"I thought hiking was going to be fun."

Me too, Awol thought as he watched his kid jam the earplugs into his ears and turn away.

But Awol made it a routine. Every night, before they went into their tents, they did push-ups, sit-ups, and from a limb of the nearest tree, chin-ups or pull-ups. Awol planned to teach him some takedowns and other moves when the time felt right.

Several evenings later, after Kenny had done twelve push-ups without stopping, Awol asked the burning question. "As smart as you are, and given your studies in biochemistry, how in the hell did you get involved in drugs?"

"It doesn't make any difference how smart you are or what your background is; once you feel that rush, it's hard to back out."

"So?"

"I took my first pinch of coke at a frat party. I never thought I'd get hooked."

"Is the hard stuff easy to get?"

"You can get it anywhere."

"You got hooked early?"

"First time. I knew I was done for."

"That happened to me after my first beer."

"How old were you."

"Sixteen."

At day's end, they camped separately, each pitching his tent fifteen or twenty yards away from the other. Although they hadn't gotten on each other's nerves, they wanted to avoid the possibility. They converged for breakfast.

The ambush at the pass had slowed Awol, and he wondered if he would ever get back to 100 percent. He felt a numbing ache at the end of every day, not just the typical exhaustion from hiking. There was also a tiredness of the soul that made him question his reasons for continuing. Awol decided that he would try to bond with Kenny for as long as his son would stay with him and try to finish in Canada before the heavy snows, but he would not push himself to further injury. And he had to remain vigilant, especially for Kenny's sake. Awol's ex, Gloria, made it clear that she would kill him herself should anything happen to Kenny.

They tramped north into the Oregon forest a mere sixty miles east of the Pacific Ocean and clambered to a wind-sculptured ridge of mantle rock overlooking scraggy talus-based cliffs and granite walls patched with snow on the other side of the gap. In the mountain meadow of the gap, alder thickets and clusters of spruce trees grew in dark, irregular patches. Six mule deer, including a buck, picked through the heather. Kenny admired how simple their life seemed to be.

Awol let Kenny spot trail marker posts or the occasional rock arrows arranged by hikers on sandstone, but usually the narrow trail path itself was all that was necessary to stay on course. When they reached the top of the next ridge, Awol pointed to a mountain, a distant lake, and a nearby tarn and had Kenny estimate the distances and locate the sites on his map. Then after comparing his estimates with the map's distance scale, he showed Kenny how to interpret map elevations and compare them to visuals. The boy was smart and had a solid memory. Awol would sometimes test him by appearing confused at junctions or by acting puzzled when spotting yet another of hundreds of lakelets and water-filled basins. Every time, Kenny was quick to find their location on a map and orient them.

Kenny shared the lead with Blazer, who often bounded ahead on his own. Kenny liked the dog and took to feeding him and giving him water. In the late afternoons after averaging only thirteen miles a day, as Awol attended to his journal, he made a point of asking Kenny questions about the day's terrain, weather, mileage, start and finish times, geographic spots, flora, and fauna. Before sundown, they would review the guide and appropriate maps for the next few days. Awol put Kenny in charge and had him highlight the routes in yellow marker. While glad to answer questions, Awol was wise enough not to hold court and blab on. Kenny absorbed information quickly, and like him, he preferred quick and specific answers.

"Do you ever call Linda?" Kenny asked one evening.

They had reached Mazama Campground next to Crater Lake Lodge. Mounds of last-winter snows, where front loaders had made piles weeks ago to clear the parking lot, melted in the sunny sixty-degree weather. They sat at a picnic table at their tent site eating ice cream. Blazer lay underneath by Awol.

"I'm in the dog house."

Kenny smiled. "What happened?"

"I got drunk. Threatened all sorts of stupid things. Made an ass of myself."

Kenny nodded.

"Don't let an addiction trample your life, Kenny. You should be relieved that you only experimented with drugs and got temporarily hooked. I think you can walk away completely. Not me; I'm told I might have deeper issues that serve to derail me from time to time."

"The war."

"Yeah."

Awol grabbed his water bottle and got up.

"How long do you think you'll want to stay on the trail, Kenny? Don't feel this is something you have to do to please me."

"I think I'll finish Oregon. Maybe cross over into Washington, so I can say I hiked to there."

"Oregon is neat," Awol said. "The Cascades farther up won't be too difficult, but the range gets steeper in Washington."

"I noticed that in the guidebook. I might try my hand at some big climbs."

"One needs to build up to it, Kenny. You're young, but even so, pacing is important. You never want to do too much, too soon, too fast."

Kenny watched his father amble to his tent and knew what he'd do next. Every night, as if on the clock, his father dug out his journal, sat by his pack, and wrote. He watched him check his fancy watch with built-in timer, altimeter, and compass. His father always knew where north was—he confirmed it with his compass several times a day, and each time he would take a moment to look east, west, and south, as he did now. His survival knife was always in his left pocket and connected by a rawhide shoelace to a carabiner latched to a belt loop. The keened blade had saw serrations—useful for building a fire in extreme conditions or making a survival hut, he'd said. His quick-draw Buck knife he hid in his other pocket. Kenny knew his father played dumb sometimes about their exact location and that he was testing him. At first this annoyed Kenny, but then he played along, knowing his father excelled at navigation and orienteering.

CHAPTER THIRTY-SIX

PAULA AND ALVARADO WERE SEATED on opposite sides of a chessboard in Palm Springs, though the pieces remained in the box. She'd been delivered to Alvarado's private hacienda, which overlooked a golf course bordering a llano that stretched to purple mountains.

"Come, *mi querida*, let's watch the sunset." Alvarado led her by the arm onto a second-floor balcony. Overlooking the shrubbed promenade, which included blooming manzanitas with their clusters of pink flowers, they sat in cushioned wicker chairs next to freshly watered palms and acacia. Frank Sinatra crooned at low volume.

Paula watched a cloud on the horizon turn from salmon pink to fiery orange. "This is simply gorgeous, Luis."

Alvarado took something from his pocket and pulled back a frond beside him, exposing a foot-long iguana. He dropped some seeds into the pot.

"Would you be good enough to give these to Cisco? He's right next to you."

Paula took what looked like sunflower seeds and spread the plant leaves at her side. Cisco, a longer and larger iguana, cocked an eye to Paula as she tossed in the seeds.

"Are these your pets?"

"I have two Gila monsters at my hacienda in Mexico that are my pets. But I'm fond of all lizards." From his other pocket, Alvarado pulled two jojoba nuts and secreted them to his mouth.

The blood-red sun brought distant towering rock walls into relief and drew out tans, reds, and whites. Neither spoke as the sun disappeared behind the mountains.

Alvarado led Paula back to the chessboard and sat her down. He grabbed two different-colored pawns as Paula interrupted.

"No, Luis. It is your turn for white."

An hour and forty minutes later, Paula had gone through four cigarettes and managed to draw the game by perpetual check.

"Damn you. Damn you!" Alvarado said.

Paula excused herself and went to the bathroom.

When she returned, Alvarado smiled. "Rude of me. Please, let me see to your comfort." He picked up her goblet and gave her a menu, written in Italian with English subtitles. "My chef is in my kitchen downstairs. Choose whatever you like; meanwhile, I will refresh your wine."

After an exquisite dinner of osso buco with arugula salad, Alvarado returned the conversation to chess.

"We have a deal, my dear, but it is unclear who owns who for the night."

"And you're about to tell me that this dilemma can be solved in only one appropriate fashion."

"Correct. And it is my turn for black. You look tired, Paula."

"Correct."

"You will not lower your standard for me."

Paula's eyes burnt him. "Mr. Alvarado! Hear me when I say, I will never give up in the game of chess. Not to anyone, and especially not to a man."

It was a furious struggle, but two hours later, after using the assembled game skills of a lifetime, Alvarado got her to the endgame. There he found that critical king move that would enable him to gain the opposition. *How fitting*, he thought. *Capablanca himself would be proud.* Three moves later, with élan, he lifted his king and set it a space ahead of his queenside advancing pawn in direct line to her king.

"Very good, Luis. You have the opposition." She toppled her king.

Luis refreshed both wines and lifted his glass to her.

"To the royal game," he said. "Salute!"

"Salute."

"Freshen up and be back here as you are in twenty minutes."

She returned in fifteen. Alvarado finished splashing water on his face from the bar sink and dried off with a towel. He folded the towel, placed it neatly on the metal edge of the sink bowl, pulled down his shirtsleeves, and rebuttoned. He walked over and sat down across from her; the chess set had been put away.

"What I want from you is information. You will tell me everything you know about Mr. Lombardi, and you will keep this conversation secret. Start from the first time you ever heard his name."

Paula adjusted her dress, pulling it down to cover her legs.

Alvarado tried not to notice. "Do you understand?"

"Your instructions are clear. I am surprised by the request."

"Do you work for Mr. Lombardi?"

"Well, no."

Alvarado stared at her and didn't speak or move a muscle. She crossed her arms and looked to the window.

"Look at me, Paula, and listen carefully. I look for reasons to kill people."

"Luis, why are you threatening me? I expect you to fuck me!"

"Of course you are employed by Lombardi!" Alvarado thundered. "I will not be insulted."

Paula's face blushed and her lower lip quivered.

Alvarado waited. "We have our deal. Correct?"

"Correct."

"My instructions remain the same. I want you to tell me everything you know about Mr. Lombardi. Bear in mind, I don't give anyone second chances. I—"

"I've noted that in your chess, Luis."

"And I don't like to be interrupted. Suppose—"

"Luis—"

Alvarado jumped up and raised his hand to slap her face. Paula ducked and covered. A minute passed before she withdrew her hands and peeked up at him. He held a finger to her. "Never . . . ever . . . interrupt me."

Nearly an hour later, when Alvarado had exhausted all possible avenues and could see that she had no more specific knowledge, he posed a proposition.

"You have done well, Paula. And I confess that my earlier remarks"—
he hesitated—"and actions were crass." He smiled and spread his palms
to her. "Please forgive me."

She said nothing, but leaned back against the couch and closed her
eyes. *She is exhausted,* Alvarado thought.

"*Mi querida,* we both need sleep. Before we lay together into our
pleasant dreams of the night, I want you to take me up on an offer.
For our next meeting—which will be our rubber match, by the way—
I'm going to ask that you get more information about Mr. Lombardi
and his associate, Frank. We can discuss the specifics I have in mind
tomorrow morning, but I'm prepared to reward you handsomely for the
information. Deal?"

"Deal."

No hesitation, Alvarado thought. Good.

"And now, it is I who offer to be at your service for the remainder of
the night. What is your wish?"

"Sleep, Luis. Sleep sounds good."

CHAPTER THIRTY-SEVEN

PAULA RETURNED TO LAS VEGAS with a mixture of relief and dread. She was glad that Frank wasn't picking her up at the airport—she needed time to think. She resented both men as much as she feared them. Lombardi would instruct her to go back, and Alvarado expected her back; their rubber match was set up for next weekend. Paula, ever the chess player, thought ahead. Both men were paying her outrageously and, with her own savings, if she could hold on a bit longer, she'd be able to accelerate a long-held dream. Despite her fears, the money, the opportunity, was too good to pass up.

BARCELONA WAS BACK IN THE drylands. That he could tolerate, but Verdugo kept him sleeping with one eye open.

"You are lucky I haven't gutted you and hung *you* on a tree, Barcelona."

"I swear, Verdugo, when I got to him he was dead—it is a *milagro*."

"You will never cross me again and live to tell about it."

"Verdugo, I didn't—"

Smack! "Not another word. Don't speak to me again, unless I ask."

Barcelona was reassigned to the first route in the cartel's PCT operation. He reasoned that Verdugo hoped he would try to escape back to Mexico so that Verdugo could kill him. Barcelona steeled himself not to make that mistake and forced his wife and family out of his mind whenever he looked south, especially when he crawled through the border tunnel. *All in time*, he thought. *All in time*.

He was one of six regulars who worked the border, one of six who smuggled a drop past the averted gaze of Yolanda Sanchez and hauled it up to Verdugo or to his associate, Gomez. Sometimes he was instructed to drop off at Snow Creek Road; other times he was to drop off at the canyon head a mile south or at another junction a mile north. Times were varied—three, four, two thirty—but it was always done in the wee hours of morning. One blink of vehicle lights meant he was clear; two blinks meant not to advance. That had never happened to him. Sometimes different vehicles would show, but most always it was a Jeep or some type of small four-by-four. Once, shortly after being reassigned, Barcelona was stopped by Border Patrol. He feared the worst as he presented his PCT papers and permits. The young official made a call on what looked like his personal cell phone while the larger phone in his vehicle emitted static, interrupted by words of other patrollers. Barcelona was released, and the BP vehicle sailed away. He feared Verdugo would punish him, but nothing was said or done. He could not take the chance of being caught again.

It was the beginning of August, and even for natives who had lived in Mexico all their lives, the heat was unbearable. Barcelona moved only at night and in early morning. He knew every barrel cactus, every saguaro, so he had no trouble navigating at night. During the day, he knew where to find shade for sleep and rest. He was trained to tell anyone who might stop him that he was section-hiking the PCT and had judged conditions badly—that he only had to make it to Idyllwild or some such place. But he was never stopped again. Three times he had encountered illegals at night; two times they rushed away. The other time they approached him. "Stay away, or I will report you," he'd said to them in Spanish. He had eight months to go, eight months to stay away from trouble, to focus, to avoid Verdugo's wrath.

Farther up the PCT, and in various national parks, certain rangers and officials were paid off by Alvarado's and Lombardi's men. It was the job of the commanders, people like Verdugo in southern California and Nino in Oregon, to keep the wheels greased in Yosemite, Sequoia, Kings Canyon, John Muir Wilderness, Lassen Volcanic Park, Mount Hood Forest, North Cascades National Park, etc. Rangers never bothered to check the contents of the opaque food vaults anyway. As long as hikers had them, they met the requirement. If they hiked without them, they would be cited and fined if caught in bear country.

Here at the border, Barcelona viewed himself as a paramecium on glass, under a microscope. No place to run; no place to hide. Accomplish your mission or else.

CHAPTER THIRTY-EIGHT

KENNY WAS THE FIRST TO spot him. They were camped thirty yards east of the PCT near Willamette Pass. At nearly eight in the evening, Awol was fingering fox fire on decaying timber, wondering when the fungi would give off the green luminescent glow implied in the name, when he saw Kenny wave to a hiker who looked like he had just emerged from the old Oregon Skyline Trail. Awol watched the hiker give a nod without waving back and hustle on.

"He doesn't even look tired," Kenny said.

Awol looked at his guide. Shelter Cove Resort was a couple of miles away, and he wondered if the man had come from there. The hiker looked too clean and refreshed for the load he was carrying—an extra tall pack that loomed over his shoulders.

When they broke camp next morning, Kenny sensed a shift in his father.

"What is it? You've been quiet since last night."

Awol pursed his lips.

"What's the secret? I figured you're working for the feds, Dad."

Awol looked at him. "I was, but not anymore."

"Why are we out here, then?"

"Because I wanted to clean out your head and body and spend time with you. And I want to hike to Canada. I've wanted to hike the PCT ever since I finished the Appalachian Trail. And when I finish this, I'll probably set my sights on the Continental Divide Trail, which goes right over the Rockies."

Kenny was quiet as they poled side by side.

Awol looked again to Kenny. "Most of all, I wanted to become closer to you, Kenny. I wasn't there when you needed me."

"I doubt you could have helped me then."

Awol looked around him. "Now I'm wondering if this was such a good idea."

For the next half hour as they walked, Awol told his son the details behind the ambush. Kenny listened, and finally Awol pulled off his pack and sat on it. Kenny sat down on a stump.

"I didn't want to get you involved in this mess. I'm telling you now so you will stay alert. Be on guard; our lives could be in danger if they know I'm back out here."

Kenny was jabbing a pole into the duff and smiled. "Can I tell Jill?"

"Jesus Christ, no, Kenny!"

"Okay, take it easy."

"Jesus, Kenny. I don't know why I thought . . ." he whispered and looked behind him again. "Look, drugs are being hauled up the entire PCT. I know what these mules look like; you just waved to one. You need to get off the trail."

"No way, Dad. Not now. With or without you, I need to see this through. You, of all people, should understand that."

Awol stared at the ground, silent while he worked out his thoughts.

"Dammit. Stay with me for now, but if I sense it getting worse, I'm marching you off the trail and putting you on a bus back home. While you're with me, I need you to keep your eyes and ears open. And this conversation remains private. Got it?"

Their hiking continued without incident over the next week. On the sixth night, they set up camp in a saddle along the Cascade Divide. It had gotten late. The moon was up as Kenny went to hang their food bags, picking up a rock along the way to tie to the rope he would fling over a suitable limb. They had, as was habit, already eaten several miles south and were far enough from those bears that would smell their lingering cook site aromas, but bears were everywhere.

Awol finished setting up and turned to Kenny, who was still under the tree where he'd hung the food bags.

"I see a good limb right where you're standing."

"Fuck! Dad!"

"Man up, son. Let's go." Awol jumped up and grabbed the limb. "You beat me by one, you can skip the push-ups."

Awol did five chin-ups, not bad for a guy recovering from a broken arm; on a good day, before his accident, he could pump out fifteen. He dropped to the ground. "I gave you a break. Not back at full strength yet."

Kenny jumped up and started.

"Full extensions, Kenneth. I want full extensions."

Kenny dropped off after four, grumbled, and walked to his pack.

Awol opted to let it go. He'd have him finish his other exercises in the morning and insist on a complete workout tomorrow night, even if it meant stopping early. *If I can build up his confidence, the boy won't ever need drugs*, he thought. Awol did six one-armed push-ups and wondered when his bad arm would allow him to complete a one-armed push-up on that side.

Awol had been thinking about Sacco and wondered if there was anything new on his end. He retrieved the satellite phone from the bottom of the pack and was surprised to learn the detective had left him a message two days ago.

"Awol, call me if you get this. Keep it confidential. If I don't answer, hang up."

Awol called, but received no answer. Later, after they had set up tents and Kenny had gone to the brook to fill water bottles, Awol tried again.

"Awol. Where are you? This shows Oregon."

"I'm back on the PCT. Only my wife and son know."

"You're crazier than I thought. You out there alone?"

"No. But I don't want anybody to know my son is with me. Okay?"

"Understood. Seen anything?"

"Saw what I think was a mule a week ago—young, fit guy with the same kind of oversized pack. I don't know if he was Hispanic, but the pack was a tip-off, and he was all business, moving smartly at eight at night."

"Hmmm."

"What did you call me about?"

"What can you tell me about your friend Barcelona?"

"Why do you ask?"

"I'm near certain that the new Border Patrol official at Campo is on the take. A person matching the description you gave of Barcelona at Silver Pass is back at the border."

Awol told Sacco all he could. "So you're back on the case?"

"No. And that's why you have to keep every word of this confidential. I'll get canned."

"Got it."

"From what I can tell, Barcelona's hauled in the Sierra as well as the desert. He knows the operation, the people. I'd like to turn him, but he's killed one of our men and left you half dead."

"To turn a cop killer is against policy?"

"Never seen it done. Keep in mind, for us to even have a chance of negotiating with him, he would want conditions—one of which, I'm sure, is to avoid life in prison. That ain't going to happen."

"His wife and kids?"

"That might help us."

"What's your next step?"

"Not sure. I'm all alone here. I'll keep you posted. Call if you see anything else worth noting."

In the days that passed, Awol continued to impart outdoor knowledge to Kenny whenever he could. They discussed the number one hiker virus, Giardia, and Awol showed him how to, for survival, purify rain puddle water, to first sift the water through a bandanna then treat it. "If you can't get Aquamira, use a pinch of powered bleach. If you run out of that, boil the water until it bubbles." At the end of each day, before going into their tents, Awol quizzed him on the next day's route: Where would they find water? How many miles between water stops? How high were the elevations? Where would the tough spots be? What were the names of passes and mountains and the distances between? What would the weather be like? The boy took to it and was prepared for the ritual. Later, Awol might hear him scribble in the journal Kenny had bought in town or hear him rifling through maps and guides. Kenny took charge of planning each day's route and showed good sense most of the time. So it came as a surprise to Awol when Kenny planned too hard a day, but Awol said nothing as they labored over late afternoon peaks.

"Okay, I overdid it."

"That's all right. What's your B-plan?"

Kenny glanced around—even Blazer lay down between them. "How about we eat right over there?"

"Sounds good."

When Kenny questioned him about Desert Storm, Awol intended to hold back; but for whatever reason, he didn't—or couldn't. He told him that he was dealing with problems he'd had in the war and that long-distance hiking had been therapeutic.

"Can I ask what problems, Dad?"

"I accidentally shot and killed a man."

"The enemy?"

"No."

"What happened?"

"We were ambushed, taking fire, and there was a lot of confusion." *And now I distort the truth again.* "It was strictly an accident. But I've been fucked up ever since."

"Were you . . . did they . . . ?"

"No one ever knew—except me."

"Did you know him?"

Awol looked straight at the trunk of a pine. "Yeah. He was in my unit. Two days earlier, I'd almost gotten him killed. He threatened payback, and I feared him. I've wanted to contact his parents, try to explain. His mother was Pennsylvania German, just like mine, your grandmother. His father was black. But what would I say?" Silence. "Kenny, let's keep this private—only between us, okay?"

"Does Mom know? Or Linda?"

"Not what I just told you. Your mom and I never talked about it. Linda has been trying to get me to open up for a while. She knows something happened, but I've had a hard time talking about the specifics."

"It'll stay private, Dad."

A riffling breeze picked up. It smelled of evergreen with a tinge of smoke, reminding Awol of New Hampshire in the fall, the gondolas at Loon Mountain, the tram at Cannon. He settled.

"The mountains and hiking have always curbed my desire to drink."

Awol sneaked a glance at Kenny. "Maybe you don't think of drugs out here."

"That incident, is that what makes you want to drink?"

Awol shifted his legs and leaned back to pine. "The buzz feels good. Takes my mind off things."

"It was a total accident, Dad."

Awol looked to Kenny and tried to smile. "Thanks."

They had finished their evening meal, and the two sat there; neither felt like tramping more miles to set up camp.

"Do you remember those air rifles I bought for you and Gregory?"

Kenny chuckled. "I don't know where mine went. It might be in the attic at the house."

"That was the last time I saw you and Greg."

"I remember getting them when you came out. My stepfather went on a business trip and told us, Gregory and me, that you were coming because you loved us and that we needed to be on our best behavior for you."

"Damn good of him. Maybe your parents didn't think the gifts were appropriate."

"Mom didn't. My dad, I mean Richard, set up an area in the backyard where we could shoot and let us put soda cans up on a sawhorse."

"It's okay for you to call him dad. And I'm glad he did that."

"I got mad at Greg one time and told him I would pop him in the ass. Mom took the guns away after that."

Awol said nothing. But that night he spent a long time writing in his journal. As he crept out of his tent in the middle of night, he heard the caterwaul of what he suspected was a bobcat and then the strident hoots of a barred owl. Stars teemed above him, just as bright as in the desert, but in a smaller section of sky. A night wind shook the trees, and leaves rustled in the limbs as Blazer looked at him and thumped his tail. It became quiet again. He heard Kenny's light rhythmic snores and understood that, despite the quiet and peace, somewhere out here runners were delivering addiction. Addiction that fucked up the young and ruined their lives. He stared for a long time at Kenny's tent.

CHAPTER THIRTY-NINE

"**S**O," LOMBARDI SAID, STARING STEADILY at Paula, "what can you tell me?"

"I have little, and I'm afraid you will be disappointed, but I'm making progress."

Lombardi turned a palm to her. "Give me what you've got."

Paula had taken a day to comb through Mexican papers and news magazines at the city library, plus she'd drilled down into the name Alvarado and found online archives referencing "chess-Alvarado-Mexico City." In his youth, Luis Alvarado was a budding chess player, and she'd managed to pull up a few old clippings with pictures. The articles and pictures provided family background, homestead, and names of early friends and opponents. These she showed to Lombardi, along with her own typed profile of the man.

"He wants me to think he is Italian, but with a name like Alvarado . . . yet we find from this article that his mother is part Italian. In his condo, he's hung Italian paintings; he serves Italian food and wines . . ."

"This is hardly a start, Paula. I need specifics. I need current info."

"Yes, of course. I did overhear him talk to a 'Verdugo,' but he stepped out of the room and I couldn't get the gist of the conversation. I saw a cook and a housemaid when I left. Both looked Hispanic . . . common in Palm Springs, I'm sure. Sorry I don't have more. As you can imagine, he is very secretive."

Lombardi stared her in the eye. "You're right—I am disappointed. You have to try harder. And get me the names of his cooks and maids. I have people in the area. When do you see him again?"

"Two weeks."

Lombardi gave her an envelope.

Frank was fast asleep in Paula's Las Vegas townhouse. He'd been child's play for her. One level-eyed look, a touch, a promise to keep it discreet, and he was hers. And now, by the looks of it, he was out cold for at least the next twenty minutes. She went to his jacket, which she had deliberately hung on a hanger in the foyer closet, and found a small address book. She closed the bedroom door to Frank's snores. The auto-light of the closet was sufficient for her to copy down names and numbers: Tony, Nino, Orlando. She checked other pockets, returned a set of keys, found a matchbook that read Sal's Hideaway, and copied that name and number to her pad. She tucked the pad into her coat pocket at the other end of the closet and shut the door. She wouldn't be able to access his wallet tonight, but she had time in the days remaining before she returned to Palms Springs to discretely dig into Lombardi's background with unwitting help from Frank and her other Vegas contacts.

Two weeks later, she was back at Alvarado's and losing at the royal game. She'd been lured into a trap in the middle game, her forte, and was scratching and clawing to find a way out. She'd come to detest Alvarado, his slick play, his brio, his over-the-top effort to come across as an intellectual. But she was scared to death of him—in life and across the chessboard. The man was a calculating sneak. His vocal annoyance at himself as he mounted a queenside attack, she now realized, had been a diversion. He had been closing in on her king all the while. On the twenty-eighth move, behind a piece, feeling suffocated and at her worst, she resigned and toppled her king.

"Bravo," she said.

Alvarado looked angry for an instant, because he had wanted to crush her fully. He recovered. "Thank you, Paula. Your variation in the Sicilian I have not played in fifteen years. It brought back good memories."

They put the pieces into the box and Alvarado removed the set and board while Paula went for her notes—she knew what was coming next.

Alvarado refreshed their wines and wiped the table. "Let's get to the business at hand."

She recounted to him all she knew of Lombardi, gave him written names and numbers, and discussed Frank at length.

"Frank is one of your lovers?"

"We have a business relationship."

"But he's made love to you?"

"Yes, if by that you mean sex, and quick sex at that."

He smiled. "Good that you are honest. That's treating me with respect."

Paula finished by giving Alvarado her unsigned, typed profile of Lombardi, which he now scrutinized after donning his glasses.

He folded the paper and went to a cupboard over the wine sink behind her. Paula watched him watch her as he quietly took out a notebook and placed her report inside it. From the available light, she saw all this from a reflection in the glass patio door—she didn't have to twitch a muscle.

"Very well, my dear. Go to the bedroom and freshen up. I'll be in shortly."

As soon as Paula entered the bedroom, she locked it, knowing she had a snitch of time. She opened drawers, checked the end tables and the closet—*nothing*. Not wanting to chance another second, she unlocked the bedroom door and went to the bathroom. There she also secured the latch, poked around the linen closet, looked under the sink. In the medicine cabinet, she found pills—Methylprednisolone and Celebrex. She ignored the fine print but read and reread the prescriptions and the name of the doctor and pharmacy. She closed her eyes and committed the information to memory. As she heard the bedroom door open, she flushed the toilet and unlatched the bath door.

She did her level best to tire him out during the night. Flush with his victory, he was up to the task—initially. As he "owned" her according to her original rules, which she now regretted, he enjoyed making her do beastly maneuvers, tiring her out as well. But she'd seen it all before; this was, after all, her business.

"Once more, Luis—for me. You are a bull. How do you say bull in Italian?"

At half past three, she took a daring chance. Convinced he was dead asleep as he wheezed full-rounded snores, she left the bedroom, slowly shutting the door, and stepped to the cupboard over the wine sink. She took down his notebook. By the light coming in the window, she wrote in a small pad, which she kept hidden in her purse. She found the names and numbers of Border Patrol, Gomez, Rodolfo, Verdugo and wrote as fast as she was able. She found a slip of paper at the end that read "Yolanda Sanchez, BP" and wrote that down. Paula thumbed to another page and found a ledger with dates and numbers. She transcribed numbers and locations for the most recent date. She was about to close the book when she found a page scribbled in Spanish, dated a few days ago: *Barcelona— expendable. Find way for him—Sacco—X.*

Back at her townhouse the next night, Paula closed the blinds, secured the doors, and went into her bedroom with a plastic bag. She put on her bathrobe and crawled into the bed and found an old movie on TV—*The Barefoot Contessa*. She hadn't seen it in a long while. By the light of the flickering TV, she savored her treat, a cream-filled chocolate donut. She did her best to lose herself to the movie, but her thoughts kept returning to Alvarado and Lombardi—she was scared. She needed to hold on just a little longer. She had cringed when Alvarado invited her to his place in Mexico but realized that was her chance to cash in on her dream. She'd played him like a Strad: "Luis, I can't leave the country or be gone that long. My business."

"Nonsense, my dear. Aren't I paying you enough?"

Paula had used all her wiles to convince him—*I made a mistake in the Sicilian . . . next time*—that the only way she could make it happen was for him to advance her the week's money. In the end, Alvarado gave her the money.

She wished she had bought a second donut, understanding she needed to spend extra time at the gym, time she didn't have, to work off the calories in the one she just ate. On the television screen, the contessa threw a coconut at her rival. Paula's thoughts returned to Frank, who was not happy about her going to Mexico. Lombardi thought it was a good opportunity for information but ramped up the rules, requiring her to check in every few days by calling an untraceable number. In the end, he handed her the envelope of cash.

Of the two, she feared Alvarado more, but Lombardi was in her backyard, and the Mafia always got the job done. *And now I'm involved with Frank.* More than in any chess game, she found herself trapped.

Paula thought about going to the kitchen for more to eat. She'd have to spend all next week at the gym. *No!* This was her chance. She had to be tough. When the movie finished, she turned off the TV, got out of bed, and went for her gym bag.

CHAPTER FORTY

AFTER CROSSING THE UPPER SALMON River, Awol grabbed Kenny's forearm and squeezed. "Bobcat, two o'clock. See the short tail?"

"Oh, wow," Kenny said as they watched the spotted reddish-brown cat, double the size of his mother's large tabby, slip into woods near a spur trail. "First one I've ever seen."

Kenny noted from his map that the spur trail led to a lodge in the Timberline ski area. They were in Mount Hood National Forest, and the chance to eat prepared food at the lodge made him push to take the shortcut there. Awol had noticed the short spur trail on the map this morning, but hadn't suggested it. If he pampered anybody, it was Blazer.

With Kenny in the lead, they entered the A-shaped rustic lodge and, after going through a cafeteria line with their trays, selected a table near a window. Another young man read a newspaper at the opposite end, also at a window. The rest of the tables were empty. The manager said Blazer could join them, but at noon, when it got busy, the dog would have to go outside. From the window they could see a snow-topped Mount Hood and the surrounding forests, a thick, pristine wilderness of fir, oak, and pine. What looked like ski trails, with spindrifts of wind-driven snow near the top, wound down a closer mountain. A working lift offered "Scenic Gondola Rides" to the summit.

After several minutes, the young man approached with his folded newspaper.

"Smart-looking dog. What kind is it?"

"Belgian Malinois with a pinch of shepherd," Awol said.

The man smiled and reached down to pat Blazer.

"He likes having his ears rubbed," Kenny said.

"I had a shepherd once," the man said. "He was a great dog."

"What was his name?" Kenny asked.

The lanky man twisted a chair around from the adjacent table and sat down. "King."

Blazer had now moved to the man's side to let him play with his ears. Kenny and Awol ate.

"You guys live in the area?"

"No," Kenny said, "we're hiking the PCT."

"Oh." He looked at their equipment while he stroked Blazer. "I've done some sections of the PCT."

"Yeah? Where 'bouts?" Kenny asked.

"Mostly in the Three Sisters area. But I've done Crater Lake, too."

"Crater was spectacular," Kenny said. "How about that miniature crater within the big cone?"

"So you guys going into Washington?"

"That's the plan," Kenny said.

"You can make it. Weather will be good until September, but you should try to hit the border as soon as possible when you reach the Cascades."

Awol shifted in his seat but said nothing as he glanced at Kenny. Something about the guy bothered Awol, though he couldn't put a finger on it.

"I might not get that far, but my dad here . . ."

The man smiled. "You going all the way, sir?"

Awol made a big deal of wiping his hands with the napkin and burped. "Maybe." He turned his body, forehead crinkled, and looked straight at the man before turning back to Kenny. "You ready to saddle up?"

"In a minute, Dad."

Kenny wiped his face with a napkin. More people came into the lodge. "Are they strict about IDs here? I'd love one of those Coors over there."

"Consider it done," the man said. "They'll card me; the drink is yours."

As the man went to the counter, Awol barked at his son. "Jesus Christ, Kenny!"

"Aw c'mon, Dad. Keep your shirt on."

The man returned with three bottles. "This round's on me."

"Thanks, dude," Kenny said and clinked his bottle with the man's, while Awol stared at the bottle in front of him. Awol liked his beer ice-cold, and he watched tiny flecks of ice slide down the side.

"It's only one, Dad."

Awol cracked his knuckles and abruptly stood up. "You finish that one drink and then haul your ass outside. This ain't no party. C'mon Blazer." Awol walked away.

THAT AFTERNOON, TULIO LOMBARDI RECEIVED a call from his godson and listened a few minutes before speaking.

"You mean the guy with the dog that the spic tried to whack?" Lombardi said.

"Yes," Nino said. "He's hiking with his son."

"Are you positive this is the same man and dog?"

"Yes. The man is injured. He can't turn his neck very well. Limps. His face is still marked up, and his beard doesn't grow in a scarred spot. Plus, one of his arms doesn't hang right. It's him. The son's just a student, scrawny, doesn't look like a threat. What should we do?"

"Absolutely nothing, and don't breathe a word of this to anyone—not even to your associate up in Washington. But track them."

"I'll have to pull someone to do that."

"Do what you have to, have someone take your place, but monitor the situation and keep me updated every day. Right now we have someone Alvarado wants, and it could be my ace in the hole."

"I have some other information for you."

"Which is?"

"Alvarado's mule, the one involved with the rockslide and the more recent incident--he could be working for the feds."

"Who's your source?"

"Jaime, the central California commander."

"I know who Jaime is. He reports to Alvarado. Why would he tell you this? And why would Alvarado keep the mule if Jaime thought he was working with the feds? It doesn't add up."

"Maybe Alvarado's letting the feds think they can use Barcelona as a mole."

"No. That's way too complicated—even for the chess player. How did this conversation with Jaime develop?"

"He called to acknowledge my promotion. I asked him what he thought about the Silver Pass fiasco. He said that Barcelona screwed up, that he should have made sure the guy was dead, and because he didn't, it meant he was probably working for the feds."

After pacing his den a number of times, Lombardi admitted to himself that he could see the logic in Jaime's opinion. That meant Alvarado would have thought it through as well. If the man with the dog, and now the son, were also working for the feds, then the entire operation was in danger. Forces would be accumulating now to bring it down. Lombardi knew Alvarado wanted to run the overall operation. He was setting him up; he would figure a way to blame Lombardi and take over. Lombardi picked up his cell and called Frank.

"Is she on the plane?"

"I'm coming back from the airport now, Boss. The plane left on time; I watched it leave."

Lombardi winced. "Find some way to get to her and instruct her to call me at once. It has to be before she meets Alvarado. I must speak with her."

The next morning, Frank sat in front of his boss on Lombardi's patio.

"Again," Lombardi said, "why the fuck hasn't she called?"

"I tried to reach her as soon as I got your instructions. She didn't pick up, so I left a message."

"Have you been fucking her?"

"Boss." Frank held up his palms.

"Answer my question."

"Yes, once, only be—"

Lombardi slapped his cranberry juice, and the glass tumbled to the patio bricks. Frank sat rigid.

"What did I tell you about mixing business with pleasure?"

Frank made to pick up the broken glass.

"Leave it!"

"Would you believe me if I told you she initiated it?"

Lombardi stared at him.

"So help me, Boss, on my mother's grave—I didn't start it."

Lombardi's phone vibrated, and he took it out of his breast pocket all the while eyeing Frank.

"Mr. Lombardi. If there has been a change in plans, why haven't I been informed?"

With effort and a clenched fist, Lombardi said calmly, "Suppose, Mr. Alvarado, you tell me what you are referring to."

"Where is Paula?"

CHAPTER FORTY-ONE

AN ICY MORNING BROUGHT TIREDNESS and discomfort to Nino as he hiked over hoarfrost. The needlelike ice crystals should have cautioned him, but tragedy rarely issues a warning. His Uncle Tulio had been clear: keep track of them, and keep it quiet. He would not let him down.

Nino was at the top of Ramona Falls, where he could see either their approach or departure. He'd sneaked in during the night, right after phoning his uncle. All he wanted was to find them, tail them. He would inform his uncle when they headed into Washington. Nino had figured they would have hiked no more than ten miles after their lunch yesterday at the lodge—the logical camping spot being at the base of the spectacular Ramona Falls.

Spying from a lip of cliff just above the cataract, Nino saw the dog first. So did the bobcat, who wanted a closer look. In the shivering cold of an early morning, the bobcat leapt to the basalt rock Nino was crouching behind. Seeing the cat spring, Nino thought the cat was attacking him. He reacted on impulse and stuck his poles up in defense. The cat's shoulder hit a pole with sufficient momentum to tip Nino toward the falls. Nino scrambled to secure his footing but slipped on rime and tumbled 120 feet onto the basalt rocks below. His scream startled Blazer, Awol, and Kenny, who looked up in time to see Nino bounce off rocks and plunge to the bottom. Just as the flush of water from a faucet will clear debris in a sink, the deluge of water forced Nino off a rock, pushed him under the maelstrom, and bubbled him to the surface a minute later, fifty yards in front of Awol.

"Kenny!" Awol shouted.

Kenny had already waded in downstream and tried in vain to grab the hiker. The man drifted farther downstream, to a bend that Awol reached first. He and Blazer pulled the body off a snag and tugged it to shore.

They recognized the man from the lodge. As Awol detected a faint pulse, Blazer licked the man's face and an eye fluttered to half-mast. Kenny grabbed the man's hand. "Hang in there, dude, hang in there." But a few seconds later, the eye glazed to sleep. Forever.

CHAPTER FORTY-TWO

LOMBARDI SUMMONED FRANK. "PAULA HAS defected."

During Lombardi's phone conversation with Alvarado, Frank had cleaned up the mess on the patio and filled another glass with cranberry juice. He waited in the kitchen until his boss finished the phone call.

Lombardi barely glanced at the new glass of juice Frank set on the table. "Did you see her get on the plane?"

"No, only to the security gates. It was as far as I could go without a ticket. But I was able to see the manifest, and the plane left."

"Confirm that she was on the flight." He seethed with anger. "I'm sure the spic is keeping her for his pleasure in Mexico—and that she's more than happy to return his pleasure." Lombardi glared at Frank. "By the way, Mr. Alvarado wanted me to tell you that next time you visit Sal's Hideaway, have a drink on him."

Frank's face turned ashen.

Lombardi watched Frank shuffle out of sight and a few minutes later heard the rumble of the Expedition as it exited the gate. He listened for the tiny beep signaling the gate had closed.

The conversation with Alvarado had turned ugly. Lombardi had accused Alvarado of luring Paula to Mexico and trying to use her against him. Alvarado countered that Lombardi deceived him by keeping her off the flight and alleged she had taken operational information from him and given it to Lombardi. Both made counterpunches, and Alvarado ended the call saying, "Mr. Lombardi, this is the second time you have threatened me; it will be the last time."

Lombardi picked up his cell and, after a short wait, was connected to his boss, Mario Cedrone, in New York. "We have a problem," he said. "Alvarado has a runner who has flipped. His name is Barcelona, and he works for the feds."

Leveraging this piece of information, Lombardi moved forward with his plan. "That's right," Lombardi said. "Yes. But I'm having trouble working with the man. . . . Yes. . . . Okay. . . . Yes."

That afternoon, Frank called Lombardi. "She was on the departure manifest. They have her ticket stub."

"Then the spic's got her, and you can kiss her ass good-bye," Lombardi said.

A day later, in the middle of the night, Lombardi's cell phone vibrated.

"Mr. Lombardi? It's Tony from Oregon. Do you know where Nino is?"

Two hours later, at 4:00 a.m., unable to reach Nino and with a sour feeling in his stomach, Lombardi decided to bypass Alvarado and reach down to one of his commanders. A show of power was in order. Paula's notes had shown that Verdugo was Barcelona's direct commander.

"Verdugo, *Sí*."

"Where is my godson?"

"Who's this?"

"This is Mr. Lombardi. You tell Alvarado that if I don't hear by noon tomorrow where my godson, Nino, is, I'll have Barcelona executed."

––––––––––––

"HOLD IT. STOP," FRANK SAID to Tony the next morning. "Are you sure?" His hands were shaking hard enough to need both to hold the phone.

"Unfortunately, I'm certain. Nino is dead. The two people and dog he was tracking found him just below Ramona Falls. I'm afraid to call Mr. Lombardi."

"Do you have the drop?"

"Yes, but I'm out of food. What should I do?"

"Stay out of sight and do nothing until someone gets back to you. You won't starve."

Frank knew he had to give the devastating news to his boss in person—he owed him that. He raced across town and swung through the gate at ten minutes to noon. He spotted his boss on the patio, seated at the iron table, with nothing in front of him but his cell phone.

Lombardi watched Frank approach him, noting the lack of color in his face. Just then, his cell burred.

"Alvarado, this better be good."

"You will find your godson in Cascade Locks. At the morgue."

Lombardi took one more look at Frank's ashen face and threw the phone at him.

CHAPTER FORTY-THREE

Aｌｖａｒａｄｏ ｓｎａｐｐｅｄ ｈｉｓ ｐｈｏｎｅ ｓｈｕｔ. He'd heard the catch in Lombardi's throat before he hung up. *Maybe the stupid wop doesn't have Paula after all.* He summoned Verdugo, pacing the veranda, with a wave of his hand.

"Sit."

Verdugo sat down at an angle to him. He looked like a mutt that was puzzled as he beseeched his master.

"Pull your chair closer. In front of me."

Verdugo did as ordered and coughed. As the silence stretched, he coughed again.

On the end table next to Alvarado sat a carafe of wine. With the steady hand of a surgeon, Alvarado poured two glasses and handed one to his commander.

"Tell me everything you know. Start with the untimely demise of my counterpart's godson."

For the next half hour, Verdugo talked.

"You did not know they were back on the trail?" Alvarado said.

"No, señor, I didn't."

"Your connection to Tony is unusual, don't you think?"

"Yes, but I was trying to help you by getting any information I could, to help you up north with Lombardi. I asked Jaime to snoop around. He got Tony's name, and I connected with him."

Alvarado ignored the patronizing and took a sip of wine, his unblinking eyes all the while on Verdugo.

"When Tony—I've never met him—called me, he was loco," said Verdugo. "Said he was camped in a thunderstorm, freezing. No food except for some shitty loganberries he was able to pick. Said he was wet and chilled and couldn't even start a fire. He told me again that after he reported Nino's death to Frank, Lombardi's man, he was told to stay put with the drop. Asked me if I knew what was going on. I called Jaime just before I called you, but he knew nothing about it."

"Who killed Nino?"

Verdugo raised his palms. "I don't know. Maybe an accident, maybe the feds. Nobody knows."

Alvarado caught the tremor of Verdugo's pinkie. He was glad Verdugo had closed his mouth; his lack of saliva exposed the crud on his yellow teeth. *Uncouth and aging. He may have to be replaced*, Alvarado thought.

He refreshed Verdugo's glass. "You did properly, Verdugo. And, after consulting with my sources, I was able to find out where bodies are brought in that area. I informed our Mr. Lombardi."

Verdugo returned a weak smile as he reached to clink Alvarado's outstretched glass.

"We shall, for the moment, forget about the PCT," Alvarado said, "and discuss a plan for finding my Paula."

CHAPTER FORTY-FOUR

Eᴀʀʟɪᴇʀ ᴛʜᴀᴛ ᴍᴏʀɴɪɴɢ, Bᴀʀᴄᴇʟᴏɴᴀ ʜᴀᴅ been given a drop by Verdugo. He was mortified that he had to crawl through a tunnel back into his homeland to get the drop. How he wanted to flee in Mexico, but he knew Verdugo was waiting for that and hoping he'd try. Verdugo no longer spoke to him, and this continued to be a source of worry. No matter how hard he tried, after two or three words, Verdugo told him to shut up.

Things were much smoother with Yolanda Sanchez, the Border Patrol official near Campo. Barcelona noted that he hauled only when Yolanda was on duty. BP shifts varied, a new tactic by the feds, he supposed, to avoid establishing patterns. One time, several weeks ago, Verdugo skidded the Jeep to a stop while on his cell phone. "She's not? A damn good thing you told me—I'm only three miles out!" Verdugo swerved the Jeep around and kept glancing in the rearview mirrors. He said to Barcelona, "Today, you will weed my garden." Even then Verdugo hadn't come near him. He'd told him to sleep in the shed, but later Verdugo's assistant brought him a bowl of menudo and a manta that looked and smelled like it had been used to bed down a sick donkey.

Barcelona thought back to Yolanda, a more pleasant subject. She remembered him from that first day, she'd said, when she'd directed him to the PCT. It was clear she was flirting, and yes, he was tempted. She was pretty and kind. But Juanita. And his children. He'd stopped to look back at the border after leaving with the drop and saw Yolanda looking at him from her BP vehicle. *I'm doomed to hell anyway,* he thought, and blew her a kiss.

CHAPTER FORTY-FIVE

FRANK HOBBLED TO THE CAR, holding his handkerchief over his bloodied nose. He looked back and saw his boss blubbering like the schoolyard bully who can't have what he wants, who thrashes and flails, a victim of inner demons. Frank called New York and was put through to the headman. "He went ballistic on me. . . . Yes. . . . No. . . . I'm afraid he'll bring us all down—he's out of his mind. . . . Okay. I'll do my best here and wait 'til he arrives. . . . Yes."

Frank returned to the courtyard. "Boss, listen to me, please. I'm under orders to stay here and protect you."

"You caused my godson's death. I've never been to Sal's Hideaway. You let that bitch . . ." Lombardi reared. "Get out of this house, or I'll kill you right now."

Frank backed away.

"The family business is on the line, Boss."

"Family! Don't talk to me about family," he said and started to cry, covering his face with liver-spotted hands.

Frank told Lombardi's assistants that he would remain in his car outside. "Come and get me if you need help. Give Mr. Lombardi medication now to calm him—that's an order straight from the top."

Later, in the car, trying to deal with a crushed nose that needed to be reset, Frank was summoned to pick up Richard Magnante, who was arriving shortly by private jet from New York. On his way to the airport, he realized he'd forgotten all about Tony and his drop.

THAT NIGHT, DETECTIVE SACCO RECEIVED a direct call from Awol.

"Did you hear about the hiker death up here in Oregon?"

"Can't say I did. Give me the details?"

"We met the so-called hiker the previous day at a lodge while having lunch. He asked questions as if he were an ordinary civilian, not a hiker."

Sacco turned his TV down and went to his desk.

"I think he was tracking us and somehow he fell into Ramona Falls. I fished him out, but he was DOA. I looked for ID and found a notebook on him, which I should have given to the authorities."

"I'm listening."

"It has names and numbers, a picture of some guy, some stuff I don't understand, and then this: 'Jaime thinks Barcelona works for the narcs. Tell Uncle T.'"

"Get to a post office and overnight that notebook to me."

"All right. It's drying out; the covers got wet, the inside should be okay."

"What else can you tell me? Who is the dead hiker?"

"His name is Nino Volpe, from Oregon. Another note says: 'Pick up Tony, Saturday—4:00 a.m.'"

"Hmmm. It's now Sunday. I wonder where Tony is."

"I bet he has something Nino wanted."

CHAPTER FORTY-SIX

AFTER SHOWING HIM THE NOTEBOOK Awol had sent, Sacco convinced his chief that there were runners border to border on the PCT and was reassigned to the case. He then called Awol, who agreed to assist providing that details of Kenny's drug involvement--he was accused of dealing--were expunged from all records. "I'll do everything I can," Sacco had said. "You know I will."

The next day, Awol, Blazer, and Kenny stepped onto the Oregon side of the Bridge of the Gods leading to Washington State. Midway across the massive iron bridge, they halted in the pedestrian walkway and looked up and down the Columbia River. The Columbia was the lowest elevation on the entire trail—175 feet. Awol realized he'd descended from the highest point, Forester Pass—over 13,000 feet in the Sierra—down to this river. A red-and-white paddle wheel ferry thrummed below. Blue and red parasails floated to the west. Wind surfers angled east. The day was gorgeous, full of sun and clear skies. Awol put his arm around his son as they looked across the river into Washington.

At the end of the bridge, Awol saw some picnic tables in a bower of jack pine off the road and walked to them. The burnt smell of nuts from a street vendor tinged the air and made Awol think of his youth and chestnuts over the campfire in Cub Scouts. Blazer chased a cottontail that zigged, zagged, and disappeared over an embankment.

"Kenny, welcome to Washington. You have accomplished your objective."

"Thanks. Something on your mind?"

Awol turned to face his son. "I've agreed to work with the feds some more. Sacco called; he's back on the case. I'm putting *you* on a bus back to school."

Kenny looked at him. He turned back to Blazer, who had returned from his failed hunt, and played with his ears as Awol watched.

"If I go back, why can't you go back? Tell them you've changed your mind. You shouldn't be out here alone. You're not fully healed."

Awol sat down next to Kenny and put his arm around him. "Kenny, this has been great. But it's time for you to go back and see Jill and get the hell out of my hair on this one."

The boy sighed and stood up. "Are you in danger, Dad?"

"I wouldn't ever bullshit you, so I won't answer the question."

"It's a stupid question. We called the police and made a report. Our names are a matter of record."

"That's right. Look, can we make this easy, Kenny?"

"You know, I'm starting to like the trail."

"I've noticed the bitching's declined."

Awol put both hands on Kenny's shoulders and looked his boy hard in the eyes. "C'mon, you owe me your safety. And I want you to hit those books again. It's your future."

Kenny looked back long and hard. "You'd better call me if you get in a tight spot, or I'll be really pissed."

Awol watched his boy amble back to the bridge; he'd bus out of Cascade Locks. The scraggly hair gave a tug on his heart, but Awol could see Kenny had filled out some and walked with more confidence.

Awol turned back to the PCT and poled north. Several minutes later, on a bluff overlooking the Columbia—where several long-billed great blue herons fished below him—he spotted Kenny nearing the end of the bridge. He could see his head move between the iron-slanted trusses. His boy looked across the river as he cleared the landing, and Awol waved his pole, but Kenny didn't spot him. Kenny disappeared as Awol gulped and heaved in a breath of Washington air. He stared at the spot where he'd last seen his son.

CHAPTER FORTY-SEVEN

Felix Rojas, the head of the Mexican cartel, and Mario Cedrone, the head of the New York Mafia family, met in a sleepy town in upstate New York. Each brought two trusted associates to the prearranged meeting. After listening to each other's story, after considering the implications, after evaluating all questions raised by their associates, the following major points were agreed to: Lombardi was in no shape to run his portion of the operation; he would be removed. Nino would be replaced by Richard Magnante, a bright, capable capo from Providence, Rhode Island. As no one was yet suitable to take over for Lombardi, Luis Alvarado, for now, would run the entire Pacific Crest Trail operation. There would be no change in payments and share.

Cedrone brought up the final points—the hiker working for the feds and the mule, Barcelona. Lombardi had claimed that Barcelona was either a mole used by the feds, or he was used by Alvarado to such a reckless extent that Barcelona had compromised the operation. They were unanimous that although the hiker with his son and dog had aroused suspicions, to eliminate them now would attract more media attention to the trail, the last thing they needed. Let it wait. Rojas admitted that he had heard about unfinished business ascribed to Barcelona that had endangered the operation. Barcelona would be eliminated. All the associates shook hands, and the meeting adjourned.

The next day, Magnante informed Frank that his services were no longer needed. He was to report immediately to New York for debriefing and reassignment. In New York, Frank learned that Lombardi had been retired. Frank was castigated for his indiscretion—mixing business with pleasure. He was told that his only chance for redemption lay in finding Paula. She knew too much. He had one month. He dared not ask what would happen after that.

Thus it was a gift from heaven, Frank thought, when two days later he heard a familiar voice on his cell.

"Frank."

"Paula? My God, are you all right?" Frank plugged a phone cable into a tracking device. "I was so worried about you. Please tell me you are safe."

"I'm sorry for your discomfort and the mess I've no doubt caused."

"May I ask where you are?"

"I'm in Chile."

"But the manifest said you were on the plane to Mexico."

"I know. After the boarding agent scanned my ticket, I waited in the tunnel. When she was distracted—a family with kids—I walked out."

"Wait, you never even went to Mexico?"

"No. Four gates down, a flight for Chile was leaving an hour later. I bought a ticket and got on that one."

"Paula . . ." He sighed. "When are you coming back?"

"I'm not planning to. And if I did, it would never be to Las Vegas."

"So, what are you going to do?" Frank looked at a tiny screen that read Chile and pumped a fist.

Frank listened to silence and wanted to ask more questions but sensed her suspicions.

"You were always straight with me, Frank. I figured I at least owed you a call. This is a new life for me. I wish you all the best, Frank."

At least Frank had something—she was definitely in Chile. Surely the family had connections there.

Paula didn't close her phone, the special one Alvarado had given her with an untraceable number, but removed the battery, which she dropped down a street drain at the curb. A few blocks later, she dropped the phone through another drain. She heard the plunk as it hit water. She walked two blocks to a bus station and from there took the local to the first of several trains she would take that day and through the night.

She'd enjoyed that summer she had spent in Chile, but in her reading and research, often late at night or in the wee hours of morning, she'd dreamed of another mysterious and exciting land. She was looking forward to meeting her class and teaching them English—in Lima. Peru!

CHAPTER FORTY-EIGHT

Barcelona crawled into the United States through the cartel's tunnel under the border fence. He gave a last tug on his pack and, after strapping the pack on again, stuffed the tumbleweed and yuccas back into the hole he'd just squirmed out of. He was looking forward to seeing Yolanda. She was the only tangible warmth in his life right now, and he had convinced himself that Juanita would understand his loneliness. Verdugo now gave Barcelona instructions through Gomez. Although Barcelona was thankful that he didn't have to endure Verdugo, he was troubled when Gomez butchered words like he'd lost his teeth and let on that Verdugo had beaten him senseless. Gomez, old and tiny, lived in a rathole and worked nonstop for Verdugo. Barcelona, with less than eight months to go and already on the outs with Verdugo, worried himself into thinking he was a marked man.

"Hello, Yolanda." He didn't suppress his smile. "You look pretty today."

Yolanda smiled from the driver seat of her Border Patrol vehicle as Barcelona leaned to the open window. She had her hair in a low bun and smelled fresh from the shower, had made up her eyes, and had on a light shade of lipstick. She moved a notebook to the backseat. "Would you like to get in?"

Barcelona went to the passenger side of the white vehicle with the BP green stripe. He laid his pack and sticks in back and entered. He grinned at her and then turned and looked straight ahead through the window, unsure of his next move. She meandered east over a flat, dry surface of dirt, sage, yucca, and the occasional tumbleweed.

They'd been silent for several minutes when she placed a hand on his thigh, just below his shorts. It made Barcelona dizzy. That human touch to Barcelona, a man who for over four months had locked down his emotions, a man who took himself to his physical limits every day, stirred him to a frenzy. He had to lean back and close his eyes.

"I have to keep moving. They have spotters that fly overhead." Yolanda's main job was to look for illegals.

"I don't want you to get in trouble."

"They won't see you from a helicopter, and this stretch I patrol is overlooked"—she turned to him and winked—"by me whenever you haul."

Barcelona tried to feel special. "So you don't report anyone here?"

"I don't report you, Barcelona, and others like you, but otherwise I report and arrest anyone else that comes across illegally."

Her English was accented, but she spoke confidently in a throaty voice.

It wasn't long before she put her right hand over his crotch. "I can creep along here—so it's okay." She looked to him and smiled warmly and pressed the automatic lock button. "It'll be okay. Go ahead."

Barcelona unzipped his fly, and she went in with her hand. He pulled the bandanna from his head and shifted closer.

Yolanda worked him slowly, tenderly, as she crept up the straightaway, ostensibly hunting illegals. Her warmth, her touch, her assured grip reached his innermost core, and it wasn't long before Barcelona exploded into his bandanna. Yolanda continued stroking through his spasms, pulling through every last drop. And, when he was done shaking, she still held him. Barcelona zipped, and then for reasons he didn't fully understand, he put his face into her shoulder and sobbed.

He recovered soon enough, and as she began to turn back, he put the shift lever in neutral, hugged her, and kissed her full.

"Now, Yolanda, you shall drive back slowly and leave the rest to me."

He moistened his finger with saliva and hugged her while easing his hand into her panties. He made every effort to be slow, tender, gentle. With both of her hands on the wheel, with his left arm around her, stroking her breast, he slid his finger into her while whispering Spanish into her ear. The vehicle crept along in the predawn darkness, and

Yolanda experienced an orgasm as powerful as any she'd ever had; but more than that, she felt it as a return of affection, of thanks, of humanity. And when she was done, he too remained inside of her so that she was unhurried, unrushed.

"Next time, we'll find a way to . . ." he trailed off.

"But this was good," she said.

"I thank you dearly, Yolanda." They'd come back to where she started.

"And I thank you," she said.

He smiled at her. "And now I have time to come up with better ideas. Next time, I promise, it will be the way God intended."

She scanned the sky and then smiled as he leaned over to kiss her on the cheek. He retrieved his pack and poles and went to the driver side.

"*Vaya con dios,*" she said.

His pack on, Barcelona leaned down to the window and kissed her lips. He put a hand on her cheek. "*Dios te bendiga.*"

Barcelona poled north, turned to her once and raised his sticks, then poled north again with vigor. He was behind schedule.

LUIS ALVARADO WAS SUPREMELY DELIGHTED with the news. He was now in charge of the entire operation. With composure, with gratitude, with forbearance, he thanked his senior and anticipated the day when he, himself, would run the cartel. Until then, there was work to do. He summoned Verdugo and Jaime, his central California commander. They were to join him in a meeting in Las Vegas with the northern California commander; Mr. Magnante, who now commanded Oregon; and the Washington commander. Alvarado intended to see how these people operated and to establish ground rules. Although he was told his position was temporary, he was led to believe that if the operation remained smooth and productive under his watch, there would be no reason to make further changes. Before they left, Alvarado pulled Verdugo aside and told him Barcelona was to be killed.

"Consider it done," Verdugo said. "But I'd like to do it myself; can it wait until after your first executive meeting?" He smiled at Alvarado, as one standing in the presence of eminence.

Alvarado allowed that would be possible, provided his order was carried out immediately upon their return. Verdugo's eyes glistened.

After the meeting—which had not solved where Tony was nor his missing drop—Alvarado, in disguise with a beard and glasses, sat at Sal's Hideaway. He felt his cell vibrate and took the first call to Tulio Lombardi's line. He'd told the northern commanders that, in an effort to keep business as usual, they could continue to use that same number that now rang in to him. He was amazed the dumb wops agreed to it. Smiling, he said, "Instruct me, Verdugo, should I answer 'Lombardi' or 'Alvarado'?"

Verdugo chuckled and ordered another round. He was comforted that his boss confided in him. Jaime had been dispatched to work with Magnante. If Verdugo could be the one to find Paula, he'd be assured of Alvarado's good graces.

"Who is this?" Alvarado said into the phone by way of a greeting. Alvarado sniffed his wine, a delicate Chianti he'd been told, and held the goblet to the light. Suddenly he put the glass down and touched Verdugo's wrist.

"Yes, I know where Tony is and I have his drop, but no one has gotten back to me," Alvarado said.

"Before I tell you that, I must know who you are," Alvarado said.

"Because I've taken over for Mr. Lombardi. I'm in charge now." Alvarado moved the wineglass in a circular motion to swirl the Chianti.

"Barcelona? No, you are not Barcelona. If you are, you work for the feds," Alvarado said.

"Answer me this—would you be Mr. Sacco?" Alvarado asked.

With that last statement, Sacco closed down the phone. He removed the handkerchief from his mouth and thought for a long time. When he'd said, to whom he thought was Tulio Lombardi, "You don't sound like the Mr. Lombardi I talk to," the person countered that he had taken over and was now in charge. Sacco studied Nino's notebook, sent to him by Awol, and referred again to his notes. He had called most of the names in the book and had kept recordings of the conversations in addition to his notes. He played back the recording he got of his call to Lombardi four days ago:

"Where is my godson? I know it's you."

And when Sacco tried to engage, this was the reply: "Who the fuck is this? Get me Alvarado, or I'll fucking mutilate you."

So there had been a change. Sacco confirmed a different voice than Lombardi's; he had just talked to a different man, one with the trace of an accent. The mention of Barcelona had unnerved the man. He replayed that part of the conversation and noted two elisions in his speech. He concluded that Barcelona was his only in. Because Barcelona knew the operation, the people, and how it was run, Sacco had to protect him. Sacco stuck the handkerchief again into his mouth, opened the phone, and punched in the number for Yolanda Sanchez.

CHAPTER FORTY-NINE

BARCELONA WAS HALFWAY TO HIS drop site at Falls Creek when he felt his cell vibrate. Only three people had his number—Alvarado, Verdugo, and Yolanda, in case he had to abort. This had to be urgent.

"Barcelona, it's Yolanda. Can you hear me?"

"Yes. What is it?" Barcelona, back on schedule, couldn't afford another distraction and was wondering if he had made a mistake with Yolanda.

"Listen to me. A man called to tell me you are in danger. He said," she spoke lower, "they are going to kill you."

"What man?"

"He wouldn't give his name but said you were supposed to kill some man with a dog, and because you didn't, you are going to be eliminated." Barcelona heard Yolanda's voice catch. "He said Alvarado isn't wasting any more time."

"I'll have to give myself up."

"No! Why would you do that?"

"If I don't, they will murder my wife and children—I don't care about me."

"I do. That's why I'm calling you."

Barcelona crouched and peeked around, ensuring he was alone. "You told me you used to live in Tijuana."

"Yes."

"Do you have a friend there who can hide my family?"

"I do have friends there. Where does your family live?"

"I don't know if this is right for me to do. I'm a bad person, Yolanda."

"I'm not so good either. And even if you give yourself up, who's to say they still won't kill your family? Let me help you, Barcelona."

"You are right. They may be on the way to seize them now, before they come to get me."

"I will call my friend Eva right away if you promise me you will make your escape now, this very second."

Barcelona gave her the address and thanked her.

He shut down the phone, took out the battery so he couldn't be traced, and dug out his map. He figured out their plan; they would intersect him at Falls Creek or on the way in. He knew two other things: They, even Yolanda, would expect him to escape south, back over the border. No one would expect him to head north. And, if he had any chance at all to save himself, he would have to cut his pack weight to the bare minimum. Barcelona knew every rock and yucca on this route. He fixed the spot in memory, counted twenty-six strides southwest to a stunted paloverde, and dug with bare hands at a shaded spot. He dug down nearly three feet, the last foot using his bandanna to cover gouged fingertips. He took out the canister and secured it in the grave. He smoothed off when finished and covered the area with sage and tumbleweed. When Barcelona put his pack back on, he felt he could run hurdles. He consulted his map one more time and, by dead reckoning, trotted northwest, away from Falls Creek.

VERDUGO WAS TENSE. IT HAD not gone well at Sal's. In trying to regain his full stature with Alvarado, he had been able to confirm that Paula had once worked there and was known by a few of the wait staff. Verdugo had approached the staff to inquire about Paula, and when he'd found a girl who knew her, he invited her to their table and introduced her to Alvarado. Alvarado promised to pay her handsomely for information, whereupon he was told Paula was in Chile teaching English as a second language and Spanish to nonlocals. Verdugo pitied his boss, who, for once, was at a loss for words. Unable to extract further information, Alvarado flushed red as he flopped a hundred-dollar bill on the table and walked out. It seemed to be Verdugo's fault. Added to this was Alvarado's unrest at the telephone call he had taken for Lombardi. Alvarado didn't know what to make of it, but he'd managed to turn the phone conversation back to Verdugo's handling of Barcelona. "I told you to kill that man with the dog. You gave the job to Barcelona."

Verdugo parked his Jeep at Falls Creek and seethed. He was two hours early, 2:00 a.m., and, by Jesus, he would show Barcelona how to kill a man. He shut down the engine, holstered his pistol, and took out his hunting knife. After exiting the vehicle, he pushed the lock button and pressed the door closed. He circled southeast and picked a spot at a bend where he could ambush Barcelona. He crouched and waited. He was early, but he wanted no possibility of being too late. Besides, now he could build to the task and relish the moment.

I should be hearing footsteps soon.

Barcelona is running late.

Where the fuck is he? The prick is going to pay.

I'll skin him alive.

At 4:45 a.m., Verdugo realized that Barcelona must have taken a slightly altered route, off the PCT, and was probably at the junction waiting for him by the Jeep. *No matter—I'll kill him there.*

Verdugo crept back toward the Jeep, right into the spines of an ocotillo. He stifled a curse and pulled the stalk from his thigh. *Barcelona is never this late.* In a half hour, light would inch into the eastern horizon. He arrived at the Jeep and shined his flashlight all around it—no other tracks but his own. A sickening feeling took hold of Verdugo. He rubbed his temple and beamed the light back to the PCT, from where Barcelona had always approached. He walked back to the PCT and swung his flashlight. "Barcelona!"

Verdugo trotted back to the Jeep and fumbled for his keys. "The fuck?" He couldn't find them. He beamed the light through the window into the vehicle and saw the keys on the seat. Enraged, he punched out the window. He called Yolanda, who confirmed Barcelona had left on time.

Later that morning, desperate, Verdugo called Alvarado.

"He didn't show, señor."

"Explain yourself. Who didn't show?"

"Barcelona. I went to get him like you told me to."

"Then you scared him off—you clunked around like Pancho Villa and—"

"Señor, I was—"

"What did I tell you years ago about interrupting me?"

Silence. Verdugo remembered the day an assistant had interrupted Alvarado twice in a row and was summarily silenced with a bullet to his head.

"Don't . . . ever . . . interrupt me . . . again."

Alvarado pocketed his phone and knew, of course, what had happened. Barcelona had been tipped off. Alvarado also knew he was now in the chess game of his life. The situation was bleak: a million lost up north; a million on the line down here; and Barcelona, who should have been eliminated a week ago—as instructed by his cartel chief— running free. He looked down at the chessboard. He was reviewing that first game with Paula, that brilliancy that he had lost, and wondered what she was doing at this moment. He remembered how he went dizzy after she said, "I don't want a queen; give me a horse." He reached for his quirt and fondled the braided leather. *When I find her, I will horsewhip her until she can't screech, salt her wounds, and slit her throat.*

Alvarado received one other call that afternoon. He'd hoped it would be Verdugo, informing him that Barcelona had been captured, the drop saved. Instead he listened to his one superior: "I need to confirm that my orders were followed. Has this man, Barcelona, been eliminated?"

CHAPTER FIFTY

Awol PLUNGED INTO WASHINGTON AND deep into the Cascades. He tramped through forests of oak, pine, and Sitka spruce and hiked into high valleys of moraines peppered with glacial erratics, those rocks and conglomerates that had been dragged and left by the ice age and looked strangely out of place. Topping a drumlin, Awol popped astringent but edible red berries from a madrone into his mouth and felt relieved that Kenny had left and was out of danger . . . but he missed him. Even Blazer looked subdued as he padded along.

The previous night, Sacco had called to tell him that the notebook was helpful. Awol had to admire how Sacco, disguising his voice, had made calls and found out that Nino had played a larger role than the ordinary mule. But the capper was that Sacco had managed to alert a woman that Barcelona was in grave danger. Awol suspected that Nino's people figured Barcelona had dumped Nino over the falls.

YOLANDA, THROUGH HER FRIEND EVA, was able to secure Barcelona's wife and two children. It would have to be temporary, Eva had said, but they could stay with her for the next couple of weeks. Eva lived with her sister on the other side of town, and they had room in their parlor. According to Eva, Barcelona's wife was distraught and wondered how she could get her children into school when sessions resumed. Yolanda left Barcelona a message telling him his family was safe and that she would try to make further arrangements over the next weeks.

Two days later, Barcelona's wife sneaked back to her former apartment to grab a check she'd been expecting. She knew it would be risky, but her children were safe, and the longer she waited . . .

The following night, Eva told Yolanda that Barcelona's wife had disappeared, that she could not be responsible for these children, and that if his wife didn't return, she and her sister could be in danger. Yolanda, sensing a reversal of her own fortunes, told her friend to hold on, that she would get back to her. Yolanda didn't call Barcelona—and concluded she could not risk calling him again.

CHAPTER FIFTY-ONE

"TELL ME YOU HAVE EVERYTHING in order," Alvarado demanded.

Verdugo winced. He had driven farther north to a semisecluded spot with a commanding view and was scanning with binoculars when he took the dreaded call from his boss. Previously he had called Yolanda and instructed her to call him at any sign of Barcelona. His calls to Barcelona had been ignored.

"I'm looking for him, señor."

"My chief is waiting, as am I. Call me every three hours, on the hour. Do not plan to come back here until you have righted matters. Understood?"

"*Sí, sí, señor.*"

Verdugo's hands shook as he closed down the phone. It was now midmorning. As the day lengthened, things for Verdugo could only get worse. The GPS-chipped phone was useless if the prick wouldn't answer.

Verdugo punched in Barcelona's number again and left a message.

"I got news for you, Barcelona. We have your wife and kids. You'd better call."

Twelve miles north, Barcelona replayed the message. *It's a bluff— Yolanda says my family is safe.* Nevertheless, Barcelona worried as he trudged ahead under the grueling sun, two hundred yards west of the PCT.

At the next call into his boss, Verdugo felt iced when Alvarado roared into the phone, "Find him or else!"

"He had to have sneaked back over the border, señor," Verdugo said.

"Is Barcelona a marked man in Mexico?"

"*Sí.*"

"By us as well as the police?"

"*Sí.*"

"Does Barcelona have permits allowing him to travel the length of the PCT?"

"*Sí.*"

"Does he have a cleared passport to enter Canada?"

"*Sí.*"

"Then use your fucking head!"

Verdugo was exhausted and bone dry as he tramped back to the Jeep—the Jeep with a busted driver window, which allowed dust storms to consume the vehicle. He slammed his fists onto the hood, wanting to tip the frigging Jeep on its side and walk away to an oasis that had beer and leggy women; instead, he crawled inside the dust-stormed vehicle and stewed.

Verdugo called Barcelona again; this time, he left a voice mail he was sure wouldn't be ignored. "I'm in Tijuana, and I have your wife beside me. Pretty little thing . . . for now. If you want to see her alive again, you have five minutes to return my call."

Barcelona listened to the message and immediately called Yolanda. She didn't pick up. He called her twice more in quick succession, telling her it was urgent—but she didn't answer. Feeling he had no choice, after four minutes he responded to Verdugo.

"So you have decided to call me after all, Barcelona."

"Put my wife on the phone."

"I will, but you will ask me nice—you don't instruct me, Barcelona, you see—"

"Put her on now!"

"See what I mean, you are not being—"

Click.

Verdugo got the fix and located it on the map. North–northwest. *He's flying, but I have the Jeep!* Verdugo called Alvarado ahead of schedule with the news.

"You know what's at stake," Alvarado said. "I trust you will redeem yourself."

Alvarado suspected Yolanda Sanchez was complicit; she'd been the new piece on the chessboard. He ordered her cell to be exchanged and a bug placed in her apartment. If his suspicions proved correct, she would be hard to replace. She was efficient in her work, Medina had said, and tough in handling the normal illegals arrested. And that border point was crucial. With Captain Medina out of the picture, Alvarado had toyed with the idea of trying again to turn Sacco. Alvarado thought back again to the call he had received at Sal's Hideaway in Las Vegas. Sacco was worth one more try.

Yolanda heard the desperation in Barcelona's messages. She wanted to pick up, but she had been in this business long enough to know how her bosses worked. If she was at all suspected, they would torture her to death and mark her with the dreaded X. She was tough but not stupid. She had a strong liking for Barcelona; that is why she had saved his family and was working hard to arrange for his children. But if they had his wife, what could she do? She felt sorry, but his wife was out of her hands. She would contact him when his children were safe. She would work extra hard at her job, give them no reason to suspect. And most importantly, she would handle anything to do with Barcelona privately, from the one pay phone she knew of.

Barcelona dipped and rinsed his bandanna in the mud puddle. When he'd spotted the larger yucca plants and the slight browning of sand, he made a search, dug down, and was rewarded. This would be enough water to refresh him and keep him going. He retied the bandanna around his forehead and kept replaying the phone conversation in his mind. Verdugo didn't have his wife. He reasoned that Verdugo used the ploy to get a lock on his location. The more Barcelona thought it through, the more he realized Verdugo wasn't in Tijuana but was, instead, coming after him. It troubled him that Yolanda didn't answer—perhaps Verdugo had *her*. He checked his map and looked for a place where he might see an approach in several directions. He found a spot, but it took him east, away from water, and he'd been tramping through one dry arroyo after another. Barcelona, low on water in this barren and penurious land, turned west.

CHAPTER FIFTY-TWO

VERDUGO KNEW ALL THE BACK paths usable by a four-by-four. He had, at one time, tracked illegals and offered them up to his boss; that's how they'd gotten Rodolfo, Alvarado's other assistant. Verdugo raced across the land northwest to an area sufficiently ahead of where Barcelona would be. He slowed as he neared the spot, hid the vehicle, and sneaked to a brushy lookout north of the one creek, a soccer field's length away. He scanned with his binoculars and estimated he was a good hour ahead of him. He figured Barcelona's method would be to blaze west along the PCT. That would enable him to access water caches maintained for PCT thru-hikers by the Sierra Club and to scrounge food.

Two hours later, Verdugo was in fits. He was due to give a report to Alvarado, and he wanted to give him good news. He waited another fifteen minutes, scanning around, then called his boss.

"Have you thought of the possibility that he's ahead of you?" Alvarado said.

"It would be impossible, señor; I've allowed extra for that. He carries too much."

A silence hung between them. "Unless . . ." Alvarado said.

Verdugo put a hand over his eyes. "It is possible, señor, but—"

"I suggest you think hard about that possibility. Before you do anything to him, you make sure you confirm where that drop is. His wife is being brought to me now."

Helplessness consumed Verdugo as he waited another twenty minutes. He could conclude only that Barcelona had buried the vault earlier and made record time on the trail. Verdugo realized the million-dollar drop was now on his shoulders. No wonder Barcelona was flying. But he wanted to be sure Barcelona wasn't in the area; once Verdugo left here, he wouldn't come back. He tried to estimate how a pack weight diminished by twenty-seven pounds would translate into distance, but the mathematics of it confused him. He refocused at another spot on his map that he felt would be ahead of Barcelona and kept poking the spot on the map with his finger, rocking from leg to leg as he stood by the Jeep, mumbling. He spat in the dirt, refired the Jeep, and skidded north.

BARCELONA FELT THE VIBRATION AND saw that it was not Verdugo.

"Barcelona?"

"Yolanda!"

"Listen, Barcelona, this is the last time I can call. Your children are safe—you can talk to them at the number I gave you."

"Where is Juanita?"

"She has not come back to Eva's apartment, Barcelona. She's gone, but she knows that her children are safe."

"Where did she go when she left Eva's?"

"I don't know, Barcelona. She may have realized that the best way to protect her children was for her to hide somewhere else."

"Or they have her."

"We don't know that. I'm sorry, but this is the last time I can call you."

"Bless you, Yolanda."

Barcelona called the number he had memorized. An older-sounding woman picked up. After answering questions that confirmed he was their father, he was able to talk with his children. Overjoyed to talk with Papa, they wanted to talk with Mama, too. He told them to be happy. He told them to study hard and become smart, that he would test them on their lessons the next time he saw them, after giving each of them presents. He told them to be good to people, to say their prayers, and to go to church. He listened to their questions and answered what he could. He was giving them his love when his battery ran out. Barcelona looked at the dead phone and thought about other things he wanted to say to his children. But more than that, he wished he could hear their voices again. He removed the battery and tucked the phone away.

Barcelona's first thought was to escape. Maybe he could find a road and hitch out. But he hated the thought of leaving Verdugo alive for another second. And Verdugo's death would be a big loss to Alvarado, whom he hated with every ounce of his being. His children were safe. He didn't know about Juanita, but he couldn't just keep running away. No, running away was out of the question. Barcelona took up the map. After concentrating for several minutes, Barcelona turned and poled southeast.

Late afternoon, Barcelona, ear to the ground, could make out a faraway rumble. It started and stopped, but finally he heard it more clearly—to the north. According to his training map, the four-by-four paths in that direction were faint and rarely used. *It has to be Verdugo.*

Verdugo hadn't slept in nearly two days. He'd just missed sliding off the desert-cracked berm into a gully by inches. Unable to continue in his right mind, he pulled into a shaded area for a quick nap, keeping his hand on his holstered gun as he leaned back in the seat. He woke up two hours later as the sun lowered into the horizon. For a moment he forgot where he was and knuckled his eyes.

Not twenty yards away, Barcelona hid in a draw camouflaged under sage, tumbleweed, and mesquite. When Barcelona had heard the rumble stop, knowing Verdugo used binoculars, he had crept far to the west and then north to come around behind him. Over an hour later, he thought he could see Verdugo in the vehicle. Barcelona had removed his pack and laid it with his poles as he crawled into the draw.

Shortly before twilight, Barcelona watched Verdugo exit the vehicle and unbutton his fly. He could see a gun holstered on his right hip and his knife clipped at his left hip. Barcelona uncovered himself and crawled to the Jeep. He made it to the back tires and eased out his knife. Barcelona grimaced because Verdugo had just finished, but the instant Verdugo reached down to rebutton, Barcelona leapt onto his back and wrapped his legs around his hips, covering his weapons.

"Don't move, or I'll slice your throat."

Verdugo stilled as Barcelona—clinging to him, knife at his throat— reached around him with his left hand and removed his gun. He threw it behind him and then slipped out Verdugo's knife, throwing that behind him as well. Barcelona kept his left leg in front of Verdugo's legs as he dropped off and tripped him to the ground.

Barcelona stepped back a half pace, closer to the weapons. "Where is my wife?"

"I don't know, Barcelona. Only Alvarado would know that."

"Get him on the phone."

Verdugo went to reach in his pocket, but at the last instant, scooped sand, flung it into Barcelona's face, and lunged.

CHAPTER FIFTY-THREE

ALVARADO STOOD ON THE UPPER veranda and looked to his rookery behind the gazebo. A falcon and two kestrels were nesting. On the opposite side of his mansion, workers clipped hedges, trimmed lianas and shrubs of rabbitbrush, tended flowers. Other workers mulched gardens in front of the ramada. He wondered why Verdugo was late with his report. *It had better be because of good news.* He was about to return to his office when Rodolfo, a look of dread on his face, bounded up the outside veranda stairs.

"There's been an accident, señor. The woman, she threw herself onto the stone of her cell headfirst."

Alvarado's lip twitched. "Impossible."

"We found this note in the corner. She must have charged at an angle and plunged her head into the jamb where the iron door meets the cornerstone. She's unconscious."

"Tend to her! See that she lives." Alvarado swiped the piece of toilet paper from Rodolfo's hands. In streaks of blood it read: *ROT IN HELL.*

Alvarado waited another five minutes, attempting to calm himself, before calling Verdugo.

"What has kept you?" Alvarado hissed.

"This is Barcelona. Put my wife on the phone." Barcelona had his bandanna tied to cover a puffed eye.

"Put Verdugo on the phone, and I'll repay in kind." Alvarado worked to lock in Barcelona's location.

"I have the drop. Put my wife on the phone, or you will never see the drop again."

Alvarado secured the fix and went to the large map pinned to the wall behind his desk. He pressed a button to summon Rodolfo.

"Where is Mr. Verdugo?"

"Where is my wife?"

"Tell me where you are, and I'll have your wife brought to you in exchange for the drop and Mr. Verdugo."

"I need to know my wife is alive."

"And I need to know the same for Mr. Verdugo."

Barcelona could think of no alternative; he gave Alvarado his location.

"I'll have her there in three hours," Alvarado said.

Alvarado's men raced to the border at Campo. Yolanda watched as a woman on a stretcher was loaded into a van. Rodolfo attended to her in back of the van, and two of Alvarado's men in front drove north to meet Barcelona. Alvarado gave instructions from his villa and remained in continual contact.

Barcelona took Verdugo's phone and called Yolanda.

"Yes, Mr. Verdugo?"

"It's me, Barcelona. Alvarado is supposed to send my wife to me, do you know—"

"They just put her in a van; she is on a stretcher, Barcelona."

"A stretcher? Is she okay?"

"I don't think so. Her eyes were closed and her head—"

"What about her head?"

"It was bumped out. Bandaged."

Barcelona accepted that his life was over. He didn't have the drop—that in itself was enough for them to chop off his limbs and bleed him out. They would threaten to murder her in front of him to get the drop if she wasn't dead already, and if he took them to the drop and they released her, what was he to do with his wife on a stretcher? He put his head in his hands. Then he looked at the crumpled Verdugo.

Barcelona finished his work. His children were safe—his dear Juanita was as tough as nails and would never give them away. He owed it to her to survive and eventually reunite with their children. If Barcelona stayed here, they would both end up dead. Perhaps Juanita had gone to God already. One thing was certain—he had to leave this instant if one of them was to survive.

Barcelona took Verdugo's weapons, binoculars, wallet, sunglasses, and all his clothes and boots and hid them under the seats in the Jeep. He retrieved his own pack and sticks and threw them in the back. After gathering up Verdugo's maps and notebooks and putting them in the glove box, he found the ignition key and took one last look around. He picked up Verdugo's sombrero, which had rolled into the ditch, and carried it to the Jeep. For the weather ahead, Barcelona would need more than a bandanna. Barcelona didn't need to consult any maps; he knew exactly where he was going. He drove north into the playa on Jeep roads that would eventually lead him to a place where he knew Alvarado and his pistoleros would never find him. Yes, he would be taking a long way around to get back to his children one day, but the immediate objective was to disappear, to isolate. Barcelona looked north, north, and north—to the High Sierra.

CHAPTER FIFTY-FOUR

AWOL CAMPED BELOW THE NORTHERN side of Cispus Pass, at the river. He fluffed Blazer's ears after he finished writing in his journal and then pulled out his fleece.

"You miss Kenny, Blazer?"

The animal shook his tail and rolled onto his back. Awol tugged on the fleece and hooded up. He scratched the dog's belly as Blazer closed his eyes and wagged his tail in the dirt. "I miss him too. He cooks better than I do." He continued to scratch and pat the animal and thought about going back down to see both sons one more time, after he finished hiking the PCT. "We'll see Kenny and Gregory when we finish—okay, boy? And Lulu! We'll see her too."

Blazer thumped his tail.

That evening, Sacco called.

"I've been approached by the other side."

"No shit." Awol sat up straight against the pine. "Who?"

"He didn't give his name, but I did you a favor."

"What?"

"I told him I screwed it up with you, that you are out of the picture and had nothing to do with the dead mule, that you are just making an effort to finish the trail—stubborn fool that you are—and would be going home once you complete it."

"Did he believe it?"

"I told him I wouldn't consider any type of offer unless he left you alone. Said I owed you that much."

"What do the thugs want you to do?"

"He asked me to help find Barcelona."

"And?"

"I got one month from my chief. After that, we arrest the little guys."

"Which means the overall operation lives."

"Right. I need to find Barcelona."

"Why does this all hinge on him?"

"They believe he worked for us—and they are hunting for him."

"What do you want me to do?"

"All I want you to do is keep an eye out where you are and come identify him when we think we've found him."

"What makes you think Barcelona will cooperate? Assuming we find him."

"What's his alternative?"

"Where do *you* think he is? Maybe he went back to Mexico."

"No. They would have found him there already. I'm going to try to learn more. Stay alert and wait for my call."

ALVARADO WAS REVIEWING HIS HOLDING areas, which were padded, but in this particular cell, which he reserved for women, the pads didn't curve around the stone jamb that met the heavy cast iron door. He was fingering the caked blood where Barcelona's wife had hurled herself as Rodolfo's voice came through the cell phone.

"Señor?"

"Yes."

"Barcelona is not here."

Alvarado heard fear in Rodolfo's voice. "Where is Verdugo?"

"Señor, I'm afraid to tell you . . . Verdugo has been murdered."

"How?"

"Señor . . . Señor . . ."

"Send me a picture. Do it now."

When he downloaded the picture, it was Verdugo all right—gutted and hung by his own riata from a Joshua tree. There was an X marked in blood on his forehead.

CHAPTER FIFTY-FIVE

BARCELONA WAS RELIEVED TO SEE the gas gauge at three-quarters full. He figured that Alvarado would try to find him on four-by-four paths in the drylands, that other vehicles with Alvarado's thugs were hunting for him now. He prayed he was far enough ahead of them. Once out of the desert, he pulled to a secluded spot and found a map in the glove box. He wasn't used to driving on highways and without a license felt it prudent to stay on secondary roads. While studying the map, he reached into Verdugo's food bag and pulled out a banana. He drank his water and found a bag of macadamia nuts. Before leaving, he resoaked his sand-gritted eye with his bandanna.

Barcelona drove on with heavy heart. Juanita. He told himself over and over that she would want one of them to survive for their children. He prayed to God that she was in a coma, not suffering, and would die without waking. He tried to put Juanita out of his mind, but he kept seeing her awake in the desert, on a stretcher, alone, under a murderous sun. No matter how he tried to angle it in his mind, he knew he'd caused Juanita's death. All he could do in the end was ask her forgiveness and swear that he would make it up to their children. The worst thing he could do now was get caught by Alvarado.

After midnight, Barcelona, with doused lights, coasted into the back lot of Hector's Collision. He used a screwdriver from Verdugo's tool kit and removed the license plates from the Jeep. He crept over to a wrecked Dodge Ram, still hooked to a tow truck, and swapped out the plates. He drove for two more hours before pulling into a rest area and willing himself to sleep. He was awakened when a night gust blew in through the Jeep's busted driver-side window. He refired the Jeep and drove on.

In the morning, he charged his phone just enough to listen to his messages. Three messages, all from Alvarado. The final one said:

"This is your last chance. I have your wife. If I don't hear from you, I, myself, will tie her to my special cross and use my personal machete."

Barcelona knew he was making a mistake but couldn't control himself. He called.

"Put her on the phone."

"Hold on."

"You have five sec—"

"Eeehhhhyyyya, 'Berto?"

"Juanita! Is it you?" Barcelona skidded to a stop at the side of the road.

"Eyyyaaah *sí*, 'Berto . . ."

"It doesn't sound like you. What date did we get married?"

"Eyyaaahh, 'Berto . . ." Click.

Barcelona shouted into the phone. Not caring that they had locked in his location, he tried to convince himself that it wasn't Juanita; it didn't sound like her, but she could have been in intense pain. Yolanda said she looked banged up. *If only I knew for sure.*

An hour later, Barcelona used Verdugo's phone to call Yolanda, praying that she would pick up. He had only one last question, and then he would—

"Yolanda. It's me. Please answer me one question. Did they return with the woman on the stretcher?"

"No. I'm sorry."

"Thank you for being truthful. Are my children still safe?"

"Yes. Don't call me again. Verdugo didn't come back either. Another man has been asking me questions. I have to disappear."

My children are safe—God be with you, Juanita.

Barcelona was certain Alvarado had lied to him, that he couldn't skin Juanita alive, but now Alvarado had a fix and his men were after him in earnest. They would expect him to stay on the road, but he had other plans. He checked the map, deciding on Kennedy Meadows, where he began hauling after his promotion from the desert. A few hours later, he stopped in a little crossroads town, got gas using Verdugo's cash, and filled his water bottles with a hose at the back of the station. He rinsed his eye and removed the bandanna he'd slanted over it. After pulling out a mango and the last of the grapes from Verdugo's now-empty bag, he drove across the street to a mart to buy provisions. Barcelona wished he could do his laundry but didn't have the time. Instead, in the men's room he changed into Verdugo's shirt and turned his own briefs inside out. Verdugo's pants were too big, but Barcelona stowed them in his pack anyway, along with the food he'd bought. He'd also purchased hair bleach and clear reading glasses. He stashed the revolver and a box of bullets in the bottom of his pack but left the extra knife under the seat. Popping a can of Jolt, he continued north.

At dusk, before reaching the road he'd been aiming for, Barcelona gassed up one last time. There were no guardrails on this winding, uphill road to protect drivers from a huge drop into the abyss. The ground was so rocky, any drilling would serve to destabilize it. Barcelona pulled over and waited for complete silence. He'd selected a spot, and when he heard no motors and could see no headlights, he drove to the edge—a sheer mile-deep drop into a canyon with nothing but rocky crags all the way to the bottom. He grabbed his pack and sticks, put the Jeep in neutral, and left it running. Once outside, he pushed the vehicle and sent it over. Barcelona threw on his pack and ran to the opposite side, clambered over a rock, climbed up into smaller rocks and spruce, and soon disappeared. He heard the vehicle bounce several times and then explode. He turned once, several minutes later, and saw oily smoke from his higher elevation. He'd made sure the cliff by the road had been barren of trees; all that rock would prevent a forest fire. The pungent smell of oil and gas wafted into the night.

He bushwhacked in a fury. Normally such physical exertion would focus his thoughts—escape! But he kept thinking about Juanita and his kids, and how he was responsible. Finally, he was able to use his sticks, but he was sick with worry about his family and the mess he'd gotten them into. Tears mixed with sweat as he stifled shouts and curses.

THE NEXT DAY, SACCO CALLED Alvarado, who had given him a special number. The plan for now, Alvarado had said, was for them to work together to locate Barcelona. Sacco's intent was to string Alvarado along, and he had perfect news for that purpose. They'd found Verdugo's vehicle, presumably driven by Barcelona, but the vehicle wasn't a Jeep. It was a wrecked pickup at Hector's Collision. Alvarado was puzzled but thanked him for the information.

The following day, Alvarado received another call.

"We found the Jeep. A ranger in the Sierra told us it went off the side of a cliff and exploded," Rodolfo said.

"Any sign of him?"

"No, señor."

"Did you go down and check the vehicle yourself?"

"We can't do it, señor. The police have closed the area and—"

"I don't care. Get down there at once and report back to me what you find!"

That evening, while updating his superior, Alvarado was given other news.

"Mr. Cedrone called me from New York," the cartel chief said. "Mr. Magnante located Tony, the mule that missed the drop, and the drop has been recovered."

"Why wasn't I notified? Magnante is under strict orders—"

"Not any longer. Mr. Magnante is replacing Mr. Lombardi. It is set up like before, and Mr. Magnante is your counterpart. You will give him every courtesy. Do I make myself clear?"

It took Olympian control before Alvarado—the schemer, the chess player—could utter, "*Sí.*"

CHAPTER FIFTY-SIX

Bᴀʀᴄᴇʟᴏɴᴀ'ꜱ ʜɪᴋɪɴɢ ꜱᴛɪᴄᴋꜱ ᴊᴜᴍᴘᴇᴅ ᴀʟᴏɴɢ the path. Emboldened, he saw no reason not to hike north on the Pacific Crest Trail. He didn't, for the moment, have to worry about Alvarado's central California commander, Jaime. Unlike Verdugo, Jaime's counterpart in the south, not once did Jaime get on the trail when Barcelona hauled here, and he'd always sent someone else to switch out drops. Barcelona's blond-dyed hair and clear, marginally magnifying glasses, which he wore near the tip of his nose, gave him a new look. He put on his headlamp and, with the aid of a near-full moon, poled north over a wooden bridge. Two miles later he crossed Crag Creek, scaring two deer. Not until he reached the south fork of Kern River, eleven miles north of Kennedy Meadows, did he take his first break. He drank like a racehorse from the river and sat at the bank eating a peach and a pear. He checked his watch—10:00 p.m. *A four-mile-an-hour pace; good for this section.* He had muled this area several times and was relieved he'd made it back to craggy forest and isolation. Here, a person couldn't be easily discovered—especially if they didn't want to be.

Barcelona's adrenaline gave out at midnight. At Monache Creek Bowl, he camped at a level spot in the saddle, twenty yards off-trail. He was nineteen miles from where he'd sent the Jeep over the edge.

Barcelona wished he had his tent—the nights were cold in the Sierra—but when he'd been sent back to work the border, Verdugo had taken it. After he finished redyeing his hair, he said the first of a nightly prayer for Juanita's soul and then he prayed for his children. When he finished, he tucked farther into his sleeping bag and, eventually, slept.

Over the next two days, Barcelona reverted to caution and bushwhacked north. He neared the trail only when obstacles forced him to, and then he made sure to be extra vigilant. He doubted Alvarado would have sent men this far ahead. This was a no-man's-land; he could be anywhere. His pursuers were more likely to cruise access roads, guessing he would try to escape. His plan for now was simple: distance himself from the Jeep, disguise himself, and stay off the trail as much as possible.

He would avoid towns, but staying near the PCT enabled him to access them for emergency needs. He put out of his mind the oversight that he wasn't carrying the required bear vault for food—*the irony*, he thought—but all his other papers were in order. The biggest problems he foresaw were avoiding the mules behind and in front of him, and, of course, Jaime. Although Alvarado kept mules separated from each other, one would meet a compatriot at drops, and one mule was generally recognizable to another. To avoid being taken for a mule, Barcelona, whose pack already looked smaller without the vault, disguised it further. He discarded the day pack on top of it, where he used to keep his food, cut off straps on the main pack, and plastered the pack with duct tape.

At the windblown Kearsarge Pass, eighty-five miles north of the ditched Jeep, Barcelona hiked through burn and had no choice but to stay close to or on the trail. The wind still blew, and he understood how the fire had spread. He'd smelled smoke all day but chose to push through the weather-twisted pines when he convinced himself the fire had burnt itself out. A controlled burn, he hoped, as he hiked in unbelievable desolation. Charred trunks, black skeletons of once stately trees, burnt firs, fireweed, and debris slowed him down and, in many instances, barred his path. Barcelona listened to total silence. *Not even in the desert is it this quiet. Terrible.*

The next morning, north of the burn and a mile past Glen Pass, Barcelona, too late to make an evasive maneuver, came face-to-face with two rangers.

"Did you hike through the burn?" one of them asked.

"Yes, sir."

"See any flare-ups?"

"No, sir. I didn't."

"Looks like we did something right," the other ranger said to his colleague.

"Can I see your permits, please?" the first ranger said.

"Certainly."

The first ranger reviewed Barcelona's permits while the second looked into his pack. After a moment, he held it up for his colleague and pointed inside. Barcelona's heart thumped as he remembered Verdugo's loaded gun and the box of bullets he'd thrown in the food bag.

"Where is your food vault, Mr. DeLeon?"

"I don't have one, sir." Barcelona's mind raced ahead as he watched the ranger rummage the pack. "I have a pistol and some bullets in there. Are there rules about that?"

Both rangers looked at him. "There certainly are," the lead ranger said. "You should know that. Let me see your gun permit."

The other ranger dug deeper.

"I wasn't aware of the US rules."

"You are not in Spain, Mr. DeLeon, you are in the USA."

"I see." Barcelona tried to look apologetic and despondent. "I don't have a permit, sir."

The second ranger held up the revolver and opened the breach. "Loaded," he confirmed.

The lead ranger took up the revolver and examined it. "Where did you get this, and why?" he asked Barcelona.

"I bought it from a hiker going south about a month ago. For small game if I had no food. And for protection against bears in an emergency."

The lead ranger shook his head and looked at the box of bullets the other ranger showed him.

"You are on your way to Canada?" the lead ranger asked.

"Yes, sir."

"Now, how in the hell would you expect to cross the border with this?" He held up the gun.

After a few seconds, Barcelona said, "I don't think I thought it through."

"We need to confiscate your gun and ammo and make a report."

"Yes, sir. I'm sorry about this, I—"

"In addition to a citation and fine for not having a food vault, we should take you to the police to make the report there. You're lucky we don't have the time."

Barcelona sat down on a stump. "Jesus."

In the end, he signed and dated a report that his firearm and ammunition were confiscated. He paid the food vault violation in cash but didn't have money for further penalties. He had sixty days to remit the money to the address noted. If he did not, he would be officially summoned according to US Customs law, and the Spanish Embassy would be notified.

THAT EVENING, DETECTIVE SACCO READ the report article describing a Jeep accident on the road to Kennedy Meadows. He reread the part where the Jeep was unrecognizable from the half-mile-long tumble and explosion. No body had been found. He called Awol.

"What do you think?" Sacco asked.

"He jumped out or was ejected. Did they find ripped clothes or something?"

"They've searched—no blood, no threads, nothing except what was in the vehicle."

"You thinking what I'm thinking?" Awol said.

"I am. I'm having the plate they found on the Jeep run tomorrow. If it matches the plate that should have been on that Dodge Ram at Hector's, I bet he's hiding in the High Sierra."

When Sacco received a call the next day on the plate match, he called several ranger stations in that area and to the north. He asked about anything unusual, any citations, hoping that the particular rangers he talked to were not being greased by one from Alvarado's gang. They had nothing useful to report, and Sacco restrained himself from asking for further help.

Two days later, one of the rangers called back from Independence, a small town nestled in the Sierra. Just yesterday, a Roberto DeLeon—a student from Barcelona, Spain—was cited for carrying a loaded firearm and not having a food vault. The one word that Sacco repeated to himself again and again was Barcelona. Sacco was educated about thru-hikers' fixations on trail names. Awol had said that thru-hikers would most times not even learn of a fellow hiker's real name throughout an entire long-distance hike. *Is Barcelona a trail name for DeLeon?* He called Awol.

"Interesting. They said he was blond? With glasses? The guy I know has black hair. He didn't wear glasses, but I guess that's all changeable."

"Well, he doesn't have his gun anymore."

"So what's your plan?" asked Awol.

"I need to find this guy; if he's who we think he is, he knows the key people and how they operate. I'm coming out with an associate. I'll call you when we find him, and you can identify him."

"I'd rather join you now to help look for him."

"No way. My ass is on the line here. You are not officially involved."

"Exactly my point. I'm no longer connected with you or the SDPD. I'm just a citizen out here on my own."

"Look, Awol. I appreciate that, as an ordinary citizen, you may be trying to help, but you are no ordinary citizen. You've been trained and hosted by us. Even your dog's been trained. If my boss hears about this, he'll have me take you in for interfering with a police investigation."

"I'll have to take my chances. I'm not going away, Vincent. I know I screwed up before, when I was connected with you and the division. Now that I'm officially removing myself from your responsibility—"

"Awol, do I have to call Linda?"

"Won't be necessary; I'll tell her myself."

"Figures."

"Look. I have to do it for Kenny and all the other kids. I'll stay out of your way. But when I get something solid, this ordinary citizen will be contacting you."

After Awol hung up, Sacco thought it through. He was on thin ice and was told to report any and all details to his chief. Permission for Awol to help him pursue Barcelona would never be authorized. Sacco figured he would play dumb and not tell the chief. But there was someone he could call. After rifling through his notes, he found the phone number for the main UCLA dining hall and punched it in.

"Manager Kenny, please."

CHAPTER FIFTY-SEVEN

Barcelona was in a quandary. He needed a different phone, he needed money, he needed food. That night, smelling what he determined to be a campfire—there was a waft of sausage and onion in the air—he bushwhacked toward it and was able to use a camper's phone.

"No, I can't send you any money," Eva said. "I should be paid for tending your children."

"You are right. I apologize for asking. Before I speak with my kids, is Yolanda okay?"

"I haven't heard from her. Now, I have to wake them. Hold on."

But the kids were tired, and hearing their father's voice didn't create the joy it had that first time a few days ago. Where was Mama, they wanted to know. 'Berto, the younger of the two, left the phone, and Barcelona, heartbroken, said goodnight to Trini.

Barcelona camped a mile north of the hikers, well off-trail. Survival instinct kept Barcelona isolated but near the trail; access roads to get out were tempting, but Alvarado would have men patrolling those, and the Americans could have put an APB out. He felt safer in the wilds where nonhikers would never find him.

Blazing a new trail in the forest wasn't like in the desert. It was grueling, as he contended with roots, brambles, understory, debris. Barcelona's pace was cut in half, and sometimes it took him over an hour a mile when he was in lower, denser elevations, as he had to keep checking that he was in striking distance of the PCT. But much of this high section was ridge between peaks. He was exposed during these stretches, many of which were over a mile long. When he ventured out to the crest, he would first scan with field glasses and then pole through as fast as he could. The mental stress exhausted him more than the physical. At Mather Pass, which was over twelve thousand feet elevation, he scanned the area; he didn't find anything unusual, just a few day hikers. At the fork of Kings River, he was back in sufficient forest cover at eight thousand feet and made camp over a hundred yards west of the trail. Inflamed with worry, he twisted and turned in his bag throughout the night.

CHAPTER FIFTY-EIGHT

Awol, AFTER STUDYING MAPS AND reviewing scenarios in his mind, made a decision. Based on Awol's travel time to get there and Barcelona's fastest possible pace since the Jeep accident, he would scout a position well ahead of where Barcelona could be. Traveling by Amtrak and bus, Awol determined he could reach Mammoth Lakes, California, in fifteen hours. He would set up four miles north on the PCT at a place called Reds Meadow. *Perfect*, he thought, *there is even a store for provisions.* Barcelona was wanted by both sides. Awol aimed to find him first and then give him to Sacco.

On a day of flurries and gray skies, Awol went through his motivations. Yes, he wanted to set a good example for his son, who had been trampled by drugs and thugs. No matter what happens to me, Sacco will clean the slate for Kenny and look out for him. Yet Awol was still haunted by the firefight in Iraq, where he shot and killed one of his own men. *I hope by accident.* He felt honor bound to put himself at risk for the rest of his life.

Awol got a ride all the way back to Cascade Locks and from there bussed to Klamath Falls, Oregon. In Klamath Falls, he and Blazer took Amtrak to California—luckily, he'd kept papers identifying Blazer as a police dog. They'd just stepped off in Sacramento and were on their way to the bus when Awol felt a hand on his shoulder.

"Hi, Dad."

What kept words tangled in Awol's throat was his son's attire. Kenny was in full hiking regalia—pack, poles, sun hat, and a broad smile on his face. In the weeks since Awol had last seen him, Kenny had filled out; he looked healthier, purposeful. Blazer jumped up and put his front paws on Kenny's chest and yipped. Kenny fussed over the dog while Awol found his voice.

"What the hell are you doing here?"

"Classes don't start for almost a month; I miss the trail."

"Bullshit. I'm glad to see you, but you'd better not be thinking of joining me."

"Actually, Dad," Kenny said and smiled, "I am. And guess what? I've been working out. I'm up to thirty-five push-ups and six chin-ups."

Awol walked in a room-wide circle and came back to him.

"Did Sacco call you?"

"Yep. Said you'd mentioned Amtrak, so it was easy enough to figure out where to find you."

"Jesus. Kenny, we've been all through this. No. You can't join me."

"Dad, I'm coming. If you don't want me—"

"Of course I'd like to have you, but not in this circumstance. It's too dangerous."

"I'm an adult now. I'll camp nearby, but I'm coming."

Awol looked at his son a long while. "Your mother used to tell me I was the most stubborn person she knew. Looks like you're holding that record now."

His boy smiled again. "Looks that way."

"Why are you so determined to do this?"

"You did me a big favor. And you are my father."

After a moment, they both looked down at Blazer, who shifted looks between them. The animal yawned and stretched and sat down between them but looked to his master for his next move.

"Well, if I can't stop you, let's at least make our bus."

CHAPTER FIFTY-NINE

Barcelona hoped he could make it to Canada before winter, even with the bushwhacking. He'd been told that there was no Border Patrol facility where the PCT entered Canada—he could walk right in. But then what? And how would he get out when he wanted to leave Canada? And more importantly, how was he going to get his kids? For now, he had to keep pushing north. But the farther north he went, the more he felt like an elastic band being stretched beyond its limit; his heart wasn't in it. His homeland was tugging him south, and it felt like he was running away from his kids.

On his maps, Barcelona saw that he was nearing Mammoth Lakes, a sizeable town seven miles northeast. He didn't need supplies yet but noted that in four miles he would reach Reds Meadow. The map indicated a store there, practically right on the PCT; he would have to blaze around it.

Awol, Kenny, and Blazer headed south on the PCT. It was still summer, and although the forests were green, nature was preparing for fall and the coming winter. Leaves on beeches, aspens, and oaks felt stiffer to the touch; winds blew more frequently from the north; skies were a deeper blue and ready for early season snows. It was good to have Kenny back, but Awol felt vulnerable, imagining eyes behind every tree, particularly when they emerged into a glen or whenever they crossed a stream. And he got tripped up on thoughts of Gloria and Linda—what the hell was he doing with Kenny out here? He had enough problems.

"When we approach Reds Meadow, we look for a place to set up," Awol said.

"I know. You keep telling me."

"That's because I need to make it clear that my mission here is to determine if this is the guy Sacco is looking for. He's wanted by both sides. I know what he looks like, and I'm gonna make sure you do too."

"And," Kenny said, "if he is Barcelona, you call Sacco and let his team handle it."

"Correct. He's arrested, taken off the trail, and you go back to school."

"And you go home to Linda."

Awol took a deep breath. "Right. If she'll have me."

They watched Blazer sniff and dig around a stump. Father and son scanned the view of mountain peaks, varied rock formations, and lake basins, all conspicuous signs of glaciation. Rock formations included otherworldly fang-toothed granites and an absurdly balanced pile of three boulders that looked like they were ready to spill into the trail.

"There's an old Pennsylvania Dutch expression," Awol said. "'You grow too soon olt und too late schmart.' I'm not going to let that happen to me."

Kenny smiled and poled off again beside his father. "Linda seemed okay at the hospital. She introduced herself, and I got to talk with her when you were in the coma."

"I can't tell you how happy I was that she came out to see me. What did she say?"

"She asked about school, so I told her about UCLA. She asked about Greg, whom she hadn't met yet."

"She's still mad. And she deserves to be. We've had more than that one incident."

"She didn't mention any incident."

"Linda turned my life around. We've had some very good years. I thought I could handle a little drinking, and it all started to slip away."

Awol stopped, turned to Kenny, and planted his poles between them. "You're looking good, Kenny. You escaped a huge bullet."

Blazer was happy to be on the trail with them again. He ran with quickness, energy. He tracked scents, rooted around thickets, and zipped off at oblique angles, returning with his tongue hanging out. He would lead them for a while and then bound off again on a new scent.

Awol stopped and studied the terrain as they came to Middle Fork.

"See that bridge across the river?" Awol said. "Hikers will make noise with poles and boots over that. And many will get water by the bunchgrass and sedge."

"So we should set up near here?"

"Yes. Reds Meadow is four miles south. A hiker on the run doesn't need to ford here; he'll chance the bridge. It's a good spot to watch; hikers will camel up."

"I'll scout to the left for a place," Kenny said.

"Okay, I'll get the right."

Blazer ran off and took a dip in the river. Two girls with daypacks were crossing the bridge and laughed as Blazer shook himself and scattered water on them.

"Over here, Dad."

Awol tramped southeast sixty-five yards from the trail and looked on approvingly. At a slight elevation, they could look down at the bridge, but they would be hidden by gnarled and weathered blowdowns amid growing firs. The spot was dry, and they could get water out of sight at a bend in the east.

"Excellent spot. Let's set up."

That night, as they ate a late dinner, Kenny looked at the bridge. Awol had hung his binocs about his neck and was also facing the bridge.

"At night we won't be able to distinguish hikers, Dad."

"No, but we'll hear them. I can even hear Blazer scratch over it with his paws."

"So what are you thinking?"

"We'll work in shifts. I'm going to describe him as best I can and tell you what to look for. During the day, we hang here and use regular binoculars. At night when we hear someone, we can creep closer, over by that oak, and get a better look as the hiker approaches. With this."

Kenny took the scope and looked at it.

"Night vision—I bought it special," Awol said. "You've got first shift; wake me at two."

"Gee, thanks."

"You insisted on coming out here, Kenny, and I'm counting on you to do as I say. Now listen while I tell you everything I know about this man."

Awol was on shift when he heard footsteps on the bridge. He'd been reading *Jarhead,* a marine's memoir. He'd seen the movie and had sympathized with Jake Gyllenhaal, who played the unfortunate marine. Awol clicked off his headlamp even though it couldn't be seen from the bridge--he and Kenny had checked. He cut to the knoll twenty yards up from the trail. Lying behind a blowdown, Awol squinted into the light of a half-moon and saw what looked like an apparition moving on the bridge. He looked through his night vision scope and could see right away the tall pack that stuck up behind the hiker's head. Awol focused on the face. *No. Not Barcelona—too short. But he sure looks like a mule.* Awol recorded the date, time, and made notes in his log. He wondered if Sacco and his man had arrived yet. Awol reminded himself to avoid contact with Sacco until he had found Barcelona. His mind raced to Kenny. *Jesus, if his mother knew.*

CHAPTER SIXTY

AWOL CHECKED HIS WATCH. IT was time for Kenny to take over. He packed up and strode to Kenny's tent. Just as he said, "Kenny," he felt a grab from behind and instantly a pistol to his ear.

"Don't move, gringo," a man said.

Awol watched a second man, masqueraded as a hiker, open the tent flap and shine a light inside. He held a pistol in his other hand.

"Out. Now," he said.

"Blazer, git!" Awol hissed. The dog stilled for a second. Another "Git!" and the dog took off into the brush, just as Kenny emerged from the tent.

"Tie the kid up," the first man said in accented Spanish. "Make a wrong move, gringo, I shoot," and he poked the pistol farther into Awol's ear.

After he tied Kenny's arms behind him, he did the same to Awol. Now the second man tied bandannas covering their eyes. The first man took two handkerchiefs from his pocket and balled them up. "Open," he said to Awol and stuffed one of them in. The other he stuffed into Kenny's mouth, and both were led into the woods. Awol had counted sixty-five steps when he heard a vehicle door open.

"Weren't you supposed to get the dog too?" a new, gravelly voice said.

There was no answer. After Kenny was stuffed into the passenger side and Awol into the rear, one of the first two said, "We tell Alvarado the dog ran when we made our move."

CHAPTER SIXTY-ONE

Awol could sense Kenny's fear radiating from the passenger seat. Next to Awol, the kidnapper—sitting directly behind Kenny—had lit a cigarillo, and Awol cringed as the smelly tobacco smoke was blown into his face.

"You like your dog, eh, gringo?"

Awol said nothing.

"That man we left back there—he gut your dog, and maybe when you get hungry, we let you eat, no?"

Awol wanted to kick the man, but instead he turned his head away as they bumped along in and out of ruts. It was clear the path was narrow, because occasionally branches would scratch along the side of the vehicle.

Soon the ruts cleared, and they started to climb. Gently at first, then the driver downshifted and the climb became steeper. Awol could sense moonlight to his left when he angled his head up. When he glanced to the right, it was utterly dark. That told him they were heading north into the Ansel Adams Wilderness.

Awol, as best he could, probed the floor with his feet. He stuck one under the seat and felt something loose with the toe of his boot. He kept his foot on it, and when the man next to him became animated with the driver, speaking in Spanish, he moved it out nearer the door. Though his hands were tied behind him, he was able to fish around the side-door pocket while the two argued. He pulled out what he assumed were sunglasses and, with quiet effort, was able to stick them in his back pocket.

They were climbing steeper still when the vehicle slowed and veered off the gravel road to another rutted path. Awol's guess was that they had been traveling about twenty to twenty-five miles per hour, and they'd been driving twenty minutes. He estimated they were now doing no more than ten miles per hour. When the vehicle finally stopped, Awol figured a half hour total time at about eighteen miles per hour average speed. Nine or ten miles—in the middle of nowhere.

The rear doors opened. As Awol stepped out, he faked catching his foot in the doorframe and wheeled backward. The kidnapper pulled him up just as Awol grabbed what felt like a small screwdriver from the floor of the vehicle.

"Your leg asleep, gringo?"

Awol grunted. Though he couldn't see, he tried to sense Kenny. He heard the doors slam, and the vehicle took off. Awol grunted and stamped a foot.

"You dancing, gringo." He unholstered his pistol and whipped the rag from Awol's mouth.

"Where's my son?" Awol hollered.

The kidnapper smiled as another Hispanic, dressed in US Army fatigues, came up and stood next to him with his hands on his hips.

"I want my son."

The new man said, "That will not be possible. Our orders are to secure you. Where your son goes from here is not my business." He spoke with hardly an accent.

Awol slid the item taken from the vehicle into his other back pocket.

CHAPTER SIXTY-TWO

Barcelona NEARED REDS MEADOW MIDMORNING of the next day. He had seen two day hikers earlier on a secondary trail, a guy and his girl toting small backpacks with Dasani bottles stuck in the side webbing. The guy, dark complexioned and about Barcelona's size, sported a Padres baseball cap; the girl wore a Reds Meadow T-shirt.

"Nice hat," the guy said to Barcelona.

Barcelona removed the sombrero, which he'd unclipped at the sides and flattened to differentiate the hat from how Verdugo had worn it. "You like it? I'll trade you for your Padres."

"Yeah?" The guy took off his cap and tried on the sun hat. He looked at his girl. "What do you think?"

"It has personality. Try clipping up the sides." She stepped over and did it for him. "Cool," she said.

"You sure you want to give it up?"

"Sombrero's yours," Barcelona said.

The guy gave him the Padres hat. "Thanks, dude."

Several miles later, Barcelona reached a swollen stream, which he figured to be Minaret Creek. From here he could blaze closer to the PCT; there was a bridge spanning one of the wider forks, so he wouldn't have to ford. Though the water gushed furiously—the result of continuing snowmelt—at the last second Barcelona chose to avoid the bridge; this appeared to be a popular hiking area, and he needed to take precautions. He took off Verdugo's shirt and stuffed it to the bottom of his pack. Barcelona pulled on one of his tank tops, forded the rock-channeled stream, and continued blazing to the northwest.

Barcelona hiked over the eleven-thousand-foot Donohue Pass and camped that night near Lyell Fork crossing in the south end of Yosemite National Park. Looking at a snow-crested ridge not far from the famed peak, El Capitan, he put on all the clothes he had and bundled himself into his bag a hundred yards off the PCT at a bend in a stream. His immediate goal was to make it through Yosemite and get to northern California, an area unfamiliar to Alvarado and his men. But northern California was still 360 miles away, and here, Yosemite was patrolled by rangers who would check for food vaults.

A vault wasn't easy to steal if you were avoiding people. Day hikers without them could be excused, but Barcelona didn't look like a day hiker. He used his razor by a glacier-fed mountain stream to shave black whiskers, but he looked grungy, used, like he'd been on the trail a while.

He'd been able to yogi fruit and leftover trail mix from a group of day hikers he'd spied, and he got a used tarp from a tourist camper. But his food bag was getting low. He convinced himself he could hike ninety-five miles to Echo Lake over the next three days even without food, but he didn't like the prospect of plodding this bleak, windswept land of crumbling rock and scree. The lack of nutrients and rest was ruining his condition as well as his psyche. He listened to the flow of the creek; instead of its murmurs relaxing him, it made him homesick. He didn't know a soul in Canada. The farther north he hiked, the more helpless he felt. His mind pulled him south, homeward, to his children. It was then that he had an epiphany. *Why do I run?* he asked himself. *It's senseless and hopeless.* He decided to isolate as long as he could on the south side of Donahue Pass, away from rangers in Yosemite. *I'll wait Alvarado and his goons out—they'll never find me—and then head south. Canada? Where was my head?*

CHAPTER SIXTY-THREE

ALVARADO CALLED HIS BOSS. "I have who we need to negotiate."

"Which means?"

"I have not yet found Barcelona, señor, but I have two key Americans in my captivity, so if the US agents find Barcelona first, we will force them to trade—the two Americans for Barcelona."

"And what do I say to my counterpart in New York who thinks Barcelona has been eliminated?"

"You can tell him that Barcelona cannot defect to the US. That we just need a little more time to eliminate him."

Silence.

After having laid it on the line, Alvarado felt a tinge of relief. The banjo wall clock ticked away as he closed his eyes and waited.

"You have disappointed me greatly, Luis. You, if anyone, should know that I don't break or delay a promise. You will eliminate Barcelona and find the drop within two weeks, or you will be permanently removed. Now if you will excuse me, I have an important call to make."

DETECTIVE SACCO, WHO HAD HOPED to hear from Awol by now, was talking with rangers in Mammoth Lakes. He asked them again, "So has there been anything suspicious in your area?"

"We did have a report of stolen food in one of the campground vaults," Ranger Lloyd said. "That happened once before, about a year ago. It was just a mix-up that got sorted out."

Sacco rubbed his chin. "Okay, here's my card. You know about the gun confiscated by rangers south of here. Call me if anything different or unusual happens."

That night, thinking over the possibility that someone might be scrounging for food, Sacco called Awol. *That's strange*, he thought. *He usually picks right up.* He decided not to leave a message at the prompt. In the morning, first thing, Sacco called Awol again. When he didn't get an answer and was again prompted to leave a message, he squinted his eyes, knowing that's one thing he definitely would not do.

ALVARADO DISCUSSED MULES WITH HIS central California commander, Jaime. Normally, Alvarado insisted on anonymity with his mules, but the situation was far from normal. The operation was at stake and his job was on the line. The number one objective was to flush out Barcelona; he knew too much, including where a million-dollar drop was. He wanted to get to Barcelona first so he couldn't detail the PCT operation to US authorities. Alvarado downloaded a picture of Barcelona and instructed Jaime to show it to all his men that muled the High Sierra. "Tell them whoever finds and executes Barcelona within the next ten days will get a ten-thousand-dollar bonus." Alvarado ignored, for now, the million-dollar loss.

CHAPTER SIXTY-FOUR

AFTER TYING AWOL'S LEGS AROUND a pole and his upper body to the same pole which held up one end of a room-sized tent, the kidnapper removed Awol's bandanna.

"I've got to pee," Awol said.

Awol noted the kidnappers look, which seemed to say, *I forgot about that.* "Too late now. Later."

"Why the hell tie my chest to this pole if my hands are already tied?"

"Shut up!"

There were two cots in the tent, both near the back, one on each side. A kerosene stove hummed and occasionally clicked six feet in front of Awol, next to the other pole holding up the square tent. His backpack lay inside the tent near a battery-powered lantern. Door flaps disappeared behind a plastic rainfly. The flaps could be pulled together and zipped. The rainfly looked like it was rigged and not part of the tent.

Ten minutes later, Awol heard a vehicle pull up and a door slam. The first kidnapper came back, ducked in around the rainfly, and spoke Spanish to Awol. Convinced that Awol understood nothing, he continued in Spanish with his compadre.

Awol, who had taken two years of Spanish in high school, wished he had paid more attention. They were speaking too fast, but he could tell they spoke of Kenny and *perro,* which he knew meant "dog." They both said the name Alvarado. He picked out a few other words, one of them *acantilado,* which he remembered seeing on a Spanish map of the High Sierra. He was pretty sure it meant "cliff." He calculated: the driver with Kenny was gone thirty minutes, round trip, driving at what had to be about ten miles an hour. Kenny was about three miles away, probably in another tent on a cliff. Awol could see the sense of them separating him from Kenny. It would be hard enough to find one, either Awol or Kenny, doubly hard to find two. And this way, Kenny and Awol couldn't trade information and connive. *If I could only get to Sacco*, Awol thought. It would be unbearable to face his ex, Gloria, if anything happened to Kenny; she'd lynch him herself. *Not to worry*, he thought. *If anything happens to Kenny, I'll lynch myself first.*

Soon they stopped speaking and looked at him.

"You need to take a piss, gringo?"

"Yes."

One untied him from the pole and walked him outside into thick woods as the other trained his pistol on him. He stood there, his hands still tied.

"You want I should pull your pisser out?" one smirked.

"No. Let me do it."

"You be careful," the other said as he untied his hands. They took him around to the back of the tent. "And while you're here, you shit too. We only do this once a day."

"Just need to pee." But Awol made himself look vulnerable standing there as they watched his back, and he deliberately didn't get his stream going.

"What's the matter, gringo, you lie to us? Or you nervous?"

One of them lit up, and Awol got himself going. What they didn't realize was that Awol kept shifting his eyes to absorb every possible detail of his surroundings. He'd noted the direction the mud-plastered brown Jeep was parked and which way it would exit. He moved his eyes that way and saw the rutted path go downhill. He moved his eyes to the mountains northwest of him where the path surely went and peeked through branches. At what he estimated was three miles out, he saw a cliff. Kenny had to be—

"Zip it up, gringo. We don't got all day."

Back inside, after retying his ankles together around the mast but before retying his hands, he was given a bowl of oatmeal mixed with water along with a plastic spoon. *Just like on the trail*, he thought and then realized it was his own oatmeal and his own spoon they'd taken from his pack. He looked at his pack, open and empty and thrown next to one of two camp chairs. The other chair was outside the tent.

"Is my son okay?"

"We don't answer questions, gringo," the smoker said. "But I'll answer just this one. He sits down tied like you." *Another tent*, Awol thought.

The other kidnapper came over to retie his hands behind his back.

"Can I just lie back and get some rest? You guys don't need to tie my chest to this stick—how can I go anywhere with my legs locked around it?"

"Let's see how you behave, and maybe later we sit you up in a chair," the smoker said.

They tied his hands as before, propped him up again so the mast was in front of him, and tied him to it at the chest. Awol had been able, while eating, to finger what he figured was a small screwdriver still stashed in his back pocket.

They quickly ignored him, and for the second time he inventoried the tent with his eyes. Heater, knob turned to a lower level. A small backpack by the chair outside. He'd seen the smoker reach in for his pack of cigarillos and stow a small flashlight inside; there was also a water bottle in a side pocket. *Probably mostly clothing and some food inside the undersized pack.* Awol looked again on his empty pack. *Where's all my stuff?* he wondered.

Something new was lying on one of the cots—a map protected in a baggie. It was too far away for Awol to read from it, but he could make out lines and squiggles.

The floor of the tent was a worn canvas. Awol saw nothing unusual except for a suspected rip in the corner to the right of the exit. He saw duct tape sticking to the canvas, and a heavy stone sat on the tape.

He closed his eyes and feigned drowsiness. Someone moved the other camp chair to the outside and both kidnappers sat there in fleece and ski hats. He could see the smoker's hand with the cigarillo and heard the popped tabs of a can, and now he smelled beer.

He concentrated on the words he could hear. And he heard that word again—*acantilado*.

CHAPTER SIXTY-FIVE

I'M HUNGRY.

Barcelona finished the second day's rations under a contorted foxtail pine, arthritic from years of weather and wind. It looked like he felt. Although plans had changed and he was down well south of the pass and concealed, he'd prudently saved food. He'd tried stealing food from a campground food vault a couple of days ago, but the result was meager, and the one Ziploc bag of rotten fruit had been torn. It had taken time to find and prepare a perfect spot near water, and he hadn't had time to scrounge anything. He was exhausted as he slithered into his bag, under the tarp, in a saddle four soccer fields west of the PCT. He'd unrolled the end of the tarp and kept that portion under him, which prevented dampness and cold from bleeding up into the sleeping bag. In the moon-bright night, he could see the rocky spires of Donahue Pass over to his left.

He'd met two day hikers that day, on separate occasions. The first offered him water but claimed not to have any food. The second gave him a half-empty box of raisins. "You're only a few days from Echo Lake. More hikers should be coming." He couldn't believe his lousy luck. He had looked for pinyon, nut pine seeds, but those were almost nonexistent this far north.

Next morning, packed like a hiker, he was just off-trail when he saw four young women with daypacks hike toward him. Barcelona noticed them stop and huddle as soon as he drew onto the trail.

"Girls, can I possibly bum some food? Someone stole my food vault, and I'm trying to make it to Echo."

The women stood behind their sticks and gave him a wide berth so he would pass.

"What is it? Is everything okay?" he asked.

Three of them looked to the tallest.

"Did you hear about the stabbing?" she asked.

"No, I didn't. What happened?"

"It was on the news. A hiker was stabbed back at Reds Meadow."

"Really? When was this?"

"A few days ago," the tallest one said and then started to move on the trail. "A man was stabbed in the shoulder."

"So did they catch who did it?"

Behind him now, the tallest turned. "They all ran off."

Barcelona thought about this as the girls hustled away.

"Wait! Were they Mexicans?"

They all turned around, and the same three looked to their leader.

"I'm from Spain," Barcelona said.

"The victim's girlfriend reported Latinos with thick accents."

"Now I understand your concern." He smiled broadly. "And I'm sorry, but as you can see, I speak good English. Does anyone know why it happened?"

"Something about a sombrero," the tallest said. And the girls hiked away, looking back every few yards.

Late that night, Barcelona scouted the trail farther south and discovered a sign leading to a different campground. The campground was dark, but looking indirectly, he could make out three tents; he didn't see or hear anyone. He shined his mini light on a rectangular steel box ten feet to his right, scaring a pack rat. A community food vault. Barcelona unlatched the animal-proof hasp and shined his light on several bags. He took the largest, sniffed it, and swooned—*chicken!*—and stowed it in his pack.

Fifteen minutes later, he sat off-trail scarfing down a chicken salad sandwich that had been wrapped in tinfoil. He didn't feel right about it but was thankful to have substantial food at last. Barcelona figured the man who'd been stabbed was the guy with his girl who traded his hat for the sombrero, and that the police were hunting for Hispanics. *I've already been stopped and fined by rangers.* Barcelona feared arrest and deportation. Deportation meant certain death. Time was running out. He figured most knew by now that he was heading north to the border. Alvarado knew it because of his permits; Barcelona had also told the rangers, and the guy and his girl saw him head north.

Barcelona dug into another chicken sandwich and considered his plight. He'd escaped this far and considered himself lucky. It was smart to isolate; he would have hiked into a trap—especially if an APB went out looking for Hispanic hikers. It was against Barcelona's nature to isolate; he didn't like staying still. All his life he had been a mover.

He understood he would put his kids in danger if he tried to reach them, and this caused his hatred for Alvarado to build. The thought of frustrating Alvarado warmed his veins. He had the rest of his life to go back to Mexico or to go anywhere else. The mountains and wilds whispered to him; he had set up where nobody would find him. Near water. Every few days he could scrounge food here and elsewhere as new hikers came through and left after a night. Nobody would stay at the tiny campground. No amenities were offered other than the picnic table he'd seen. He didn't even remember seeing a privy. Random clothes and a beard, even if it contrasted with his now dirty-blond hair, disguised him. When things quieted, before the snows, he'd sneak out with a new plan.

Barcelona returned to his hiding spot near the creek, which flowed to a rolling upland meadow. The area was so tangled with understory he could hardly find the location. The next day, Barcelona noted from his guide and maps that there was another campground farther south. The following night, after midnight, he moved in darkness with his headlamp. As he entered the camp, he distinguished two tents. His eyes searched everywhere for a food vault. When he saw what looked like a punching bag hanging from a tree, he knew there wasn't a community vault. Hikers overnighting in the Sierra were supposed to carry food vaults, but day campers were ignorant of the rules, so he assumed this bag belonged to a short-term hiker. The bag was hung poorly—any bear could scramble up the tree trunk and paw it. Working with stealth, it took Barcelona all of three minutes to untie the rope and lower the bag. The two tents he could make out were over thirty yards away, next to a smoldering fire ring; he could smell and see a trail of smoke rising in the moonlit night and heard snores from one of the tents. Before leaving, he splayed the bag ends of the ropes and tangled them in bushes to make it look like a wild animal had hauled off the food.

Next morning, Barcelona consolidated his food; he now had enough for five days. He put all the food into his own food bag, tore and ragged up the other one, and floated it in the creek, where it would eventually disappear downstream. He turned to leave and . . . *the fuck? I've seen this mutt before.*

THE REALIZATION BROKE OVER HIM at once. The rest of his life was now. Barcelona understood that despite the no-man's-lands of mountain, lake, and canyon in the High Sierra, he was being hunted. He made a decision: he would flee no more. He expected to meet those hunting him and hoped Alvarado's vaqueros were on the way. This was payback. *I'm going to fuck things up as much as I can for Alvarado—I'm going to make him pay. I swear to you, Juanita, the* bastardo *will pay.*

CHAPTER SIXTY-SIX

Sacco PULLED OUT HIS PHONE, punched in Alvarado's number, and waited.

"Yes, Mr. Sacco."

"Where is my man, Awol, and his son?"

"I was about to call you. Let me remind you, Mr. Sacco, you told me your man was hiking up in Washington."

"So, where are they?"

"I have them both. They are safe and will not be harmed."

"What!"

"They are in separate locations. I will exchange them for Barcelona."

"You've made a huge mistake. Don't fuck with the USA, Mr. Alvarado."

"These are my terms, Mr. Sacco. Simply locate Barcelona. We will apprehend him ourselves and—"

"You and I don't know where Barcelona is," Sacco yelled. "Awol knows what he looks like and can identify him."

"I don't like to be interrupted. I'm sure he has described Barcelona to you. Find him, and these two people will be released unharmed."

"Since when do you dictate the rules?"

"Since I've learned about the close relationship you have with your sister, Angela."

"Whoa! Now, just a minute—"

"You have ten days to find Barcelona. I will not discuss anything further."

Sacco, red-faced, fumed as he stared at the phone. Alvarado had disconnected.

CHAPTER SIXTY-SEVEN

AWOL HAD SPENT A SLEEPLESS night even though he was eventually allowed to lie on his back, arms and hands tied in front of him, legs tied around the mast. They had placed a blanket underneath him and threw a shawl on top, but he wasn't thankful.

When the first kidnapper stirred, Awol said, "I've got to do more than pee."

He got no response as the kidnapper went outside to relieve his cohort. They both came back; one untied him while the other kept his pistol on him.

"Make it quick, gringo."

Awol squatted behind a boulder, but his head was clearly visible. "Can I crap in peace? If you want me to be quicker, just stand around the other side of the rock."

"You don't tell us what to do."

"You can see me. Where am I gonna go? I want it to be quick too."

They backed in front of the boulder and watched him.

Awol jerked the implement out of his back pocket and clutched it in his hand. He peeked at the small folding knife while doing his business.

Back inside the tent, Awol managed to keep the knife palmed as they retied his hands. It became obvious that they planned to feed him only once a day—just one measly packet of oatmeal mixed with water. He'd always combined at least two packets, even for a snack. He was famished but glad that they ignored him right now. Soon after, he got the knife open but waited before doing anything more until at least one of them left the tent. Two hours later, one of them got into the vehicle and drove off. Soon after, the other kidnapper walked out of the tent, probably to do his own business. Awol worked slavishly to try and cut the rope without cutting his wrist. He felt one of the coils loosen, and then it fell away. He switched the knife to the other hand and was halfway through another coil when the kidnapper returned. He made himself coffee and sat down in a chair and smoked.

Awol was desperate to get loose and give his best shot at one-on-one before the other kidnapper came back. He tried to work quietly and scuffed his feet or shifted position to mask the sound of his tiny knife cutting the rope. At last the ropes fell away. He gathered them about his wrist and kept the blade open and ready.

"Look, I'm sorry. Gotta pee," he said.

The man said nothing. Just smoked. He finished and flicked the cigarillo butt outside.

"Please," Awol said.

"Then this time I gotta pull your pisser out."

"Okay."

The man came over, laid the gun beside him, and began untying the rope connecting Awol's feet. Just as he finished and reached for his gun, Awol stabbed him in the eye. The man screeched and covered his eye. Awol picked up the pistol and shot him point-blank in the side of his head, just above the ear.

Awol stood up, pocketed the pistol, and went for his pack, which he found flattened behind food boxes. Wincing as he heard the low rumble of the vehicle coming up the path, his survival instinct told him to get out. Leaving behind the food and clothing, he grabbed a partially filled water bottle and hustled out, barely in time. He hid in brush off the ridge behind the tent and decided he would pack supplies after he disposed of kidnapper two.

That all changed as the vehicle parked and three men, one of them the kidnapper, emerged from the Jeep and slammed doors. Awol immediately slid backward down the ridge and angled himself to thicker brush. He heard shouts from the tent, which was now out of his sight, and scuttled and crab walked as best he could down, down, down the ridge to forest—all the while knowing they'd be searching.

CHAPTER SIXTY-EIGHT

Sᴀᴄᴄᴏ ʜᴀᴅ ᴀ sɪᴄᴋ ғᴇᴇʟɪɴɢ and was torn. He should call his boss immediately and fess up about what he'd done, but that would ruin him for sure; he'd be summarily canned. Alvarado hadn't said what would happen after ten days, but Sacco was sure Awol and Kenny would be safe until that time. He decided to wait one day. Alvarado would continue his own search for Barcelona. Sacco, knowing it was futile, tried calling Awol by satellite anyway. No sign of a connection, and he wondered who had the phone. *Bringing down the PCT drug operation will save more lives in the long run, but what to do about Awol and his son . . .* He knew he must do everything he could to get them out of Alvarado's clutches. He thought about calling in rangers, but at least a couple of them were on the take; that could tip his hand and get back to his boss as well.

At noon the next day, Sacco took action. He returned to Angela's to set up his own private command post. Phoning his work, he asked for several days' emergency leave so he could attend to his sister's failing health. When asked by his boss the nature of her illness, Sacco paused and said it was "very personal." Though Angela agreed to play the game for him, including corroborating support she would provide from a longtime doctor friend, Sacco accepted that his career was over if he didn't shake things loose in the few days he'd been granted by the chief.

Sacco thought again about alerting rangers but convinced himself he couldn't take the chance. Alvarado made it his business to establish contacts everywhere, and the veiled threat to Angela—which was why he now set up in her guestroom—was reason enough not to risk it. He was about to pull out his cell when it chirped, startling him.

"You have a lot of explaining to do, Mr. Sacco."

"About what?"

"Don't play dumb with me. Where is he?"

"Hey, Alvarado, I'm not Superman—you gave me ten days."

Silence. "I'm referring to your Awol, who has disappeared after killing one of my best men."

CHAPTER SIXTY-NINE

Awol HURRIED FARTHER DOWN AND away, watching his footing and trying not to be noisy about it. Only at the last second, before he was covered in trees, did he remember to look around at his surroundings. He could see the cliff still behind him at what he estimated to be three miles. He figured Kenny to be there, and with that numbing thought he stopped. He looked back up from where he'd come and then pushed on, paying more attention to what was around him. He advanced a mile farther, muscling through thickets and brambles in deep forest. He stopped when he realized he was angling away from the cliff, his destination. He looked for a place to hide and found it near a downed ponderosa.

Awol thought it through. For Alvarado and his gang to negotiate, Kenny was even more important now. But if Alvarado found Barcelona first, would they simply release Kenny? *After I escaped and killed their man?* Awol sat down and his stomach churned. He had to get Kenny. Or at least get near him where, as a last-ditch effort, he could give himself up for his son to go free.

He shook himself. "Okay, then," he snapped. "What do I have?" Awol went through every side pocket and felt through every tuck inside and outside his backpack. It took a couple of minutes; he was thorough. They hadn't taken quite everything. The tiny P-38 military can opener he pulled from a side pocket of his pack. A mosquito face net was partially stuck on the bottom of the pack, and the pack rain cover was still internally zipped and intact. A plastic bag filled with undergarments was not taken. But his fleece and shell were gone. Stolen, like his other important stuff—his tent, sleeping bag, mattress, gloves, and ski hat. He fingered out one elastic and two paper clips, and that was it for the pack. He placed the meager collection of items side by side on the ground and then knelt, pulled out the sunglasses he'd swiped, and put those alongside as well.

He'd saved the pistol for last. He took it up and checked the chamber. Nothing! He'd shot the last bullet.

He stood up, fingered the bandanna still around his neck, and plied his pockets. He still had his wallet and permits, but he remembered them taking every cent of his money. He patted his thighs involuntarily again; his survival knife and his other knife were gone. From another pocket, he pulled out the little backpacker knife with file, which he'd managed to take from the vehicle and had allowed him to escape, and laid it down in the pile. The half-full water bottle he'd swiped was also lying in the pile. Normally, Awol kept the day's guide page in his shirt pocket by his compass. Both were missing, and he remembered them taking both when he was blindfolded and searched. He looked toward the cliff and back at the measly pile. *Christ, is this all I have?* No rope to rig up some type of shelter, nothing to cook or eat with, and worst of all—as he looked at a pale sun heading west--no warmth for the night.

AWOL STARED AT THE MASSIVE rock wall in the dusk. He tried to discern the cliff at the top. Perhaps it wouldn't pose a huge challenge for an experienced rock climber, but the one time Awol had climbed something approaching this magnitude, it was with an experienced lead climber who had rope and pitons. What stared back at him was out of the question. Yet what was he to do? Everything he absorbed at that moment, every gut feeling, became more than hunch—Kenny was on top. The cartel would expect anyone arriving where Awol now stood not to climb the rock face but to traverse around the end of the rock in an easy climb—east or west, no matter—and expose himself on the back side.

Awol kept staring at the granite wall. It would be useless to try and save Kenny by going around. He'd walk right into a trap. No, the element of surprise was up there. That was the only way for him to gain a chance. But how?

Predawn. Awol scrambled to the top of a boulder and lay prone. He squinted his eyes shut for thirty seconds, the better to close off his mind from unnecessary sights clamoring for his view. In the dawn, helped by the eastern sunrise, he opened them and started from his far left. In successive sections of about ten degrees each, he first overviewed what he saw and then inspected it, tree by tree, by thicket, by rock, by crack, by anything he could distinguish. What was his best approach to the top? Awol's field glasses had been swiped, but he still had his eyes and logic. Most of all he had the experience of a longtime outdoorsman. From a distance, a hill is an illusion of steepness; it will always moderate when you get right to it. He pictured himself laying on the rocked side and climbing up. He didn't want to think of the cliff, which jutted out at the top.

Awol continued his inspection. A path to Kenny had to be ahead of him. Somewhere. He shut his eyes again for thirty seconds, reopened them, and inspected possible approaches that would lead up to the cliff. Not one thing suggested this or that way was better. Awol concentrated harder. He was tired from shivering through the night. A shadow on the rock face at one o'clock suggested a cleft. Awol advanced.

CHAPTER SEVENTY

AWOL LAY AGAINST THE ROCK surface and prayed. *God, I feel inadequate and regret that I seem to pray only when I'm in trouble and need help—like right now. Please deliver me and my son.*

Awol palmed rock and fisted any available growth, understanding that there would be fewer roots to grab as he ascended. He hugged rock and felt himself becoming more vertical as he squirmed upward. *Just don't look down!* Not often enough he found solid purchase and clung, not wanting to push off. He used that time to try and see what was ahead. He estimated he was up about fifty feet, but he could feel himself going to the right. He wondered if it was a mental ruse, as if by going to his right he could avoid going straight up. He had more than a football field to go based on an early estimate and now calculated that a shift to his left then straight up would work best. He squiggled left.

Around him, breezes blew; overhead, birds soared. Travel far enough following any point of the compass and wild animal, insect, and human would be found living life as usual—all oblivious to the scared man sweating up the rock wall. He slipped, shaking stones loose; tore up his hands and fingernails; and became frozen with dread as he neared the halfway point. Two things caused him to push on: Kenny, of course, and Gloria, to whom he'd promised no harm would come to Kenny. He was parched, but even though he had water, how was he to drink it? After clawing and squeezing stone for nearly an hour, he'd made it about halfway. He could see naked details above him in the rocks of the cliff, which hung over him. The fact that the overhang concealed him was not appreciated by Awol. *How the hell am I going to get over it?*

After another forty minutes of clamoring and squirming, his hands a bloody mess and at his physical limits, he reached an impasse. He couldn't find any handhold for his next step up, nor could he find firm rock with his feet for a push. He was distraught as he noted tiny wild flowers growing from niches in the weathered stone right next to his hands. He told himself not to panic and not to look down. He squinted his eyes shut but became dizzy, and then he did panic. Ironically, Awol considered hollering for help, as he was only fifteen yards from the cliff. It seemed to him like he was near vertical; he could never make it back down. He had no choice; his only hope was to slither to his left and pray for purchase where he couldn't see. He stretched left, straining his neck, and at the last second, grabbed rock. He prayed as he swung his feet around. Just as he planted his left leg as best he could, his left hand slipped off the rock. About to scream, he plunged both palms to the rock surface again and got his right leg and knee lodged into rock to staunch a fall. He gulped for air and hung.

Twenty minutes later, he was close to the cliff top. The good news was that he'd be able to maneuver to reach it. The bad: he was spent and didn't see how he could pull himself up and over.

Awol took several minutes to gather himself; while he did, he listened. He heard no voices, but his gut said people were nearby. He tried to discern odor on the wind, which was gusty off the top, hoping for an aroma indicating food. Nothing. He squirmed and slithered up to the escarpment. He dare not make any further noise. When he got to the chin jutting out from the top of the massive wall he'd just spent two hours climbing, he said another prayer and, miraculously, felt his body rally. Knowing that the bigger danger now was for him to think too much, much less look down, he stitched together his courage and grabbed the top of the chin. For a second he hung vertical from it, then he flung his right leg to reach the top where his hands clung. He nearly made it on the first try, and if Awol could have hollered the effort, he might have. Precariously hanging—this was it—he convulsed his leg up a second time. It caught. Now he heaved and willed himself up, up, up! He was on top. He lay there panting, afraid to open his eyes, wondering if when he did he'd find himself alive or dead.

At last he opened them. Not more than a football field away, directly in front of him, was a familiar-looking tent, all but the front hidden by brush and debris. Awol rolled left in scrub and lay prone, watching the tent. No sounds, no movement from within, but Awol sensed his son inside. As he was about to crawl closer from the scrub, the front tent flaps moved. One of the kidnappers emerged and lit up what Awol assumed to be a cigarillo.

Several minutes later, when Awol regained his wind and was about to make his next move, he heard the low and growing rumble of a vehicle and then a downshift to a lower gear. The familiar Jeep bounced around into the clearing and drove up next to the tent. Two familiar-looking armed men got out.

CHAPTER SEVENTY-ONE

BARCELONA WANTED TO DESTROY. In a rush of pent-up rage mixed with helplessness, he looked at his home hidden in scrub, which wasn't any better than a wild animal's. How did he get himself in this situation? He fumed but stifled a yell as he tracked how he'd been fucked over ever since he'd defended himself from being killed in Mexico. Unfortunately, he'd killed the son of a rich rancher. For saving his own life, he was sent to prison. He thought he'd had a chance when Alvarado plucked him out, but when he'd seen the arms and feet severed from Manuel, Barcelona knew he wouldn't be able to extricate himself from Alvarado's clutches. His wife was dead, and his children were God knows where.

Barcelona's rage built. He didn't deserve this. And he knew he couldn't wait here and hide like a frightened animal. Barcelona was a doer; he never waited. Maybe that was his problem, but that's the way it was. *Okay, then*, he told himself, *payback!* Determination washed over him and consumed him: he would do everything in his power to destroy Alvarado. And it would start now.

Two nights later, he saw his first chance. A mule—he was sure of it—poled along the PCT. That same pack, the speed and dedication to the mission. In his mind, Barcelona imagined him to be a goon from prison who indiscriminately raped and killed and who deserved to stay there. Barcelona, knife in hand, followed him from behind. The guy was tall and took long strides. Barcelona could see his thighs bulge his pants. *Yeah, athletic and tough*, Barcelona thought. *Just the way Alvarado likes his slaves.*

Barcelona mouthed his knife crosswise and tackled the mule's legs. Down he went with a thud. Barcelona couldn't believe his own frenzy. As if the mule were Alvarado himself, he banged his head into rock until he was dead. The fact that the mule could have been someone as desperate as Barcelona crept into his mind after the deed was done. He cringed at the thought that this man may also have a wife and children. But Barcelona righted all in his mind when he took the million-dollar bear vault Alvarado would so dearly miss. He stripped off the mule's shirt, knifed an X in his back, and left him in full view on the PCT.

CHAPTER SEVENTY-TWO

THE BREEZES CONTINUED TO FEATHER the trees. Birds, insects, and animals lived their lives, all oblivious to Awol's world coming apart around him. He could only watch as three men led Kenny, bound and blindfolded, to the Jeep and pushed him inside. Awol wanted to cry as he looked at the Jeep and watched the three take down the tent and pack up. *What can I do?* he thought. He considered alarming them with the pistol, but it wasn't loaded and he had no bullets. And there were three of them— Kenny could be harmed or worse. But . . . no, he couldn't take a chance against three. They'd see him coming. Or maybe just one would spot him, and in this case, one was too many.

Awol kept thinking he had to make a move—now—before it was too late. And, just like that, it was too late. He peeked at them as they took a final look around and, for a moment, he thought they would walk over to his location and search there. *Jesus!*

For the record, he did cry as he watched the Jeep pull away. He hadn't sobbed like this since he was a child, and he felt like one now as he fisted swollen hands. He ached—body, mind, and soul.

He sat up. The temperature had dropped; sunlight again headed west. He walked over to the tent site and, on hands and knees, began a thorough search. They had to have left something. He even poked about in the tent mast holes—nothing! He looked closer, nose nearly to the ground. He saw nothing but dirt and the occasional rock, an odor of urine. And now he hollered—he didn't care anymore if anyone heard him. He stood and yelled obscenities as if it was the last act he would do on this earth. What had been locked up before flushed out of him now—he couldn't stop. He finally took a breather and dropped again to his knees, not sure what to do next.

Awol walked to the cliff. *Would I? Should I? Nah, I don't have the balls for that either.* So he sat there and watched the sun set. Just as he wondered how things could get any worse, he perceived a yammer. A few seconds later, the stifled whine was unmistakable and drew closer. Awol turned to look behind him. Blazer, bruised about the snout, gimped shamefully to Awol and licked his tears.

CHAPTER SEVENTY-THREE

SACCO TOLD HIMSELF TO CALM down. *Think*. But he couldn't. He was about to give up and confess to his chief when his cell chirped.

"This is Ranger Lloyd."

"Yes?"

"You told me to call about anything unusual."

"That's right."

"Does a dead hiker, with a face so contused he makes the hunchback of Notre Dame look like Casanova, count as unusual?"

"Where did this happen?"

"Right on the PCT. He was also stabbed in the back."

After examining the body, which had been dragged off the PCT by several rangers who'd been told to wait for him, Sacco inhaled deep.

"Lloyd, I want to speak to you privately."

Lloyd waved the others away, and Sacco took him off to the side.

"I don't know who I can trust here. It appears that some powerful cartels control rangers in this area."

Lloyd crossed his arms and locked eyes with Sacco. He said nothing.

"How do I know you're not greased by a drug cartel?" Sacco asked.

"You don't know."

"Here's my question. What are all these other rangers doing here? Six fucking rangers—and sure, not one of you is on the take."

"Here's my answer. My boss from Tuolumne Meadows called me.

I grabbed the two guys in my office. The other three, two of whom I know, were here when I got here."

"So who called them?"

"I'll find out. Cell phones don't work in this section. Had to be someone with a special phone."

"Where is the nearest Forest Service law enforcement ranger?"

"Crabtree. Down in Sequoia."

"Sequoia?"

"Sequoia National Park."

"Look. Here's my real question." Sacco sidled closer and looked straight into Lloyd's eyes. "How do I know I can trust *you*?"

Lloyd threw up his hands.

"I'll tell you how," Sacco said. "You find any ranger-rat and bring him to me. Set it up. Even if it's you."

Sacco walked back to the trail but turned around to Lloyd. "I need an answer by this time tomorrow."

————————

BARCELONA WAS STILL FUMING AS he crouched into his hideout. He'd escaped after pulling off the mule's boots, taking his tent, and shouldering the backpack with the vault. At the last second, he'd rifled through the pants pockets. He left what he didn't need but took the mule's knife, cell phone, duct tape, and all the money in the wallet. He left the wallet so identification and permits could be documented, hoping the information would lead investigators to Alvarado. But he now regretted killing the young man, who'd been forced into being a mule like himself. He fixed it again in his mind by blaming Alvarado for what he'd become—Alvarado had turned him into a goon.

He felt better after eating cheese and a mango from the mule's pack and was beyond pleased when he thumbed the mule's notebook of routes, dates, names, and phone numbers. He had tons of new information. He could use it all—especially to negotiate, if he had to give himself up to the Americans. But for the here and now, he had ways to drive Alvarado loco; after hiding the vault—*that makes two, almost two million, and counting*— he studied the notebook to plan out what and where he'd destroy next.

CHAPTER SEVENTY-FOUR

WHEN AWOL LOOKED MORE CLOSELY at Blazer, he saw cloth wrapped around his right rear leg.

"Whoa, Blazer, what's this?" As he touched that leg, the dog whimpered as he went down, front legs first, and then rolled to his back. The ripped brown cloth was so worn and dirty that, initially, Awol hadn't noticed it. But it was definitely a bandage and, from what Awol could see, someone had tried to set the leg; there were twigs used as splints under the cloth.

"What happened, boy?" But Blazer just whinnied and kicked his three good legs while still on his back. Awol patted his snout, which was scabbed where he'd lost hair and pelt. Awol sniffed the snout and the dog's mouth. *Nuts? Gorp?*

After sundown, knowing he couldn't endure another night like last, Awol ripped out the pack's rain cover. It wasn't much, but it would cover his upper body. His hands were raked raw from scrabbling rock, fingers bloodied, tips and nails torn. He put fingers, several at a time, into Blazer's mouth and let the dog suck them. The dog's pack was gone and Blazer could offer up nothing, but Awol thanked the man upstairs for the animal's company and for a night's warmth laying against him, and most of all, for what he was sure would be Blazer's next help—finding Kenny.

The next morning, he took the mosquito net out of the pack and let the unquenchable thirst, which up to now he'd pushed away, overwhelm him. Water. He'd finished the swiped bottle in one pull yesterday, knowing as he drank that he should stop and save some, but he couldn't. He'd been dehydrated and could hardly move. Now, too tired to find a creek on his own, he'd use the netting to strain water from wherever Blazer could find it. Awol could survive water anywhere, now that he could strain it. He took up the empty water bottle and let Blazer sniff.

"Water, Blazer. We need water."

The dog sniffed and licked the cap, which Awol had loosened. Blazer understood and circled, nose to the ground. The dog ambled in the direction the vehicle had gone. Awol, aching and hobbling, struggled to keep up, even though Blazer was slowed with his own bad leg. Awol didn't want to walk the road, but he didn't have energy to bushwhack. At least the dog led him downhill.

A mile? The body ache and lack of hydration were taking a toll. Survival meant not sitting down to rest. He'd end up crawling. Finally, the dog veered off the road and entered forest. Awol was ready to plead when he saw and fingered drips from a boulder banked to the right. The dog kept going, as Awol leaned against the rock.

"I can't climb, Blazer."

The dog disappeared as Awol lay against rock for the second time in twelve hours. Sufficient water was nearby. But how close? On all his extended hikes, Awol had learned not to stop at the first sign, the first trickle, the first fresh puddle. No, that first sign was always a promise of more and better ahead. So he pushed himself off the rock and got himself moving.

A hundred yards later, he saw a tiny stream falling from another rock and pulled out his bottle. He let the animal go on. Awol's hands shook so much he had to lean his body onto the embankment and use both hands to try to steady the bottle under the trickle. After a minute or two he had enough for a couple of swallows, and he chugged it down. It made him only thirstier and tightened his throat. He did the routine again and after the last swallow moved ahead to find better and more.

That night, next to a tiny creek, Awol slept with his hands in his pockets, the pack along one side, the pack cover entwined around him, and Blazer warming the other side. The night wasn't any warmer than the previous. *Thank God for Blazer.*

Drizzle. Predawn. Cold! Even Blazer squirmed to get closer but then got up and meandered off as Awol shivered under the all-too-thin pack cover. Blazer came back a few minutes later, but the dog was wet. And now came rain. Awol cursed, twisted, and cursed again at new aches. His neck was sore. The lack of a pillow or something soft, yet the need for sleep, caused the problem, and he wished he'd angled some pine needles or moss or tufts of grass—something—under his head before he'd slept.

He worked his way to a crouch as the rain strengthened, gathered up the pack, and moved farther in to stand under a towering lodgepole pine. He and Blazer needed food. The dog looked at him forlornly as if to say, "What now?" But they had water. Going back to the gravel road was out of the question—the thugs would be searching and patrolling it. He thought of hiding along it and hoping for someone to come by in a four-by-four that he could flag down. But how many people came by here? On a miserable day like this? Certainly not tourists. Who could he trust? He pictured the thugs waving down any and all vehicles and asking questions about who they'd seen, where, when. No, he had to figure differently.

"Can you help me find Kenny, Blazer?" Hands on his hips, he looked at his animal. "Kenny. Kenny. Which way is he, Blazer?"

The dog looked at Awol, wagged his tail lazily, and sat.

Awol opened his pack to where his food bag used to be. He let the dog sniff, knowing that there would be no trace of Kenny, but maybe the smell of food could connect some memory to Kenny.

"You hungry, Blazer? We need food. You lead us to food, okay, boy?"

Now the animal circled around him but then led Awol back to the gravel path.

Awol let the dog go and stopped to think. He and Blazer had walked back down the mountainside, the way the vehicle left. Would the kidnappers set up anew or return to where they'd held Awol previously? The more Awol thought about it, he saw no reason for them to try to elude Awol. They had to protect only one now, a kid—raw, scared, untested. More of them together now, only one holding area. They knew he hadn't swiped a phone. If Awol tried to rescue Kenny, he'd be recaptured. Awol pondered how to contact Sacco without a cell. *But I need to fix where Kenny is. And right now I need food, sustenance.* Awol caught up to the dog again.

CHAPTER SEVENTY-FIVE

BARCELONA COULDN'T BELIEVE WHAT HE was staring at. He'd been rifling through the mule's pack contents and saved the cell phone for last. When he powered it up, he saw a picture of himself with the caption "*Estar sobre aviso:* $10,000 reward for IMMEDIATE execution of this former mule, Barcelona." *So, that's what I'm worth. Señor Alvarado, your price is going to skyrocket.* Barcelona realized the mule would have murdered him in a heartbeat, and now he didn't feel so bad about butchering him.

Barcelona consolidated all that he wanted into the mule's pack except for the extra food. That he left in the mule's food bag and treed it deeper into forest behind him. The mule's boots were too big, but he stashed them in his old pack; if needed, he could wear them with extra socks. He took up the mule's notebook and studied it in earnest.

That night, after several hours' sleep in his new tent, Barcelona penned a note, which he stuffed into a side pocket in his old pack. Then he headed out to the PCT.

SACCO SAW THE NUMBER ON HIS cell and knew who it was. "So, what can you tell me?"

"I was about to say, 'This is Ranger Lloyd.'"

"I'm listening, Ranger Lloyd."

"I'm keeping a close eye and ear on a ranger who, after thinking about it, is acting suspiciously."

"I need more."

"Best I can do right now, Detective. I can't and won't turn against an associate unless I'm sure."

"I'm not asking you to turn against anyone at this juncture. What I really need to know is if I can trust *you*."

"You can. You'll just have to take me at my word."

"And if I give you vital information and it's a mistake, more lives will be lost."

"How can I help you, Detective?"

Sacco drummed his fingers on his sister's rolltop desk. He'd gotten back late last night.

"What makes you suspicious of your ranger?"

"Calls come in on regular lines; he goes outside with his cell phone to respond. Occasional quick-whispered calls in the office."

"Maybe he's cheating on his wife."

"Divorced. Lives alone."

"What else?"

"He's been quiet. Checks his watch a lot."

"Not enough for me to take a chance of this gravity, Ranger Lloyd. Keep me updated. I'll get back to you."

CHAPTER SEVENTY-SIX

ONE OF THE THREE KIDNAPPERS sat outside, next to the same tent where they had previously held Awol. Inside, Kenny was bound hands and feet and blindfolded, while the two others pitched cards on a milk crate in front of him. "No," the dealer said, "I won't take the blindfold off, and if you even think of trying to escape, I will personally slice your eyes out." The man outside scanned with Awol's nightscope. Alvarado had warned them that he would execute them all if the young man escaped.

Alvarado's lead man put down Awol's nightscope and picked up the burning cigarillo. He took a deep drag, laid it back down, and viewed again through the scope, this time circling the tent. Howls from coyotes pierced the darkness. As he swung the scope, the howls died out and an owl hooted up the cause. He wondered if the scope emitted some type of ray causing the temporary ruckus. Jaime, following Alvarado's instructions, had told the three kidnappers they were to stay together for the duration. He needn't have bothered; they had little choice. When Jaime had driven his assistant to them with a week's worth of food and supplies, the assistant took the kidnappers Jeep and left them without a vehicle. "Needed elsewhere by Alvarado," Jaime said.

Two hours later, only Kenny lay awake on his back, still blindfolded. He coughed deliberately to see what would happen. The two inside the tent kept on snoring, but he heard muffled movements outside and heard the tent flap fall away. *Full-time guard*, Kenny thought. He knew more Spanish than his father and had deciphered that his dad had escaped. Kenny played dumb about his knowledge of Spanish and, truth be told, they talked too fast for him to absorb details. As he lay there now, he gave himself a crash course in the language. He concentrated on every verb he could resurrect from memory and then, as best he could, conjugated it. After the verbs, he'd work on resurrecting nouns in alphabetical order.

ON RECEIVING THE NEWS OF the butchered mule and another stolen drop, Alvarado contemplated coming out to the PCT himself to find Barcelona. "Mindless midget," he called Jaime. "An insult to your homeland." He had never displayed chaos with employees nor revealed his hand among any competitor, but this time he was so enraged that—after locking his office door and dousing the lights—he moved to his small chess table and kicked it across the room. As pawns, bishops, and rooks flew and bounced across the room, he accepted that he had miscalculated. But he had the last winning combination in the young man he held prisoner. The boy was to be exchanged for Barcelona in case Sacco found him first. But Barcelona knew too much and was gaining more knowledge every day. The thought of him spilling his guts to Sacco before the switch agitated Alvarado's mind more than any chess problem. The clarity was pristine: find Barcelona.

Alvarado thought it through again. He would keep the three men on the boy—more than needed, but it kept that option safe. The boy's father got by one; he wouldn't get by three, even if he did find his son. Jaime had been given a last chance to redeem himself. Alvarado concluded that his top assistant, Rodolfo, had emerged as the best man to replace Jaime after Barcelona was captured.

BARCELONA HAD WAITED TWO CONSECUTIVE nights for the next mule. No one showed. He reexamined the dead mule's map and saw that a side route to the east of the PCT extended around the area where he had killed him. He surmised that mules had been instructed to use the new route. On the third night, he waited patiently at the new route by a bend in the rocky path. He saw him. It was easy to tell it was a mule. *Who else would it be?* thought Barcelona. To Barcelona's surprise, the mule neared

him, sat down without removing his pack, and took off a boot. He shook
something out of it and was about to step back into it.

"You work for Señor Alvarado?"

The mule jerked his head up. Barcelona, sans pack, stood
nonchalantly, arms behind him.

"Who are you?"

"I think you know who I am."

The mule retied the boot.

"Stay seated and you won't get hurt," Barcelona said. "Give me
your pack."

The mule looked up and askance to Barcelona. "Jaime!" he yelled.

Barcelona twitched for a nanosecond, and when the mule lunged,
gutted him with the knife he'd been holding behind him. Barcelona
finished the work, including the X on the forehead. He hadn't even
turned around. The night was still. He knew Jaime was nowhere near.

Barcelona grabbed the newest pack and left the mule right where he
was, about fifty yards east of the PCT. This mule's boots looked his size,
and he put them into the pack. He returned to the PCT and retrieved
the previous mule's boots, which he'd hidden behind a tree only an hour
ago. He placed them on the trail and pulled up from one of the boots, so
it could be seen, the note he'd written in his tent.

Estar sobre aviso:
For immediate capture of *cobarde* "coward" Alvarado, *un peso!*
Señor Roberto DeLeon

Barcelona then arranged rocks to form an arrow—directed east—
and wrote in the dirt with a stick: *Body 50 yards.*

CHAPTER SEVENTY-SEVEN

Awol SMELLED BACON ON THE wind and swooned. He hadn't eaten anything approaching a square in days, and he felt faint. It was just after eight in the morning, and Blazer was leading them to what Awol determined to be a distant campfire; mingled with bacon, he smelled smoke. When they neared, Awol peeked between limbs and saw a grizzly and cubs meandering about a smoldering fire a hundred yards away. He watched for several minutes as the animals scrounged and knew that they would give up nothing in the way of food. No people anywhere, and he suspected they'd taken off in a hurry. It would be a lost cause even if he dared to go over and poke around once the grizzlies left. Desperate, he sat with Blazer.

"Don't worry, boy." He patted the dog. "We ain't dead yet. We'll make it." The animal yawned and stretched. Awol sensed Blazer was as hungry as he was.

Awol wasn't ready to hunt frogs and gather insects; it would be too chancy to fire them up anyway. It would be like calling to his former captors, "Hey, I'm over here." His plan for immediate sustenance was simple—wild plants and nuts. He applied a faulty analogy to the airline stewardess who advised passengers to put the oxygen masks on themselves first before putting them on others. If he wanted to save Kenny, he needed to take the time to find nutrients now.

Awol found chokeberry and chickweed. He discarded the pits in the chokeberry and worked to separate the clefted petals of the chickweed. He swallowed the plant food together. He kept looking for something to go with the acorns he'd gathered and then saw it—shrubs of hazelnut. The two times in the past he'd foraged the wilds for food, he found it more palatable to combine the nuts or the plants, and he did it again. The hazelnut blunted the tannin in the acorn and, when combined with sips of water, Awol was able to chew and ingest nutrients. All this had taken forty minutes. Though he couldn't find other edible berries, he did find the leafy lichen called rock tripe, which he picked and saved to eat raw later. With a mentally forced placebo effect, he convinced himself he was stronger, surer, abler. Blazer had been cautious. He sniffed barks and licked birch bark close to ground level and tongued gooseberry, but that was all.

During this time, Awol fixed in his mind the problem of freeing Kenny. Though he'd love to have Sacco's help, he couldn't reach him. Experience made him realize the fewer hands on the problem, the better. He had the element of surprise. No one knew where he was, and anyone looking for him would suspect he'd go to Sacco or rangers as soon as he had the chance. Awol felt more confident with Blazer beside him—*Jesus, the dog is smart!* Awol remembered what army survival had taught him: *don't try to wrap yourself around the entire problem at once; break it into parts.* He may or may not free Kenny, and though he couldn't bear the latter thought, he couldn't deal with that part just now. The first thing was to locate him! With the cunning of this animal and his own instinct, he would at least locate Kenny. Then he would focus on the next part of the problem.

"Blazer." Awol cupped the dog's head in his hands. "Kenny! We need to find Kenny. Where's Kenny?"

The animal headed back to the gravel road. Well behind, scanning constantly in all directions, absorbing all that was humanly possible, Awol followed.

KENNY WOKE TO RAIN PELTING down on the tent. He made the assumption that it was dawn from the snores and from the fact that he had to poo and pee. He hadn't had a bowel movement in two days and wondered if the quantity of food, not suitable for a wren, was deliberate. On top of being scared, he was so hungry. He wondered if he would even be able to swallow if a decent meal did pass his way again. Before finally going back to sleep, he attempted to translate the Lord's Prayer into Spanish. As a practical matter, it kept his mind off food. He also thought it would be wise to try and impress his "higher power."

The rain didn't last. When it stopped, he might have smelled them into letting him crouch outside—well removed from the tent—for not a word was spoken as he was lead to a spot by a man on each arm. Kenny sniffed the barely perceptible aroma of bacon wafting from his left, and he looked blindly in that direction. In doing so, black night gave way to dusk—so the smell was from the east, and morning light. He turned his head opposite, back to the black of night. He didn't know how he knew, but he now believed that he was at the tent where his father had been. He remembered the driver saying *tienda,* tent, before the driver dropped off his dad from the Jeep while Kenny remained in it, several days ago.

After he'd returned to the tent and was retied, he plied the dirt behind him with his fingers and kicked around the ground in front of him. He couldn't confirm the feeling, but he sensed traces of his dad, and his mind's eyes saw him now. *Escaped! Way to go, Dad.* Kenny was convinced he was on his way to get help. Sacco and reinforcements would be coming.

A while later, one of the kidnappers pulled from his pack a black radio with a long antenna. His two sidekicks watched as he turned a crank and then twisted a knob. Soon Kenny heard Latin music sung in broken Spanish. After straining his ears, he concluded the lyrics were Spanglish. Twenty minutes later, there was a news broadcast: "Las noticias, Los Angeles," the announcer said. Because of the clear and controlled enunciation, Kenny gained a foothold and comprehended some of the happenings in greater LA, the weather, sports. When music began again—accordions, Zydeco—he heard one of his captors say something about a murder on the PCT. He shuddered and thought about his dad. He tried to put the thought out of his mind that his father may have been killed on the trail. He began to think that he would be taken away, across the border, never to see his mother, brother, or Jill again. He pulled at the ropes binding him and wondered how his father managed to escape. He was hungry, sore, helpless. Most of all, he was hungry.

When his father came for him, he'd have to be ready. Prepared. What could he do to get ready? *There must be something.* He needed to get the blindfold off.

CHAPTER SEVENTY-EIGHT

IN ALL HIS OUTDOOR EXPERIENCES, Awol never missed the chance to make fire. He excelled at making fire in wilderness, and he'd accomplished the task in sundry ways when he had to, once surprising even himself. The irony—here he needed a fire for warmth and to boil water to leach nutrients from plants, but he dared not make one. He was too close; they'd be watching, listening, smelling for any signal of another human. And he was the only human they could possibly be expecting. When Blazer had led him to the rutted path that began the climb up the mountain, Awol knew. Kenny was now where he had been. Awol sat off-road eating the rock tripe raw, contemplating his next move. *All right, let's say they are expecting me. They don't know I found Kenny at the cliff. They think I simply escaped and am huddled up nearby, like I am. But what does Sacco know? And how can I be sure Kenny is here?*

"HEY! SOMETHING'S WRONG WITH MY eye. I need the blindfold off."

Kenny heard the flap open and measured steps nearing him that stopped.

"Listen, please. Do you have medicine here? I know about injuries. This eye is going to get worse if it doesn't get some light."

"Medicine! Ha! Jose, you hear that?"

More steps. "Take it off and let me look at him," a gravelly voice said. *So that's Jose.*

They unwrapped the blindfold. Kenny had an easy time of squinting and blinking, half thinking that maybe something *was* wrong.

"What eye?" asked Jose.

"The right one. Your left."

"Stop blinking. Looks okay to me."

"It's not. Can you at least keep the blindfold off for a while? If you don't have eye drops—"

"Shut up, kid, or I smack you, and then we see how your eye feels."

Kenny stared at him with his left eye but kept blinking the right eye.

Jose turned to his partner standing beside him, and Kenny saw the third kidnapper step in. "Give him fifteen minutes, then put it back on," Jose said.

They went out. Kenny eyed a map on the cot to his left. Boxed food was next to the cot on his right. What looked like a water can sat next to the food. Two full Nalgene bottles of water were next to that. Then the lantern. No third cot, therefore full-time guard. No weapons in sight. Had his father been tied here? He inspected the ground around him and saw scuff marks. Now he noticed two short, hair-sized strands of hemp.

He heard steps as he was trying to memorize the map on the cot, like he'd seen his father do with maps. The heart of ever-narrowing mountain elevation squiggles showed a red X at the peak, and he assumed that's where they were—here. He glazed at a tent wall as Jose's partner retied the blindfold. "Not so tight," Kenny pleaded. And, mission accomplished, the blindfold was tied looser.

At night, when the lone camping lamp was turned off, someone removed the blindfold as he feigned sleep while on his back. His legs were always tied around the post, but at night they gloved his fingers before securely tying his hands in front of him. *If it wasn't for these fucking gloves,* Kenny thought. But the gloves gave him one advantage. Sitting up in the pitch-darkness, gloves prevented suspect scrapes and blackened, torn fingernails as he dug quietly down into the earth just between his legs by the mast. When he felt the round of a palm-sized rock, he confidently pried it loose with a gloved hand. It took over an hour, but he was able to place the jagged stone back into the hole and cover it with loose earth for easy accessibility. He moved his thighs back and forth to spread the excess dirt. He finally slept, with his right thigh lying over the hidden hole. This night, for the first time he could remember, he dreamed in Spanish. He was hollering to his father in Spanish about something and kept pointing his hand west. Blazer seemed to understand, but his father looked puzzled.

Next morning, when the gravelly voiced Jose and another man led Kenny behind the tent, Kenny, though blindfolded, turned his head west. From the west he heard the honks of wild geese that his father had educated him about. Their honks diminished, and he wished he were flying south with them.

CHAPTER SEVENTY-NINE

To SAY THAT ALVARADO WAS enraged when he received news that a third mule had been found murdered, stabbed, slashed with an X, and without drop would be like saying a father was enraged when he learned that a former trusted field hand had mutilated his sons. He stared at the messenger.

"What's that you have in your hand?"

"Señor, I'm told I must give this to you."

Alvarado snatched the piece of paper and read Barcelona's note.

"Kindly turn around," he told the messenger. "Face the doorway."

The messenger did as instructed.

"You will forgive me, of course," said Alvarado as he pointed the revolver at the back of the man's head and pulled the trigger.

Señor Alvarado didn't say another word for the rest of the afternoon in his separate Palm Springs office. He oiled his revolver; packed his Winchester rifle, ammo, and four days' worth of food; filled three canteens; and grabbed his whip. He retrieved his disguise from a valise but not his traveling chess set. He thumbed his chef to leave and made his own special chili, which he'd finished eating at his desk in his office. A large painting of his father was on the wall facing him. In the desktop-sized, gold-framed painting, the tiny Alvarado looked about five years old and sat in his father's lap. Alvarado reminisced about that day as he sipped wine, worked his mouth with a toothpick, and stared at the painting. They had sat in that spot watching his father's horses from a mesa on the Alvarado homestead while the artist drew.

That evening, when his valet looked in timidly at Alvarado—still seated in his office with a half-finished carafe of wine—Alvarado finally spoke. "Fuel the Jeep; connect my horse and trailer. Oats for four days."

Two hours later, after the valet had finished fitting Alvarado's disguise and packing his Jeep and trailer to his master's orders, the valet accepted an envelope from Alvarado. "Keep everything a secret. I'm indisposed for four days. If things remain the same when I return, I'll give you another envelope." Alvarado grabbed maps and some other official-looking papers, made a phone call, locked his office, and drove north into the night.

Six hours later, tired but alert from pills and extra strong coffee, Alvarado had made it to the base of the Sierras in southern California. He parked in a special "Ranger's Only" lot and pulled out a phone designed to work with portable repeater towers in the area.

"Meet me in exactly one hour--just you and a trusted driver," he said into the phone.

Alvarado power napped the hour and awoke to headlights in the lot. He waited until one of two men he could see walked over. Then he stepped out.

"Where is Señor Alvarado?" the ranger asked.

Alvarado walked sidewise to the man and turned him so their backs faced the sedan behind him. "Tell him to douse the lights." After that was done, Alvarado slipped him an envelope. "Before I pass on Mr. Alvarado's instructions, he wants you to look into the envelope."

The man's eyes widened as he counted American hundred-dollar bills, while Alvarado inspected the moon. After pocketing the envelope, he looked at Alvarado.

"Did you bring what Señor Alvarado asked you to?" Alvarado said.

"Yes."

While the man went back to the sedan, Alvarado led his horse from the trailer. When the man returned, Alvarado unzipped the garment bag and checked it. "Good. Take this Jeep and trailer to Reds Meadow. Park it by the west fork of the river. Divert trail rangers into Yosemite as much as possible; if anyone asks, tell them I'm on special assignment by the government to check out things on the PCT."

Alvarado patted one oat sack and walked around the magnificent palomino to check the second, which was tied to the other side of the saddle. "Keep your radio on at all times. Leave now."

The man thumbed his driver to leave.

When both vehicles had disappeared around the bend, Alvarado tied the horse to a nearby tree and took the garment bag behind it. Five minutes later, he was in ranger uniform complete with hat. He stuffed the garment bag into a trash receptacle, put the clothes he'd changed out of into his saddlebag, and untied the palomino, who was already hoofing ground anxious to please his master. Alvarado patted his neck—"*Sí, Caballo*"—and mounted. He reviewed the map again under a penlight and selected a path angling into forest. Soon the forest path widened, and after a trot he broke Caballo into a slow canter under a bulging moon.

CHAPTER EIGHTY

Awol RIGGED UP A MAKESHIFT shelter deep in forest. He needed to save his energy, but he could smell rain coming, and he had to protect himself since he couldn't chance a fire. He'd looked for a cave or a natural dugout but had found nothing. Stopping in front of a Volkswagen-sized boulder, he built an opposite-side barrier behind him by dragging over debris—limbs and branches. There was only three feet between the rock and the built side, but it was enough space for him and the dog to squeeze in. He tore branches from trees to lay across the top and then covered that with firs and fern. It would do.

Awol knew he'd have to kill again to save Kenny. He could do that, but this time he needed to backpack out sustenance and supplies. He wouldn't bring Kenny back down here. This shelter would serve as a decoy. He would hide elsewhere and contact Sacco using one of the kidnappers' phones. He forced out of his mind the probability of them fixing his position when he used their cell. *One step at a time,* he told himself. He found more acorns and chewed on those until it got dark and the moon had risen. *How in God's name had he gotten himself into this fix?* He remembered his last words to Gloria: "You have my word, nothing will happen to him."

Awol felt he shouldn't be tested like this. Hadn't he tried to keep Kenny from rejoining him? Was he supposed to punch him out at the bus station to keep him from coming? He looked at Blazer, who was napping at his feet, conserving his energy. *A dog with a good master has a damned good life,* he thought. *Our species complicates things.* He knew one thing—he'd do his best to extricate Kenny, and he'd take a bullet in a heartbeat to accomplish that.

Night. Awol on the move; Blazer right beside him. "Blazer. We must be very quiet," Awol whispered. He stopped and crouched down to the animal, thinking his quads would burst. He took Blazer's face in both hands and whispered into it, "Shhhh." And when the animal tried to whimper, Awol squeezed his snout. "Shhhhhhh. Quiet, boy." One more time, the same routine, and Blazer understood and stayed quiet. Awol felt a burst of confidence flood him; he and his dog understood each other.

Although he didn't have to climb a rock wall this time, Awol had to stop several times as he ascended. He wasn't out of breath; he was hungry and sore. Every ligament begged for sustenance. He'd had to tighten his belt up a full notch. He thought about victims of the Holocaust and castigated himself. So he was tired, sore, and hungry; those survivors would have laughed in his face. *Bear up, damn it. Bear up!* And then he continued on. Blazer was perfectly quiet and seemed to sense a critical resolve in his master. Awol dared not crouch, thinking he might not be able to rise, but he stooped down to Blazer. The dog licked sweat from his face. "Yeah, I love you too. Shhhh."

The climb was long and tedious, and he occasionally stumbled in ruts at the side of the road. He didn't think it would be this long a hike, nor as steep. He was enervated; the ascent was arduous, and his legs and body shook. He didn't allow himself to walk in the middle of the road. They had his nightscope. When he could see all of the Big Dipper, he sensed he was almost to the top. After one last caution to Blazer, he cut into thickets from the road and began to bushwhack to the summit. He finally arrived at an edge of shrubs and small pines, from where he could see the tent. It was as he remembered it from the tree line when he'd escaped, but he faced the side of the tent. It sat in brush about fifty yards away, about twenty yards from the nearly impassable rutted path. There was a glow from within. Blazer sat and stayed quiet.

Awol receded into forest and bushwhacked to the front, which took another twenty minutes. He lay prone and indirectly looked, as one does at night for clarity. The scene at the front of the tent looked familiar. Camp chair, man in it with hat, lit cigar, and a can of something beside him. All under a fattening moon. He wondered about his nightscope and assumed the smoker had it with him. Blazer lay down next to Awol.

"Shhhh. Is Kenny there, Blazer?" The dog thumped his tail. Of course he was there. Awol could sense him as much as Blazer could smell him. The big question was, how many guarded him? Awol was confident he could sneak up and take out the front guard, and with the guard's pistol, he could at least incapacitate another, but that was all, and outdueling just two was a huge chance. Okay, then. He'd learned that, statistically, the time for deepest sleep was normally 2:00–4:00 a.m. Raids were best planned deep into the wee hours. Awol didn't have his watch, but he would will himself awake in the wee hour. He had no choice but to get a bit of sleep, or his waning energy would evaporate and the chance would be lost. He retreated to the forest, lay down, and prayed again, but he'd hardly got his thoughts together when he fell into slumber. Blazer wiggled close to him, their bodies as one. Dog sleep followed.

He shivered himself awake. He thought it odd that he hadn't been dreaming. Maybe his mind saved the effort so all his faculties could rally. He wished his entire life was a dream. More so, he wished a dream could pitch him to his hoped-for reality: Kenny back in college; Linda, he, and Blazer happy at home. Blazer stirred under the hidden moon.

"Okay, Blazer. This is it. You be good, okay?" The animal yawned. His face was drawn; the eyes bespoke hunger. "Yes, boy, we'll eat soon. I promise."

He figured that the thugs had already searched down behind the tent and off the mountain the way he'd previously escaped. They would search that area again. They would also track by the road, the way he'd just come. From the map he remembered the front or north side of the mountain was an impossibility—too many rocked walls, no paths or trails of any kind. One could survive there for a while, but if he wanted to escape with Kenny and get to civilization, his best route was over and down the western side of this mountain. He remembered seeing a stream on the map, and there were always trails leading to rivers and streams. Even animals would make them. Now to the business at hand. He unpocketed the rock he'd selected earlier.

When he reached his former position, he ordered Blazer to stay.

It was dead quiet out, and he could hear snores. In the inky black of night, he could not make out a guard in front as he angled forward to the side of the tent. Halfway to the tent, he took out the sunglasses he'd swiped from the vehicle and placed them on the ground. Some yards farther, he dropped the P-38 can opener. Let them find those and continue to search that line. He thought of honest rangers who might also fall for the ploy and be led astray, but he remembered the lead kidnapper talking on a special radio at what seemed like regular intervals to another. The thugs would be the first to put things together and the first to search back this way.

When he saw him, head tilted back in the chair, hopefully asleep, Awol crept behind the tent and deployed his senses. Yes! He'd seen the guard's gun stuck in a holster. He thought the nightscope lay beside him. It was quiet inside except for two sets of snores, one of them Kenny's, just as he remembered it. *So maybe two bad guys.* With juices flowing, he inched around the tent to sneak up on the guard from the western side. Just as the chance came, there was a stirring in the tent and truncated snores. Kenny's! The guard perked up and sat straight, just as Awol's rock slammed into the side of his head. Awol grabbed the revolver from the holster and looked for a flashlight on the guard. Seeing none and with a cough inside the tent, he opened the flap.

"Freeze! Or I'll blow your brains out."

"Dad?"

"How many, Kenny?"

"Two in—" Awol felt a hand grab for the gun, and he pulled the trigger. The hand fell away. "Watch out, Dad!" Awol shot at movement to the left of Kenny's voice and heard a groan. Awol, in a crouch, felt a hand grab something by his knee. Awol planted his kneecap over the hand and placed the gun to the kidnapper's head. The man stilled, but when Awol reached down for the gun under his kneecap, in one last desperate attempt the man pulled it away. Two shots fired. A bullet whirred by Awol's ear. Awol's shot went into the man's head.

"You okay, Dad?"

"Yeah, what about you?"

"I'll be a lot better when you untie me."

Once Kenny was untied, Awol heard him grub for something beneath his legs. Awol looked for the lantern. Kenny had not been blindfolded, and now the boy caught sight of a human bull tearing into the tent. The kidnapper from outside, cursing, grabbed Awol from behind in a one-armed choke hold and went for his pistol, which lay next to a backpack. With a roar, Kenny charged the man from his knees and slammed a stone down on the man's head.

Awol found the lantern and switched it on. "Good going, son."

"Dad, I think that whack killed him. Look at the eyes."

Awol saw the vacant stare and that one of the man's arms folded funny across his chest.

"I think you're right. I wouldn't worry about it; he was aching to off both of us."

"Dad. They're all dead."

"Whistle for Blazer, and help me pack up. We need to take anything relevant. We must have their radios, maps, and all weapons. I'll pack food and water."

With Blazer yipping and licking Kenny, Awol gathered his thoughts. He pulled over the third backpack.

"Kenny, order number one: separate the two best sleeping bags, mattress rolls, tents, and packs."

Awol finished gathering food, including garlic paste he found—good for thwarting bugs—and all the canteens. They found two radios and two identical sets of maps and were in the process of collecting knives and ammo.

"Where are we going, Dad?"

"Order number two: Get me the nightscope and any extra clothing—in particular shells, jackets, hats, and gloves. We take anything we can wear. Stuff it into the packs."

Five minutes later, they shrugged into their confiscated packs and looked around.

"Did you see an extra flashlight?" Awol said.

Kenny went to the night guard and pulled a penlight out of his pocket.

"Excellent," Awol said as he grabbed an unwashed mess kit sitting by one of the cots. He dug around a few more boxes and found a small plastic bottle of soap. "Stuff this in your pocket," he said.

"You still haven't told me where we are going," Kenny said.

"That's because I don't know exactly, but we are getting the hell away from here." Awol ducked to the outside and looked west and up to the sky. The Big Dipper had twisted. "Follow me."

CHAPTER EIGHTY-ONE

THE BODY HAD BEEN DISCOVERED by a day hiker. He'd called 911 and was relayed to the nearest ranger station. A retrieval party was sent, and the next day, a gory close-up of the dead male—Hispanic, estimated to be in his late twenties—made the papers.

Luis Alvarado, sucking on a blade of mountain grass, reread the account. His horse grazed on the grass free but near his master, about thirty yards east of the PCT in the High Sierra. Alvarado had asked Jaime for an update. "Download the account to me, word-for-word," he'd instructed.

"I'm not sure how to—"

"You will find out how to, and you will do something else. I'm turning your command over to Rodolfo. You are to spend all your time finding Barcelona."

"We've lost mules, señor."

"I just made it clear! Rodolfo is in charge. You will find Barcelona—alive. This is your last chance. Report to me every six hours!"

Alvarado noted that there was no mention of a backpack or anything else in the news item. Just mention of the dead body, stabbed in the gut, in the back, and about the forehead. The creator of the PCT drug scheme turned off his phone and made a promise to himself. He, himself, would not take Barcelona dead or alive: only alive! He saddled up.

BARCELONA SLEPT AS HE USUALLY did—in fits and starts. He shifted in his bag and remembered being with Juanita on the beach in Acapulco at night. She had just told him she was pregnant with Roberto, and in his glee, he picked her up and carried her to softer sand behind an old wharf. He remembered their sex and how he placed his shirt over her as they nestled after, looking at stars, talking about names for the baby. Barcelona smiled in his bag as he recalled Juanita saying if the baby was a girl, she would have final approval on a name, but he could name him if it was a boy.

The following night, after a day of rest, Barcelona wormed into the tent and closed the flap to a wind that came from nowhere just as the first drops of rain sprinkled upon him. He changed into fresh clothes from the mule's pack as wind-driven rain smacked the tent. Barcelona, fully rested and unable to sleep, sat Indian style. Feeling like a caged animal that can't even pace, he put his head into his hands and thought he might cry. He missed his kids, a woman's touch. He felt remorse for the people he had killed but felt cynical and foolish praying for forgiveness. But he prayed for Juanita and their children. He prayed for Eva and Yolanda. His prayers shifted his soul to Yolanda, who was alive, a tangible human being who embodied kindness. Might he reach her once more? It was too late to call the children, and every time he did, he endangered them; Eva's phone records could be pulled. Yet it would be so good to talk with someone.

Barcelona reached into the mule's pack for the newest victim's cell and felt something underneath. It was a loaded revolver—small but mighty in Barcelona's hands. Alvarado normally didn't allow his mules to pack weapons, but he knew he'd have to make exceptions if Barcelona was to be captured. Barcelona felt a rush of confidence. He picked up the special phone and saw that it had a charge. Being in the High Sierra, he felt blessed when he saw three bars in the cell window. He keyed in Yolanda's number. He was saddened as the phone kept ringing, but when Yolanda's familiar voice told him she was away at the moment, that all messages were important to her, and to please leave one, he was smitten.

"It's me, Yolanda. Barcelona. How I miss you and . . ." Barcelona grimaced and slapped the phone shut. He couldn't believe what he had just done.

CHAPTER EIGHTY-TWO

THE MORNING AFTER BARCELONA CALLED Yolanda, he awoke in a fevered sweat. He hadn't slept well again and had listened to the intermittent sprinkle of rain on the tent for most of the night. He peeked out to fog and, shivering in the raw dampness, back-crawled into his bag, feeling wretched. But he needed to dig in at a new spot; he'd given them his location. He could wait here and take out a few, but he wanted the element of surprise for himself, so he could inflict the most damage.

He sat up two hours later and still felt miserable and feverish. Believing his problem was hunger and lack of sleep, he stepped out and pulled down the food bag, took it into the tent, and made a meal of oatmeal, fruit, tortillas, and gorp—aware that this meal could be his last. He had just finished getting packed up to bushwhack farther south when he felt a vibration from the one charged phone. He'd forgotten to take the battery out! *Yolanda?* He didn't recognize the number, but this could be Yolanda on a new phone.

"Hello."

"You are surrounded."

Barcelona looked around but didn't see anything or hear a sound. "That you, Jaime?"

"We have people all around you, Barcelona. So you might as well give up."

"That's what you'd like me to do," Barcelona said, keeping his voice low. "Anybody comes close, I sprinkle my drops to the winds. You tell

Alvarado I have the newest drop, and I know where the other two are hidden. Try to take me out and I promise you, he'll have *nada*."

Barcelona shut down the phone and took out the battery. What to do? He figured that Jaime had fixed his location. They wanted to scare him into staying put. If they had him surrounded, why would they tell him?

Barcelona wondered if he could turn himself over to the Americans but again thought of the dead federal agent and the attempted murder of another, never mind his other murders on US soil. No, at best they'd deport him to Mexico as an escaped convict wanted for murder there. Barcelona, rushing now, opted to bushwhack and thought of a new idea that would give him his best chance at maximum damage.

ALVARADO HAD ALWAYS NOTICED THAT he could accomplish his best voice impersonations when he was in disguise. He had tried to prove this fact wrong several times over the years, thinking that it should make no difference, but when he was in disguise, he was always able to nail the impersonation as he just did with Barcelona. He checked the coordinates on his map with those he'd inked on there last night after hearing Barcelona's call to Yolanda. *He hasn't moved.*

BARCELONA PICKED A PONDEROSA, BUT before he clambered up, he searched for a place to hide the twenty-seven-pound drop. *There.* Ten yards away, a lightning-scarred dead pine with a hollowed out trunk looked perfect. He pulled out dead moss mixed with wood lice, stuffed the canister inside the trunk, and then packed moss back on top.

Not unlike a rock climber grabbing and digging for purchase, his legs cut into the trunk like angled pistons. His body hugging the trunk, Barcelona inched up until, at last, a limb. His hands sticky with pitch, his head busting through riffraff branches and twigs to other limbs that he used as rungs, he climbed.

Sun peeked through fog. Barcelona had on a beige hooded shell and full khakis. The fleece, gloves, and hat were more than enough to keep him warm, at least for now. Barcelona secluded himself in a spot that gave him a bird's-eye view of not just the trail itself, but east and west of it extending twenty yards or so. To thwart dehydration, he swigged extra water from a full bottle.

After he got settled, hardly fifteen minutes had passed when he heard hiking poles. Barcelona, huddled behind the trunk, watched what looked like a bona fide thru-hiker heading south sixty feet below. Barcelona figured Jaime and Alvarado's goons would hunt near the trail and reconnoiter on it. One way or another, he would kill mules or goons coming through. For driving the *cobarde* mad, one was as good as the other.

CHAPTER EIGHTY-THREE

AWOL AND KENNY, AFTER ESCAPING and checking confiscated maps under penlight—and after snacking on peanut butter, cheese and crackers, nuts, and fruit—had found a trail down that would take them to water. They picked this route because nothing was grease-marked near it by the thugs. It wasn't the easiest way down; the map revealed that. But for Awol, fortified with food, it was most welcome. He could almost sing and hummed the "Marine's Hymn" from time to time.

"You were in the army, Dad."

"In war, the marines help the army, and we help the marines. Besides, I like the tune."

Awol told Kenny to set up the tents by the stream while he figured out next orders. In truth, Awol was in a quandary. He needed help from Sacco, but he was sure the phones he and Kenny had taken from the kidnappers were monitored by the thugs. But he needed to do something—he figured the message would be in how he said it.

"Listen closely. I'm with Alpha two. Do you copy?"

"Awol!"

"That would be Alpha one. They are somewhere in the High Sierra. Over."

"Awol?"

"Tell me how I should reach you. Out."

SACCO COULDN'T BELIEVE HIS EARS. But he understood, or at least he thought he did. Awol and Kenny had escaped or were being held captive "somewhere in the High Sierra." There were only two reasons why Awol wouldn't say more: he was on a monitored phone he'd stolen, or a gun was to his head and he was being forced to lure Sacco into a trap. But why a trap? Sacco was working with Alvarado—or so he had led Alvarado to believe. Alvarado must be more than desperate to find Barcelona; his mules were dropping like flies. Lloyd had called to let him know about the most recent murder, and this one made the news. He decided he'd call Alvarado.

"I can no longer depend on you, Mr. Sacco." These were the first words Sacco heard when Alvarado answered.

"Whether you depend on me or not, I can't control. Perhaps you don't want to depend on me."

"What is the purpose of your call?"

"I heard about the recent murder. I haven't been able to find Barcelona."

"So I should release my captives? Naught for naught?"

Sacco thrummed Angela's desk.

"Is that what you want, Mr. Sacco?"

"Might be best for you."

"Mr. Sacco, that is why I won't depend on you any further. I no longer trust you."

The phone went dead. Although Sacco couldn't confirm his suspicion, his gut told him that he wasn't being lured into a trap. The bastard would never reveal his failure, least of all to him. Awol and Kenny had to have escaped. And if that was true, Awol and Kenny, for sure, would be led into a trap.

Sacco thought through every possible angle. The PCT operation, his career—it was all on the line. His only hope of prevailing was to fess up and beg. He steeled himself to meet his boss. During the drive to headquarters, he made one last call using a different phone.

"Okay, Ranger Lloyd. I'm putting all my chips down on you, that you are honest, that you will not deceive me."

"Guess I better get ready to impress you."

"Where is your suspect, Ranger?"

"Right where I want him. Kinda under my thumb."

"Keep him there. Sometime in the next twenty-four hours, on a moment's notice, I will need you to travel quickly to somewhere in the High Sierra."

CHAPTER EIGHTY-FOUR

ALVARADO DISCARDED SACCO; HE SHOULD have known never to work with him. He'd heard Awol's attempt to disguise a message for Sacco. He would concern himself with that later; what could Awol and his son accomplish now? Might even be a good diversion for Sacco. He'd have to find them and extricate them from the wilds at the coordinates the phone revealed. It looked to be a messy project from what he could see on his map. In the meantime, he would concentrate on Barcelona. At this moment, Alvarado allowed himself to fantasize how he would do in the betrayer. Alvarado thought Barcelona might particularly enjoy a ride back inside the horse trailer, harnessed face up underneath the rear end of Caballo. He patted Caballo now as he and horse moved to new coordinates given up by Barcelona's foolish call to the one bitch that so far had eluded him— Yolanda. Alvarado considered shutting down the phone to save battery but left it on, hoping for more information. *Prudence,* he told himself.

―――――――――

Awol shut down both phones. One, he and the boy needed sleep. Two, Sacco would leave a message. *Patience,* he told himself.

The next morning, he was rewarded. There was a message left by Sacco, but he couldn't make heads or tails out of it.

"Kenny, what the hell does he mean?"

Kenny listened to the message, which consisted of letters and numbers: **Z-9-R-6-L-4-E-3-B-2-A-1**

After a few minutes, Kenny smiled. "It's easy, Dad. The letters constitute an anagram. See it?"

Awol looked at what Kenny had written down on a piece of paper. "No."

"Look at the Z."

"Aha! You think so?"

"Yeah, it's B-L-A-Z-E-R."

"So we should switch around the numbers?"

"Yes."

Awol, smiling, tried again, punching in a different frequency.

"'Bout time you caught on," Sacco said.

Awol chuckled. "That's because my smart one here was still asleep, and I wanted him to get his beauty rest. Clever."

"Alvarado is a smart cookie, but, so far as I know, he doesn't know your dog's name."

"Let's hope you're right."

"Okay, more good news. My boss carved me a new asshole, and I all but literally kissed his, but I've been given another few days to make something work. Then he pulls the plug. Forever."

"So what's the plan?" Awol said.

"I know where you are. If you follow the stream north, in two miles it widens and begins to look like a river. Look there for an access road. It'll look more like a cow path but navigable in a four-by-four, I'm told."

"I don't see it on this map."

"I'm not surprised; rangers know about it. A Ranger Lloyd will meet you there when I tell him to. I'm calling him now."

Awol walked a few paces to the side of Kenny, out of hearing, before finishing off with Sacco and pocketing the phone.

Awol, with furrowed brow, had Kenny lead the entire way. Following the stream was rough going. Kenny sensed discontent and turned around.

"Something the matter, Dad?"

"Not if you follow orders."

"Aren't I?"

"Stop here a minute."

Awol looked at him, put down his sticks, and grabbed Kenny's shoulders. "When we reach this guy, Lloyd, he's going to take you out of here. That's the first thing I want you to understand." He shook his son's shoulders.

"Dad, you're almost hurting me."

"That's because—here's the other thing I want you to understand. You are not coming back here. I order you to go straight to your mother. Understood?"

Awol squeezed harder.

"Yeah, yeah, Dad. Geesshh! Is that what you set up with Sacco just now?"

Awol took the lead.

The four-by-four hadn't arrived when Awol, Kenny, and Blazer reached the river. The two adults thought they were in the wrong place as they scanned for some type of path. Blazer led them to it. They watched Blazer rut around the river. Kenny gave a salute when the animal jumped in.

"You understand my orders?" Awol asked.

"Yeah, Dad. Do you have to keep mentioning it?"

"Right. To close the loop, here is how serious I am about it." He waited. Kenny finally looked at his father.

"I'm letting you keep the dog."

Kenny pulled his head back but said nothing.

The four-by-four pulled up. "Okay, Kenny, a hug."

Kenny put an arm around his father and wiped his eyes with the other.

"Kenny, good luck in school. And my regards to your mother and Gregory, okay?"

Kenny separated, handed him his backpack, and looked at Blazer, who had come up shaking himself dry as a ranger stepped out of the vehicle.

"The dog is yours, son, until I get back. I better not say good-bye to him. You're enough for me to handle." Kenny said nothing. He knew when to keep quiet. He wasn't going to win this one. "Please take Blazer into the Jeep and stay with him while I cover off with the ranger."

Awol shook the ranger's extended hand and noted *Lloyd* sewed onto the patch steamed to the shirt. "Did Detective Sacco explain . . ." Awol nodded to the vehicle as Kenny opened the passenger door.

"He did," Lloyd said.

"Okay then. Please take him and the dog straight to a bus station. Do you need money?"

"No. It's been settled. I'll make sure he gets on the bus. Sacco told me it was"—Ranger Lloyd smiled—"critical to your well-being."

Awol shook the hand again. "Godspeed, Ranger Lloyd."

For the second time in a month, Awol watched his son depart. The last thing he saw was Kenny holding up Blazer to the window. Kenny did wave at least.

CHAPTER EIGHTY-FIVE

SACCO HAD BEEN STRAIGHT-UP WITH Awol. They could work together for only the next few days. Sacco had promised Awol that he would bus Kenny to his mother immediately. But if they didn't capture Barcelona— the one person who could detail the scheme and provide names—Awol could be arrested for interfering, citizen or no. Sacco would be demoted, given a transfer, and this unofficial operation would shut down. But if Awol left right now, he'd said, Awol would be okay with the chief. No one would inquire.

"So you are telling me to leave?" Awol said.

"No, if you think we can get him in three days. Yes, if you don't think we can."

"I say we get him. Just think, Detective, at least *you* won't be arrested."

Awol, feeling relieved, feeling nourished just by looking at both backpacks, crouched down to consolidate. He wanted to travel light. Rather than take extra food, he decided to eat a good meal now, which would also give him extra time to formulate a plan. He thought over key items that he knew and some things that he suspected. Barcelona hated Alvarado and feared capture and return to Mexico. He loved his children. Barcelona knew US authorities were also after him; Barcelona figured if he gave himself up to the US, he would be deported and a marked man in his homeland. A seed began to germinate in Awol's mind. *If we could entice him to cooperate with us . . . but he'd still have to pay a heavy penalty, unless . . .*

"This is quick," Sacco said. "Forget something?"

"Barcelona told me how he loved his children. Where are they?"

"Don't have a clue. I see where you are going with the question, and I like your thinking. I'm on it."

Awol downed some beef jerky, cheese, fruit. *If we can only find him,* he thought. He dug out from the peanut butter jar with a plastic spoon. Sacco had told him to stay put until he had location info, but Awol wasn't going to sit around and take a nap. *What would I do if I were Barcelona? Water. I'd stay near water.* Awol hadn't seen anything suspect behind him along the stream. The stream widened considerably ahead. *That's the direction I'd go.*

ALVARADO HEARD THE VEHICLE BEFORE he saw it. He pulled his horse aside and remained mounted as he peeked through branches. An unmarked all-terrain vehicle. Dirt cowboys, he figured, but a good source of information. He rebuttoned his ranger shirt at the collar and took a commanding pose under his crisp-looking hat as he pulled into the middle of the path. After hoisting his hand ordering a halt, he had misgivings. *Too late,* he thought.

A ranger stepped out of the vehicle. "I'm Ranger Lloyd. What's going on here?"

"I'm searching for a Roberto DeLeon, alias, 'Barcelona,'" Alvarado said. He stiffened when he saw the young man and then the dog in the car.

"Where do you—who are you?" Lloyd asked.

"All in good time, Ranger Lloyd. Right now, I'm going to ask you to kindly move two paces to your left. You, inside," Alvarado hollered to Kenny. "Out!" He swung Caballo closer to the four-by-four and took out his revolver.

Stunned, Lloyd held his spot.

"Ranger Lloyd, move as I instructed. I won't ask again."

All at once, Blazer jumped out the open door and spooked the horse. The palomino reared as Alvarado shot sky and twisted sideways, almost falling off. Kenny had already sprinted for the nearest tree, and when Blazer ran to follow, Kenny kept going. He heard another shot as he dove over an embankment and, adrenaline surging, kept running for his life.

When the horse spooked, Lloyd jumped into his vehicle and drove straight for the animal. Alvarado swerved his horse just in time as he shot and blew a hole in the center of the windshield before galloping away, straight across the river. Winded, Kenny peeked behind him. He heard and saw the vehicle roar and bounce out of sight. The horse and rider galloped the opposite way Kenny had gone. Kenny kept sprinting and jogging into thickets and brush as much as his lungs allowed, trying to keep up with Blazer.

Awol and Jaime heard the shots. So did Barcelona.

CHAPTER EIGHTY-SIX

Awol SENSED IT BEFORE HE heard shots. It was in the air—things were ready to pop. *Thank God I sent Kenny on his way,* he thought. But the secure feeling about his son changed only moments later when his cell phone vibrated.

"Dad!"

"What? Where are you, Kenny?"

"A ranger on a horse stopped us and—"

"I repeat my first question, where are you?"

"He had a gun, Dad! Me and Blazer escaped."

Awol sat down—his nerves were shot.

"He shot to kill, Dad, but missed. Lloyd managed to get back in the Jeep and tore off. The other ranger galloped west on his horse, across the river, toward the PCT. I'm sorry, Dad."

"Just give me a minute here, Kenny. Just give me—so where exactly are you now?"

"East of the river. Don't worry, I'm hidden; he can't get in here with a horse. He won't come back across the river."

"Where did you get the radio?"

"Yeah, I'd taken the radio out of the pack earlier. I forgot it was in my pocket."

"Okay. Listen up. Hide yourself to the extreme; go deeper in, and do not—I repeat—*do not* cross that river."

"Okay, Dad. I know you're mad."

"Kenny, I'm not mad, I'm scared. Don't call me unless it's critical, in case they've figured out . . . Keep Blazer with you. Await further orders."

Awol lay in scrub and restudied the map. Drawing on army experience, he determined that the shots he heard at the river were a good half mile east of the PCT. *Barcelona would have heard them if he is anywhere near the PCT west of me. Could he be there? Why?* Awol pulled up the binoculars hanging from his neck and scanned. He saw nothing but some birds alight from the pines. It was quiet again. A ranger who shot at Lloyd and Kenny was heading in that direction. *Why?* He punched in for Sacco.

"Awol! Don't go away. I'm talking with Ranger Lloyd."

JAIME, ON HEARING THE SHOTS, wondered if Barcelona had now resorted to shooting mules. Unnerved, he didn't think game hunters were in the area, and the shots sounded like small arms fire, certainly not from a shotgun. The shots occurred east of the PCT; he would stay just west of the trail and move up.

Barcelona saw him fifteen minutes later. It was Jaime, alright; he always walked with a stoop, and when he stood erect, his head and neck were lopsided. Barcelona thought of a perfect way to unhinge Alvarado. He pulled out the mule's pistol and let Jaime pass below him. When he'd gone far enough, Barcelona clambered down the pine. It didn't take long for him to catch up.

"Freeze! Walk to your right, Jaime. Do something stupid, and I kill you."

He had him walk east. "So I thought you had me surrounded," Barcelona said.

Jaime said nothing, but when Barcelona reached into his captive's holster for his gun, Jaime grabbed the hand and turned, costing him a shot in the leg with his own weapon. Jaime howled and sat, hands around the wound in his thigh.

"I should have blown off your kneecap. Limp, gimp. Get a move on, or I'll do worse."

Jaime started to cry as he hobbled along, one hand covering the wound in his thigh. He looked heavenward as if hoping for an angel. "Please don't kill me."

"Not yet. I've got plans for you."

Twenty minutes later, Jaime was tied up midway between the river and the PCT. Barcelona had eyed another ponderosa and stuck Jaime in thick brush thirty yards from it.

"Alvarado! I have someone who wants to talk to you," Barcelona said.

Jaime, hands tied behind his back, sat in the thicket, his left leg coursing blood. Barcelona held the phone to Jaime's mouth and a knife at his throat. "Speak."

"I've been shot," Jaime slobbered in Spanish. "Says he's going to cut a hole in my throat and stuff it with the drop."

Barcelona spoke into his phone while Jaime begged. "You hear that, Alvarado? After I'm done here, I'm coming home to hunt you."

Alvarado could barely control his rage. "No need. We are coming for you."

"More men coming now? Great! Tell them I'm waiting, scumbag."

Barcelona slipped the phone into his pocket and looked around. More coming, he'd said. *Alvarado betrayed his usual calm with edge*, Barcelona thought. He remembered seeing a distant horse earlier from his crow's nest. *That's it!* Jaime has someone out there waiting for him. That someone will come looking. Barcelona turned Jaime backward to him and blindfolded him, then he put on Jaime's backpack and climbed the tree. After scanning, certain he was safe, he transferred Jaime's cell phone and the notebooks he found in his pack into his own.

CHAPTER EIGHTY-SEVEN

Aᴡᴏʟ ʜᴇᴀʀᴅ ᴛʜᴇ ꜱɪɴɢʟᴇ ꜱʜᴏᴛ. *Toward the PCT.* He lay hidden on the east side of the river in a spot that afforded a clear view across. Picking up the field glasses again, he headed west.

Awol blackened his face with mud before fording the gushing river. He separated his small day pack, shrugged it on, and left the main backpack at the riverbed. He wasn't able to stone-step because water covered the stones, but by expertly shifting-planting-shifting his poles—not unlike an alpine skier—he twisted through the icy waters. After fording, he shook out his boots, squeezed water from his socks, and lay prone to scan again in the direction of the shot, but he saw nothing. He'd now heard a total of three shots. Was Barcelona alive? Maybe Awol was no longer needed. He crawled into shrub and waited. He needed to hear back from Sacco.

"He's alive. I have his cell number."

Awol secured the number into his phone. "Good. I'll need it."

"Let me get back to that. Lloyd found out that the last mule killed was packing. Barcelona has a weapon. We need to rethink this."

"If you're thinking of bringing in police and other rangers, then I'll never be able to help you negotiate with Barcelona. And that's why I'm here, right?"

"Awol, this thing has gotten completely out of hand. There is some kind of cowboy ranger running around on a big horse. Says he was assigned to check out the PCT, but Lloyd says no one knows anything about this. He was ready to shoot Lloyd and your son. You have put your life in danger. We need—"

"Stop. Kenny is hidden, and he is safe. I'm in contact with him. You are blowing our only chance to bust their operation. We get Barcelona on our side, and they will call in their chips. We've come this far; we take this opportunity."

"Awol. I appreciate what you are trying to—"

"I didn't come down here to help deport a few thugs only to have the cartel back in full swing in a couple of days. Barcelona is smart; he's fluent in English. And deep down I think he has a decent side."

"Look. Awol."

"I'm not walking away, Detective. Are you going to help me?"

Silence.

"I can get a fix from here if Barcelona picks up when I call," Sacco finally said.

"Perfect."

"You need to tell me when to make the call. I could call now, but if he gets jumpy, he'll be gone before you get there."

"Okay."

Sacco had disconnected, and Awol punched in again on the new frequency. "Kenny, did you hear the shot? Everything okay by you?"

"Yeah."

"You where I told you to be?"

"Yes. I'm well hidden."

"Stay put. I'm still waiting for Lloyd to call me back."

Awol concentrated. He could isolate in the forest in the general area of Barcelona and wait it out. But if the thugs flushed out Barcelona or Barcelona flushed out the thugs, Barcelona might be killed. Sacco needed his knowledge. This was Awol's chance.

Awol looked west and, like a gator, low-crawled that direction.

Fifty yards later, Awol hesitated. He scanned with the binocs and listened. He saw and heard nothing but noted a grove of pines ahead and believed the shot had come from there. He crouched and sidled in the scrub.

Voices. Half the length of a football field away, he figured, but voices. Awol knelt down and squiggled again.

Awol felt the vibration and took up his cell.

"Ranger Lloyd here. Sacco update you?"

"As much as he could. What can you add?"

"That other ranger I've been suspicious of is in cahoots with Roy Rogers on the horse. A different ranger, one I trust, followed him when he saw him take a personal call and leave the office in what seemed like a hurry. And we just switched off; I'm following him now in a different vehicle. Guess what he's trailing?"

"What?"

"A horse trailer. I'll call you and Sacco when I find out more, but he's headin' your way."

"Keep me in the loop." Awol heard voices again and mumbled, head close to the ground, hand covering his mouth, "But from now on, we can only text."

Awol crawled again, trying not to snap twigs. With the cunning of a wild animal, he chose a five-yard route dead ahead. The voices had stopped. Awol crawled the five yards and bent an ear to the ground, but he couldn't hear anything. He was afraid to go farther, afraid the men behind the voices were listening and waiting for him. He wondered if Barcelona had left. Awol pulled out his phone and texted Sacco.

Call Barcelona, get fix, text me only

Barcelona pulled his phone and looked at it. He didn't recognize the number.

"Who's this?" Barcelona whispered.

"Believe it or not, this is a potential friend, and I can help you."

"You didn't answer my question."

"I'm from the other side."

"I don't trust you." Barcelona shut the phone.

But it was enough, and Sacco downloaded the trace and texted Awol back.

See coordinates

Awol looked at the numbers and checked it with the way points on his GPS.

Hold tight

He wiggled farther.

Where the fuck is he? Think. What would I do? Awol, approaching forest, scanned the view and heard several crows squawk from trees dead in front of him. *Trees! Of course; the bird's-eye view.* Awol calculated the handicap and the odds. *He has a gun, he's above me. He may have spotted me already.*

Awol heard a rustling and peeked to his right. He thought he could see—*over there*—a head wrapped with a bandanna wobbling in a thicket at thirty yards. *Someone is crouching—going to the bathroom? He's talking, crying. Sounds like Spanish.* Awol eased up the binoculars and scanned the thicket. Blood. A man was sitting there, but Awol couldn't see his hands. *He's tied up.*

Awol quickly updated Sacco.

He has a hostage

Can you spot Barcelona?

No. Let's negotiate

I tried. No go

Do nothing. Wait

Another text came in, this time from Lloyd.

I'm here with 4x4 and trailer. Bad ranger arrested. Roy Rogers still loose. Wait

An idea came to him. He sent a text to Kenny.

Are you still near river?

Yes

Do exactly as I say

Twenty minutes later, Awol heard the patter of an animal coming. *Yes!* Squinting up from the ground, Awol could see it perfectly. A white handkerchief waving from a stick that should be tied—*Blazer! Good boy, Blazer.*

"You once told me you like dogs," Awol yelled up. "My dog is here with the sign of truce—please don't shoot my dog."

The hostage started up in Spanish again, sounding like he was praying. But the rest was silence as the blubbering of the hostage stopped.

Awol held on to Blazer, who was licking his face. "I know, I love you too," Awol whispered. Kenny had shoelaced and duct-taped one end of a hiking pole to Blazer's collar. A white handkerchief was tied to the other end. "Okay, Blazer. Go and see"—Awol gave him a gentle shove—"go and see."

Awol watched as Blazer marched up to an open spot. He saw the dog look and sniff and then saw him run to the hostage, as the man cried, *"El salvador, Christo, el salvador—"*

"Shut your blubbering mouth!" Barcelona hollered. "One more word, so help me, I'll splatter your brains."

Awol jerked up to the sound and saw how close the tree was. *He must have seen me the whole time!* Blazer trotted up below the limbs, looked up, and--unbelievably--wagged his tail. The white flag fluttered in a mild breeze.

"Sit, Blazer. Sit," Awol said, and the animal did as told, looking up into the tree expectantly.

After a long minute, Awol reached both hands into the air, sat up slowly, and removed his hat. He pulled his knees up, wrapped his arms around them, and looked up to Barcelona's tree. Awol said nothing. The hostage was quiet.

Another minute passed without a sound. Blazer, tongue hanging from a panting mouth, scratched his front paws into the ground and yipped up into the tree.

In a sudden understanding, Awol said, "Was it you who set my dog's leg?"

"I should have killed you at Silver Pass," Barcelona said, talking through the tree to Awol.

"Why didn't you?"

"I don't know. Those were my orders. If I'd followed them, I wouldn't be here now."

"So this is all my fault?"

Silence.

"What do you want?" Barcelona asked.

"I'm not a cop," Awol began. "And right now, I'm not officially connected with this case."

"Answer the question! What do you want?"

"It's what my government wants—your knowledge, contacts, information, testimony. What do I want? I'd just like to finish my hike and go home."

"What's stopping you?"

"That's a good question. My son is a recovering drug addict."

"So that's my fault?"

Blazer lay beneath the tree. The stick and flag pointed straight up.

"Please," Awol said, "just listen. You won't be set free by the US government; you've killed a government officer, killed others, so no—that won't happen. But you told me your family is on the line, maybe—"

"They killed my wife!"

Awol pursed his lips, squeezed his knees tighter.

"I'm sorry to hear that. Are your kids safe?"

"I think so."

Awol's mind was rushing into unfamiliar terrain, but he had a foothold.

"If you will allow me to call a decision-maker in my—"

"What makes you think I'd trust you?"

"Listen! Barcelona, DeLeon, whatever, you left me half-dead. You damn near got my son killed. I'm not out here because I like you. But right now, if there is any chance for you and your children, I'm all you've got."

"I saw you crawl to that spot; I could have blasted you."

"There must be a reason you didn't. I'm thinking it must have something to do with you and your children."

"I don't care what happens to me."

"Then allow me to see what I can do for your children." Awol held up his cell phone toward the tree.

"Stand up," Barcelona commanded.

Awol stood.

"Walk up until I tell you . . ."

Awol walked.

"Stop!"

"It's okay, Blazer. Sit," Awol said. Awol stared at the hostage.

"Both my children get flown to the USA. They will stay in this country permanently and be brought up near me by someone I approve. I will stay in prison in this country, near my children."

Awol held up his other palm and called Sacco.

After a discussion with Sacco, Awol looked to Barcelona. He had come down from the tree and was patting the dog. Barcelona's gun was in a vest holster, but he carried a knife in his other hand.

"He wants to talk with you," Awol said, holding out the phone.

"No. I will speak only with you," Barcelona said. "If he isn't truthful, I will see it in your eyes and hear it in your voice. I am sorry for what I did to you. And yes, I reset your dog's leg."

Several minutes went by as Sacco explained he had to get his chief on the other line.

"Barcelona," Awol repeated. "We cannot guarantee you asylum in the United States. You are wanted for murder in Mexico; they say you escaped from prison there."

Barcelona looked so mad, Awol thought he was about to draw the gun.

"I have notebooks, addresses, numbers, and three million worth of uncut, hidden."

Awol held up a hand and spoke into the phone. After another long minute, he put his hand down.

"We will try, Barcelona. But we cannot guarantee."

"What the hell can you guarantee?"

"That your children will be flown to the United States; that they will be placed in foster care of your approval; that they will be granted US citizenship; and that they will remain here permanently until the legal age of eighteen, when, by US law, they will be free to make their own decisions."

"You swear to this, Awol?"

Awol held up the phone near his mouth and stated, "Providing you tell us everything you know about the PCT drug smuggling operation and that you will testify, yes, Barcelona. I swear."

Barcelona untied the holster and dropped it. He threw his knife to the side and looked skyward.

"For you Juanita, and Trini, and 'Berto, I give myself up."

Jaime, still tied and blindfolded, yelled out something in Spanish, and a shot rang out. Awol saw Jaime's head burst.

"Freeze!" a voice to the right of Awol yelled.

Awol jumped again and stared at a revolver that steadied on him and now swung toward Barcelona. A ranger, hat brim hiding his eyes, crouched with both hands on the gun.

Awol looked at Barcelona, at the raw hate in his eyes, while the man with the gun rose to full height.

"And you swore to me," Barcelona hissed.

"Yo!" The shout came from the bushes just behind the gunman.

The man lost his focus, and in that instant Kenny charged from behind and polevaulted the pointed end of a hiking pole into the man's head. The shot went wide as the ranger's hat, along with something in it, flipped off, and he crumpled to the ground.

For a moment there was dead silence as Barcelona stared at the ranger, who now had recognizable hair. While Awol and Kenny looked at each other, Blazer trotted over to the ranger, sniffed at a twisted eyelash, then sniffed a wig partially stuffed in the ranger hat.

"I have no idea who that is," said Awol, looking at Barcelona, who walked over to the ranger. Barcelona bent down and pulled something from the face.

At that moment, another figure, holding a pistol, emerged from the path. Before Barcelona could react, Awol held up both hands. "This is one of our guys. It's okay. Ranger Lloyd," Awol said, "this man has agreed to cooperate fully with the United States government via Detective Sacco. He is to get special handling in custody."

"Understood. But sir, I will need to cuff you," Lloyd said to Barcelona.

Barcelona, eyes glued to the fallen ranger, held up a hand. "That will be fine, sir. You will have my complete cooperation. Just give me one moment."

With volcanic voice, Barcelona yelled, "Alvarado! *Cobarde!* Open your eyes!"

The eyes quivered and opened.

Barcelona pointed. "PCT drug lord. Scumbag!"

Alvarado felt the back of his head and winced. He saw the burst head of Jaime next to him. He looked back at Barcelona, who was now standing over him, a leg on each side.

Barcelona unzipped his shorts and pulled out his dick. "Stay on your back! If you move your face or try to cover your face, I will stomp your throat until dead, right here, right now."

Too stunned to say anything, Awol—feeling something inside the lower regions of his gut, understanding that this ritual had to be played out—held up a hand to Lloyd.

"I am Roberto DeLeon!" Barcelona pissed thoroughly into Alvarado's face. "You are *un cobarde.*" Barcelona zipped and walked away.

Nobody said a word as everyone but Barcelona watched Alvarado cover his face.

Barcelona looked to Awol, and after getting a nod, he put his hands behind his back and turned around.

Once Barcelona was cuffed, Lloyd called for backup and an ambulance. They bound Alvarado. Barcelona, tears welling in his eyes, turned to Awol and Kenny. "Thank you for keeping your word. And for saving my life. Giving my children a fair shot at an honorable life, a life better than mine, is all I ask."

CHAPTER EIGHTY-EIGHT

"YOU SURE SAVED THE DAY back there by the tree, with that hiking pole. Guess I have to forgive you for not following orders."

Kenny chuckled. "I thought to myself, I better do good or I'll be court-martialed."

Awol looked proudly on Kenny. "Taking off your boots was smart; Alvarado didn't hear you coming."

"I'd like to take credit for that, but I didn't have much choice after using my laces to tie that other pole to Blazer's collar."

"And the duct tape?"

"It was on Ranger Lloyd's passenger seat. He said you never know when you'll need duct tape, so I wound some around the pole like thru-hikers do."

AWOL AND KENNY FINISHED HIKING the Pacific Crest Trail a month later, on September 20. UCLA had given Kenny a three-week extension on his summer break. After hiking by dormant glacier-clad volcanoes and snowcapped peaks in the Cascades, after climbing into a September snowstorm followed by a twelve-mile slog through calf-deep snows, they celebrated in a tavern near Manning Park, British Columbia, while Blazer rested beneath their table. Awol had just gone to the dispenser to get a refill of Diet Coke and looked back on his son, who played with Blazer's ears. Kenny looked fit and confident. Awol ambled back to his son and his dog feeling almost haughty.

Awol smiled and took a sip of Diet Coke. It tasted good, and he thought about Linda. He wondered if she'd received the trip packet and brochures for Europe he'd mailed a couple of days ago. After he'd learned that Sacco had successfully cleared both his record and Kenny's, he'd received another phone call from Sacco.

"I have something else for you," Sacco said.

"Yeah? What's that?"

"How much did you say you gave Kenny to pay his drug debt?"

"I gave him thirteen thousand."

"That's what I thought. This afternoon I mailed that plus twelve additional to Linda—in your name, of course."

"You're kidding."

"Compliments of Alvarado and his gang."

"How did you do that?"

"Awol, I felt it was the least we could do. We raided Jaime's operation first and collected a lot of cash. Before I filed a final report, I talked about it with my boss. He agreed to it but covered himself by pre-posting an award for Barcelona's capture. You won that award."

Awol pulled from his pocket a copy of the e-mail he'd received yesterday from Linda and showed it to Kenny.

"You're out of the doghouse, Dad."

Awol winked. He looked at the bottom of her e-mail. *Thanks for your letter. Yes! A changed police file with something positive going into it . . .* Karl touched the e-mail to his lips.

"Did your mom ever tell you what I did just after the divorce?"

"No. What?"

"Your mother always hated the color purple. She stayed in our house; I got an apartment. When she went to work one day, I snuck over and painted the front and back doors purple. Two weeks later, she up and went to California."

"I remember those purple doors, but she didn't rant to me and Gregory about it."

"I was drinking heavily back then, and a stunt like that was what I was capable of."

"But . . ."

Awol looked at Kenny. "I was petty. Not anymore."

After the meal, they went outside into the early evening. Stepping toward autumn-hued woodlands, the sound of crunchy dry leaves reminded Awol of home in New England. He missed Linda. Awol and Kenny sat down on a wooden slab bench warmed by moveable mushroom-topped heaters spread through the area. They watched the sun dip behind firs under a red-streaked sky while Blazer finished off the bone Kenny had brought for him.

Honeysuckle. Awol turned to his right and inhaled the aroma as Blazer moved away from his meatless bone and looked up at the two of them as though to ask, "What's next?"

"So, Blazer," Awol said, "do you want to go back and see Lulu?"

At the mention of Lulu, the hound wagged his tail and sprinted east a good thirty yards, then abruptly turned and charged back in front of them and continued west the same distance. Kenny and Awol looked at each other and laughed as Blazer crisscrossed in front of them again, shoulders lunging as if he were after wild game. Finally, the animal came to a stop in front of them and panted between licks to Awol's and Kenny's faces.

"Okay, Blazer," Awol said. "We get the message."

FEDERAL AGENTS IN THE GREATER Las Vegas/Reno area alone recovered eleven of fourteen drops, and eleven of fourteen mules were arrested. Frank fled to Saint Thomas in the US Virgin Islands, and using money he had saved in a Swiss bank account, set himself up comfortably in the foothills with a view of the exquisite Charlotte Amalie Harbor. But Frank didn't sleep with one eye open. A month after his arrival, he was shot between the eyes in his own bed.

Sacco promised Luis Alvarado asylum in the United States in exchange for a full confession with taped recordings of him detailing the complete PCT drug operation. At the end of seven sessions—when Alvarado had nothing else to tell—Sacco apologized to Alvarado, saying a last-minute snafu had occurred and he would have to be deported after all. Alvarado is serving a life sentence in a Mexico City prison that some say is under the thumb of the Cordiero cartel. He's been mixed in with regular inmates and has been denied his chess set. He sleeps with both eyes open.

Vincent Sacco was awarded several citations and had write ups in local and national newspapers detailing his bust of the Pacific Crest Trail drug operation. He was promoted to chief of West Coast Operations within the department and, when asked by a reporter if he had further ambitions, hinted that when the time was right, he might throw his hat into the political arena.

Roberto DeLeon, known by most as Barcelona, was, at the last minute, given permanent asylum in the United States. Sacco told

Mexican authorities that the only way he would agree to give up Alvarado was to gain asylum for Barcelona as well as his children. After all, Sacco reminded them, in addition to Barcelona's exhaustive detailing of the PCT operation, with added information about Alvarado's enforcement methods, it had been Barcelona who'd exposed and detailed the fraudulent prison system that peopled much of the drug scheme in the first place.

On hearing this best possible outcome, Barcelona broke down and wept. He is at an undisclosed US prison for life and sees his children once a month. He's become an accomplished middleweight in the intraprison boxing system. It is said that he's also been drawn to music. At the prison library, he has learned to read music and has composed love ballads with Spanglish lyrics.

Awol is back with Linda. He attends AA meetings weekly, and on the day marking his one year of sobriety, he and Linda renewed their wedding vows. Linda invited his sons to the ceremony. Following the ceremony, he and Linda flew to Germany, where they are now. After a memorable meal of German food, Awol showed Linda a receipt confirming his registration for six months of PTSD counseling when they return home. Awol says there is only one condition, and she has just agreed to it: while she visits the typical tourist spots in southern Germany, she will give him three days to hike alone in the Alps.

A NOTE FROM THE AUTHOR

FROM THE OFFICIAL WILDERNESS ACT, "... where the earth and its community of life are untrammeled by man, where man himself is a visitor who does not remain."

USING THE TRAIL NAME "HAMLET," I started hiking the Pacific Crest Trail from the Mexican border on May 8, 2007. I made it only to the Oregon state line that year because of a family wedding and commitments back east. I finished the PCT in Manning Park, British Columbia, on August 18, 2008. I certainly didn't witness any of what you have read here. I was surprised, however, to find no security or checkpoint where the PCT crossed into British Columbia. Not a soul was around. Anyone could reenter the US or cross into Canada at any time.

I had a wonderful experience. The beauty and majesty of the trail were awe-inspiring, and I met great fellow hikers and other fine people.